Reviews of FAMILY SECRETS

It was a beautifully written book about one woman's struggle with breast cancer, but also to rebuild a relationship with her son. FAMILY SECRETS squeezed at my heart... numerous times. It was hard to put down as I wanted to know if Alexis would survive the cancer, and if Colton would eventually let go of his father who had died, and rebuild a relationship with his mother. Well done, Donna M. Zadunajsky!

In "Family Secrets" Donna M. Zadunajsky has again weaved a plot so full of twists and turns, loss and triumph, suspense, romance, and the deep emotions of a family in denial that it keeps you highly intrigued and guessing up until the final sentence. Much as she did in her previous novel, "Not Forgotten." Donna is a true storyteller who is masterful in creating the element of surprise and achieving superb realism. The best news yet, however, is that "Family Secrets" is the first in Zadunajsky's new "Second Chances" Series. When an author captures the imagination of the reader in so many heartfelt ways, "Second Chances" are never far away, if you can survive the upheavals in your life!-Deborah A. Bowman Stevens, author and Editor-in-Chief for Clasid Consultants Publishing, Inc.

"Secrets and Second Chances" Book 1

Family Secrets

By: Donna M. Zadunajsky

COPYRIGHT

DEDICATION

To
my
dear
friend and
second mom,
Ellen Meade.
Thank you for all the
love and guidance you've
given me in all the years we've
known each other. Cancer wasn't
kind to you. It wasn't a friend that
came to visit, but the kind that came
and took you away from everyone that
loves you. You somehow beat breast cancer and then was dealt with a cancerous
Squamous cell in your brain. And last,
you were diagnosed with pancreatic cancer stage three. You're always in my
heart and in my thoughts. I love
you and miss you more
than you know!

DEDICATION

This book goes to my best friend
Gillian Fisher. God brought us together
when I needed you the most! Now, I can't
imagine my life without you. I'm really
happy to have the kind of friendship
I have with you. Because my life
would be a lonely mess without you.   You're my best
friend, I love you and
miss you more than
you'll ever
know

!

Part 1

Every great dream begins with a dreamer.

Always remember, you have within you the strength, the patience, and the passion to reach for the stars to change the world...

Harriet Tubman

It is not the strongest of the species that survives,
Nor the most intelligent that survives.
It is the one that is the most adaptable to change...

Charles Darwin

One

Was life fair? Not in the least. Not when you worked your ass off for everything you've ever dreamed of and *poof*, in an instant, with one sentence...it was gone!

Life doesn't always work out the way we want. No matter what you've done or how you've done it, something without a doubt gets in the way. You could spend days, weeks, months, even years working for the things you want out of life, only for it to be taken from you as if your dreams and schemes never existed. As if you had never tried at all...

It's funny how life seems to work out the opposite of what we want. Why bother to dream at all if they never come to fruition? *But*, if we don't have our dreams and goals to motivate and guide us, where would we be in this world? Lost, stumbling aimlessly, and not driven by desire, blood, sweat, and tears!

We've all heard the phrase, *"Life isn't fair,"* so why are we so defeated when things don't turn out our way? When everything seems to fall apart? Shouldn't we just keep trying? *"If you fall down, get back up, dust yourself off, and try again."*

But what if...*just to be fair in this unfair world*...what if we weren't meant to have those dreams at all? What if they were only to teach us something we didn't see in ourselves? What if there was something better than our dreams waiting for us on the path of life?

Two

Ever since Alexis Finley had been a young girl, she'd dreamed of becoming an astronaut. She'd wanted to explore the universe—do something meaningful with her life. She was mere inches from making her dreams come true. The grueling hours she'd spent at work; she'd practically lived there. All for this one unexpected moment in her life that destroyed everything. *It was so unfair!*

Time seemed to stand still in her heart. The seconds ticked away as she sat in the expensive brown leather chair, staring speechless at the woman in front of her. Suddenly, life as she'd known it came to a screeching halt!

It didn't matter how many times she blinked, she was still sitting in the same chair in front of the same doctor she had known for years. They'd taken a class together in college, for heaven sakes.

Alexis tried to let the words spoken to her sink in, but it just wasn't registering completely. She prayed a silent prayer deep inside herself that perhaps she had heard it all wrong. By chance, the test results were someone else's, not hers. Doctors were known to make mistakes, sometimes picking up the wrong report or reading the wrong patient's file. Had the lab made an error? That happened sometimes, too, a false positive. So why couldn't this one time be just that?

Alexis would get a second opinion, that's what she'd do! She'd say, "Thank you," and get up and walk out the door. Yet, she couldn't move, her body numb and her mind in denial from what the doctor had just said.

"Alexis, we have to start treatment immediately. It's extremely important before your condition gets worse. Time and early discovery is your ally, but we won't know about that until after the biopsy," said Dr. Sarah Ramsey.

"Are you sure it's breast cancer?" Alexis asked anxiously. Her mind was whirling. This made no sense at all! She'd been checking herself off-and-on for years, and she'd never found a single lump, not even suspected one. Had she examined herself wrong? Maybe she didn't realize something might have been a lump; maybe she'd thought it was something else, but never cancer!

Alexis had turned forty just last month, and now she'd have to have a mammogram every year for the rest of her life. *"My life,"* her mind repeated. How much time did she really have left? Panic was starting to set in.

"Yes, Alexis, I'm sure. I've checked your mammogram films and the ultrasound several times. I'm sorry, but the density of the images shows you definitely have breast cancer. There's no mistake," Sarah Ramsey stated firmly, yet warmly.

"I guess..." Alexis's throat tightened and she swallowed. "This being my first mammogram and the additional ultrasound was just...just an initial precaution, ya' know? 'Cause it was my first..." she stammered. "I thought you wanted to see me about the results in-person as a courtesy and a baseline test for the future? It didn't occur to me that anything was wrong." The room was suddenly too warm, much too warm for her liking. Sweat rolled down the back of her neck, wetting the collar of her blouse. She twisted her long, wavy, brunette hair and clipped it into place on the back of her head, hoping it would cool her down.

"I wish I was wrong, Alexis, I truly do, but I'm afraid the results show you *have* cancer. I'll call Dr. Brownski, an Oncology Surgeon at the Anderson Cancer Center in Orlando, to schedule a lumpectomy and a biopsy. He's one of the best, Alexis. We'll go from there," Sarah Ramsey offered with an encouragingly smile.

"Is there any other alternative?"

"I'm not sure what you're asking, Alexis," Dr. Ramsey frowned. "Until we have the biopsy—"

"Is there an option for a full double mastectomy?" Alexis interrupted. She watched as the doctor's right eyebrow shot up. She had caught her off-guard, maybe even surprising her.

"Well, I wouldn't suggest a mastectomy until after we have the results of the biopsy from the lumpectomy. I'm not even sure why you'd consider such evasive, extensive surgery without knowing what we're up against. Most women don't want their breasts removed because it takes away from their need to feel like a woman. As you know, a double mastectomy is done to remove both breasts. What I have seen from the images, the cancer is confined in the right breast. Most doctors won't consider a double mastectomy unless there is substantial evidence to do so. It's also a very dangerous surgery with a long recuperation, therapy, and reconstruction."

"You know I work for NASA, right?" Alexis blurted out.

Dr. Ramsey nodded, placing a lock of her reddish brown hair behind her right ear. Her intelligent green eyes searched Alexis's face as she waited for her to state her point, which the doctor couldn't quite grasp at that moment.

"Well, NASA has been considering me for the next space shuttle launch. If they knew about the cancer, there would be no way in hell they'd let me go!"

"I see," Sarah said, as she shifted in her chair.

"Do you?" Alexis's voice rose, which caught the doctor extremely off-guard. "Because I have worked my ass off for this opportunity!" The anger stage was taking over much sooner than expected, but Dr. Sarah Ramsey had seen it all before.

"I can't just sit and watch it pass me by!" Alexis shouted. She didn't know where the anger came from. It wasn't like her to jump down someone's throat for no apparent reason. Although there was a reason, wasn't there? Her dream was coming to a dead end. Thrown in the trash to be recycled. Never to be lived.

Dr. Ramsey cleared her throat. "Alexis, I know it's a great deal to take in, but this is your health we're talking about. I can't lie to NASA or keep your records confidential from them in this type of instance. Besides, NASA will have their own doctors check you out before any such mission. There could even be legal repercussions for both of us by hiding this diagnosis. I understand being an astronaut is an incredible opportunity for you, but your health is more important than flying to outer space."

Alexis grabbed her purse from beside the chair and stood up. She didn't want to sit here any longer and listen to this doctor tell her she couldn't live her dreams.

"Alexis, wait! Where are you going? We need to discuss, albeit prematurely, your options and schedule the lumpectomy!"

"I need some air." Alexis turned and opened the door, then slammed it shut behind her. She knew she was being selfish, and that her health was important, but so was everything else she'd worked so hard to accomplish. Or maybe she was just in denial about the whole thing. She was only forty years old and had her whole life in front of her. Why did this have to happen to her? Why and how did she end up with cancer? She worked out and ate the right foods. All her physical exams had come back excellent until this one. So, why her, why now?

Three

Alexis rushed down the hall and stood in front of the elevator. She poked the arrow down button with her index finger. A bell *dinged,* and the doors opened. She dashed in—took a quick peek behind her to see if Dr. Ramsey had followed her—then hit the L for the lobby. She was so thankful there was no one else in the elevator. She needed to calm down and think about what Dr. Ramsey had told her.

She took deep, easy breathes, in through her nose and out through her mouth. As the elevator doors slid open; bright light blinded her. She raised her left hand and rubbed her eyes, feeling a headache starting to surface. She walked out of the elevator and through the lobby of the medical center.

The future woman astronaut of the United States of America left without giving her doctor the chance to change her destiny and her dream. *"Just who am I trying to kid?"* Alexis screamed silently to herself.

Sarah Ramsey—she was practically a friend because they'd known each other so long—Sarah wanted to help, but Alexis just wasn't ready yet.

By the time she reached her car and sat inside, all the anger she'd taken out on her *friend* just minutes before came pouring out. Alexis Finley had always considered herself a strong person and didn't let anything get in her way, but the cancer was beyond her control. She needed to sit and think about what the doctor had said and make some decisions, even if it meant postponing her dreams. How could she give up her dreams when she was almost there?

Alexis pounded the steering wheel with her right palm, accidently hitting the horn. It blared, abrupt and loud. She didn't even glance around to see if anyone was looking at her. She didn't care if they were. She finally realized she could either sit here and feel sorry for herself, dwelling over how life wasn't fair, or she could do something about it. But what could she do?

Her dream had always been to explore outer space, and she was determined not to let anything stop her. She had to come up with a plan. There had to be something she could do and still live all her dreams, but she wasn't sure what that plan was yet. Searching for the keys in her lap, she found them and started the car, Alexis knew she didn't want to go home, nor did she want to be around other people. She just wanted to be alone and think.

It was time to come up with a new, *temporary* plan. After all, she wasn't dying...yet...or was she?

Four

Alexis drove out of the parking lot and headed towards the Martin Andersen Beachline Express. When she arrived at Cape Canaveral, she drove to Canaveral City Park. There she sat and stared at the Atlantis Space Shuttle in the far distance. Imagining the day she would climb inside one just like it and soar through the sky towards the unknown; to a whole new universe where she didn't have to think about her life and everything that had gone wrong.

Now, it would take years before she received another chance. IF—and it was a very big "IF"—she ever received another chance. That is, IF she could beat breast cancer. This opportunity was something she wasn't sure she could pass up. Her health was important to her, but so was her job, and if her boss found out, there would be no flying into outer space.

Reclining her seat back, she closed her eyes and rubbed her temples, trying to calm down enough to ease the tension headache. Her thoughts involuntarily went to her late husband, and she wished Jay could be with her. Jay would've known what to do. He could always comfort her in a way no man had ever done before or since. He was thoughtful and kind, always putting her needs above his own. God, how she wished he was here with her now!

There was never a day she didn't think of him and miss him. She asked herself as she did all the time, *"Why did he have to die?"* Then, she wondered how she had been able to cope with his death. Of course, she had continued to mourn, but she really couldn't remember how she'd got through the loss and pain of losing someone so close to her.

After the funeral seven months ago, she'd concentrated on raising their seventeen-year-old son, Colton, but she'd jumped straight back into her work. She wasn't thankful Jay had died when he did. She'd been glad at the time that Colton was almost old enough to take care of himself, but she wasn't sure if he grieved the way she did. So many nights of lying in bed crying herself to sleep; then one day she climbed out of bed and moved on with her life as if nothing had ever happened.

Colton, on the other hand had never cried; at least, not in front of her. He just seemed to isolate himself from his father's death. To a certain extent, Colton helped around the house when she worked late. He was just like his father, in some ways, always thinking of others. She was glad, but also hoped, he was getting what he needed—closure. She'd always worried about whether her son had accepted the loss of his father. But, now, it hit her that maybe she hadn't found closure, either.

Instantly, Alexis sat up, startled by the revelation, but she couldn't think about it now. She had other decisions that needed to be made, so instead she viewed the scenery around her. A man wearing a Miami Dolphins' T-shirt was walking his German Shepard on a leash. The dog stayed near his owner, looking up at him every few seconds to see if his master was still beside him. To the man's left, a young couple sat on a blanket staring into each other's eyes and chatting. The man smiled at his lover and leaned over to kiss her on the lips. They seemed to be in love, tuned into each other, as if no one else in the world mattered.

She thought of Jay again and how much in love they once had been. She missed him terribly. Her heart still ached from the loss of him in her life. Maybe if Jay had been with her, things wouldn't have fallen to pieces; maybe she'd have had a closer relationship with Colton.

However, as the years passed by, even before Jay's demise, she had spent more time at work than at home. She had, in many ways, neglected her husband and son. She put herself first and her work became her life. She did love her family, but somewhere along the way, she'd lost the need to be at home. Jay had never said anything to her about it; never mentioned she should spend more time with them and not so much at work.

Right now, though, Alexis had to stop this useless woolgathering. She couldn't change the past. She knew it was fine to think about him, but she needed to start planning her future. She had a son who was almost an adult, but he still very much needed her. If something were to happen to her, if she were to leave this world, he would be alone.

Colton was an only child with no brothers or sisters to advise him. She was his only family, which meant, as much as she hated to do it, she needed to talk to him about the breast cancer. He could reason with her, just like Jay used to do and help her make the right decisions. Yet, she was the parent, the adult, and well aware of what was best for the both of them. She clicked on her seat belt, started the car, and drove towards home.

Five

When Alexis pulled into her familiar driveway, she pushed a small button on her visor to open the garage door. She parked her car inside and climbed out. She entered through a door to the kitchen and set her purse on the table. As she glanced at the clock on the wall, she saw it was almost two in the afternoon. Colton would be home from school any time now.

She was dreading this conversation with her son and she was filled with nervous energy. She went through the automatic motions of fixing a sandwich, even though she wasn't really hungry, she knew she needed to try to eat something. She'd eaten nothing since early this morning before leaving for her *routine* appointment with Dr. Ramsey. The appointment that could change her life forever, yet, she couldn't think about that now. She just wanted things to be as normal as possible when Colton walked through the door.

She sat down after setting the sandwich and a glass of water on the kitchen dinette table. The house was quiet except for the sound of the clock ticking.

When she finished what she could eat, she placed the plate with the half-eaten sandwich in the sink and sat back down at the small table. The front door opened with a squeak, Colton was now home from school.

"Hello," she said.

"Alexis, what are you doing home so early?" He slumped into the chair across from her, as far as he could away from her, dropping his books on the table.

She hated it when he called her by her first name instead of Mom, like he should. It was something he'd started right after Jay had died.

"I had an appointment today, so I took the rest of the day off."

He said nothing to her. Was she actually expecting him to? They hadn't talked but a few words here and there to each other in seven months. Should she tell him about the cancer? What would he say to her? Would he even care? Yes, of course he should care what happened to her! *Right?*

Scattered thoughts were running wild in her head. She couldn't control them. She had never been a person to sit and analyze her life; she just went out and did it. *So why now?* Why worry about what her son would think of her? Why did she feel the need to tell him about the cancer?

She rationalized that she could have the surgery and he would never know. The cancer would be gone and she wouldn't have to say a word to him, and life as they knew it would continue. But did she want life to go on with them at separate corners? With them ignoring each other when they were in the same room? She wasn't sure. She hadn't been a real mother to him in over twelve years.

Maybe she needed to sit and think about things before telling him the truth, but hadn't she thought through all this before she came home? A nagging thought in the back of her mind surfaced, *"What if something goes wrong with the surgery? What if the cancer doesn't go away?"*

Suddenly she realized, *"It was now or never."* If she didn't talk to him now, she knew she'd put everything aside and move on. She'd keep everything inside just like she'd done when Jay died.

The words out of her mouth, however, were work-related— just like always, "I just received notice that I'll be part of the crew going on the next shuttle launch."

A look of uncertainty crossed his face. Was he happy or upset about the whole thing, she couldn't tell. They sat across from each other as she smoothed her fingers across the table waiting for him to say something. She saw his mouth open, then close.

She didn't want to sit waiting for him to speak, so she broke the silence. "Should I ask if you're happy for me?" Still nothing came. "Colton, please talk to me. Tell me what you're thinking." She kept her eyes on his, waiting.

"I think it's great news, but only because I know how bad you've been wanting to go. You've worked hard at NASA to become the next to go up, but don't you think being with me is more important than going up in that stupid space shuttle?"

"That space shuttle is not stupid. And yes, I do think you're more important, more than anything. But... But this is my dream. Haven't I always told you to live your dreams no matter what?"

"Alexis, work isn't more important than family. Why is it so hard for you to understand? Dad wouldn't want you to choose your job over your family, so why are you?"

She felt a wave of tingles pass through her body as if she'd just seen a ghost. Colton didn't talk about his father. He'd never brought him up in any conversation. Maybe this was his way of getting her to listen to him. She didn't know. "I never said I was choosing work over my family. I just...I just have other priorities right now."

"You know what, Alexis? It sounds to me like you're being selfish and inconsiderate. No wonder Dad left us!" His anger was blatant.

"Wait a minute, Colton. Your father committed suicide for reasons I don't know. I didn't make him do it, he chose to!" Alexis was angry now, too.

"Maybe if you'd been at home more he wouldn't have?" he blurted out.

"Don't you dare go there? I loved your father with all my heart, and I'm sorry you think it was all my fault he took his life, but don't you think for one second I was to blame!"

"Well, I do!" He slammed his fist on the table, causing the saltshaker to fall over and spill. He wasn't going to sit here and listen to her choose work over him—again. It was always about her, always about Alexis. He pushed himself up from the table, grabbed his books, and stomped up the stairs.

She waited a few seconds then heard the bedroom door slam shut. Now, what was she going to do? She'd planned to tell him about the diagnosis; she'd decided that before she came home. Why had everything gone so wrong when she tried to talk to him? Not only did she have to decide about her health, she had her son to worry about, too.

Six

Alone now, too, Colton dropped his books on the floor and plopped down on his bed. He was used to his mother not being around. Not one part of him felt sorry for throwing his father's death in her face. He wasn't sure if he'd said it out of anger or just to hurt her.

As he stared up at the ceiling, he wondered if he truly believed the suicide had been Alexis's fault. He hadn't been able to call her "Mom" since it had all happened. Did it even matter? *No, not really.*

In exasperation, Colton rolled over on his queen-size bed and faced the wall. He was just plain disgusted with *Alexis!* He still couldn't believe how selfish she was being, but that wasn't anything new. That certainly hadn't changed since Dad died. *Hell, she hadn't really been a mother to me since, what; I was five or six years old?*

He'd tried more times than he could remember to reach out to her, but as always, work came first. Deep down he knew that was why his father had killed himself because, honestly, what other reasons could there have been? Dad must have felt as abandoned by her as Colton always had.

His father had taught him everything he needed to know about life. Dad had cared enough to be around when he got home from school. They talked all the time and hung out together, playing basketball and other stuff.

That's why his father's death bothered him so much. Colton hadn't seen it coming. Shouldn't he have noticed something was wrong since they'd spent so much time together? Yet, the thought had never crossed his mind. *Why, Dad, why? How I wish you could tell me things like you used to! I don't know how to deal with her, either!*

Colton closed his eyes as the sadness overwhelmed him; tears escaping from his tightly squeezed eyelids. He'd be damned if he ever let *her* know he cried. His mother certainly didn't seem that torn up over it. She just went back to work like nothing had ever happened. As anger filled him, he was able to control his tears.

Yes, his father had killed himself, but there seemed to be something not quite right about the whole thing. He'd gone to the police without his mother knowing and questioned them again, but the detective-in-charge had said there was no mistake. The evidence showed suicide—case closed—but Colton was still uncertain about his father's death and started his own search. He wasn't an investigator or anything, but he knew how to follow the trail since he'd been closest to Dad. So far, he'd found nothing, and it was so frustrating! He knew there was more to it than everyone else believed. He knew his father.

Colton reluctantly crawled out of bed, picked up his books, and set them on the bed. He wasn't in the mood to do his homework, which didn't surprise him; he hadn't been in the mood for months. He used to be a good student with A's and B's in all his classes. Well, at least until his father's death.

He didn't need to study hard because it came naturally to him. Most of his friends would say he was a *geek,* instead of a jock. Most jocks he knew didn't give a crap about what grades they got in school, but he did because he wanted to get the hell out of the house and away from his so-called mother. He'd been taking care of himself for the past seven months. Now, all of a sudden, she wanted to be his friend and his mother. Maybe she could forget and forgive, but he couldn't. He knew people didn't just wake up one morning and everything was okay as if it never happened.

He combed a hand through his sandy blond hair, puffed the pillow against the headboard, and grabbed his history book. He leaned back, then changed his mind and tossed the book aside. He opened the drawer next to his bed, pulled out a folder, and started rereading the report about his father's suicide.

Seven

A few hours later, Colton stacked his books on the desk by the wall and went into the bathroom. When he came out he could hear his mom calling upstairs that it was time to eat, which was odd considering they never ate together. A sarcastic thought crossed his mind; he should write it down on the calendar like this was a special event of some kind, *the first real dinner with my mom*. He shook his head and laughed, then opened the bedroom door. He took the steps two at a time as he made his way downstairs.

His mom had the table set like they were expecting company; this was something she never did. He went to the refrigerator, grabbed a Coke from the bottom drawer, and sat down.

As they ate a simple dinner of defrosted chicken breast, vegetables, and instant mashed potatoes, the room was silent except for the *clacking* of forks when they hit the plate. He didn't feel much like talking and was hoping she felt the same.

When he'd finished, he took his plate to the sink, rinsed it, and set it inside the dishwasher. "I'll be in my room," he said before leaving.

Alexis hadn't even acknowledged his presence in the room. Colton turned and climbed the stairs, leaving her alone again.

~ ~ ~ ~ ~

Colton sat down at his desk and opened his algebra book. An hour later, he had finished his homework, but wasn't in the mood to work on the other assignments. He stood and walked over to his bed, lifted the corner of the mattress and grabbed a small plastic bag. He opened the bag and took out his last rolled joint. He would have to find a way to get some more papers for the leftover marijuana. He sealed the bag and placed it back under the mattress.

Colton glanced at the clock and saw it was almost nine. He knew his mom would be in her room getting ready for bed. He opened the door to his bedroom and looked around the corner. Her door was closed. He placed something on his bed, then grabbed his books and jacket from the back of the chair and headed downstairs, trying not to step on the boards that squeaked.

Once outside, he trotted to his car and sat behind the wheel. Colton had snuck out of the house many times before and knew to manually turn the headlights off until he was driving down the road.

Fifteen minutes later, he pulled into the park and cut the engine next to a big willow tree. He climbed out and made his way to the base of the tree. He pulled out the joint, lit up, and inhaled. He plopped down on the ground and rested his back against the tree, looking out over the lake.

Colton pictured in his mind of all the times his dad had brought him here. He felt closer to him when he was at the lake. The lake was a place he could come and escape from his life.

He took another drag, filling up his lungs. He held it and then exhaled. He closed his eyes and pictured his father sitting beside him. His dad baiting the hook and casting the line. They would sit for hours fishing in this same spot; practically every weekend since he was a small boy.

Sometimes his dad would take pictures of the fish they caught, before throwing them back in the water. There were a few times his dad would have someone who stopped to chat take pictures of them together, father and son. He wondered in that moment what had happened to those few photos of them together? They weren't framed and placed in the family room or on the wall. God forbid, family pictures were anywhere near his mother's precious art that she collected. Could his mom have put them away after the funeral? He didn't know and he didn't really want to ask her about them. *It would just give her another reason to work later,* he thought. *That was her answer to everything!*

Colton took the last hit of his joint and stubbed it out on the ground with his shoe. Moving away from the tree, he lay down on the grass and searched the sky. He found the Big Dipper and then looked for the Little Dipper that wasn't far behind. His dad used to bring him to the lake before it got dark, and they would lie on the ground just like he was now, pointing out all the constellations.

Colton fished his phone out from his jeans' pocket and glanced at the time; it was a little past eleven. He texted his friend Jake and asked if he could come over. Jake replied, *"Sure."* Colton bounced to his feet and climbed back into the car. He glanced out at the lake one last time before driving off.

Eight

Alexis reached her hand out from under the blanket and silenced the alarm clock. She moaned and rolled onto her back. All night she'd tossed and turned, only to fall asleep a few hours before the loud and annoying blare of her alarm jolted her awake.

When Alexis opened her eyes, the memories of yesterday came swarming back. Last night she'd crawled into bed, only to lie there and think about what the doctor had told her. And yet, Alexis still hadn't made a decision on what she would do. Work was what she needed to clear her mind and get things into perspective.

Alexis threw her legs over the side, slid into her slippers, then stood up and grabbed the robe hanging from the bedpost. After using the bathroom, Alexis tied the robe around her thin waist. She opened the bedroom door; the smell of fresh brewed coffee awaited her. She breathed in through her nose, and her mouth watered as if she could taste the warm coffee going down her throat. She quickened her pace to the kitchen and poured a cup, then unlocked the sliding glass door to the deck and went outside.

The sun peeked through the trees as she took a seat near the railing. Reclining back, she took a long sip from her cup. A slight breeze jostled her hair and she smiled. For a quick second she'd forgotten about all the worries of yesterday, only to have them come rushing back to dim the beauty of the morning. She sighed and took another drink. She sat outside a few more minutes, trying not to think about it, then ventured back in to refill her cup and wake up Colton.

When she reached his room, she breathed in deep before tapping on the door.

"Colton, it's time to get up for school. You don't want to be late," she said, but there was no answer.

Alexis knocked again and waited a few more seconds. When she didn't hear him respond, she turned the knob and opened the door, saying his name loud enough to let him know she was coming in. Alexis didn't have to flick on the light to know that he wasn't in bed, but she did anyway. Her eyes searched the room. His bed was unmade, which told her he'd slept in it, but when? She'd never made him fix his bed in the morning. It was his room and he could keep it as messy as he wanted. She didn't have to look at it.

Alexis coasted inside and glanced around the corner where the bathroom was. She shook her head; he wasn't in there either. She walked over to his bed and saw a piece of paper lying on the sheet, which she hadn't noticed when she came in. She picked up the paper and was about to set it on his nightstand, when her eyes glanced over the words. The note stated that he was spending the night at a friend's house.

Thoughts ran through her head. *Could this mean he left last night sometime after our talk and didn't tell me? Was he so upset that he had to leave?* They'd had differences before but she didn't remember him ever leaving. Or was Alexis so consumed with work that she didn't realize he'd left the house in the middle of the night before? She had to find out what he was thinking. They needed to sit down and discuss the rules of the house.

A *ping* inside struck at her heart. Jay had been the one to take care of Colton because she'd been too busy at work. By the time she'd arrived home every night, her son was in his room. She'd been too tired most nights to even go in and see him. Was she neglecting her son by trying to give him some space? Was Alexis without realizing it, pushing him away? If so, she knew she needed to become part of his life and fix what was broken. She felt like she'd been sleepwalking through her home life and too caught up in the excitement and pressures at work.

Alexis walked back into the kitchen and picked up the phone. She dialed her son's cellphone number and waited for him to answer. Biting her lip, the call went straight to voicemail. When the beep came, she left a message, stating she wanted him to call her. Alexis set the phone down, grabbed her cup, and went into her bedroom. She quickly showered and dressed, then hurried back to the kitchen to see if he'd called her cell.

Nothing.

Alexis glanced at the clock on the wall, grabbed her keys and purse. She wanted to catch him before he left for school.

~ ~ ~ ~ ~

Alexis drove down the road, glancing at her phone as if willing it to ring. She took the first right, drove to Bracer Street then made a left. Colton's car was parked along the side of the street. She pulled in behind it and shifted into park.

The clock on the dash read seven-ten; school started at seven-forty. She decided to wait before heading over to see if he came out of the house.

After several minutes, she grabbed the car door handle and stepped out, at the same time the door to Jake's house opened. Jake stepped out and Colton followed behind him. She closed the door and leaned against her car, waiting for him to cross the street. Her son looked at her, then away. She heard Jake telling

Colton that he'd see him at school. Colton nodded, then walked towards her. She'd told herself on the drive over not to get upset with him—to keep her cool.

"Alexis, what are you doing here?"

"What did I tell you about calling me that?"

"Why are you here?" He was not in the mood to talk to her. Why couldn't she leave well enough alone and do what she'd always done, stay out of his business, his life.

"I wanted to talk to you before you left for school. I went into your room and you weren't there. I found your note that you were staying at a friend's house."

"How did you know I was at Jake's? I'm surprised you even know who my friends are," he stated sarcastically.

"I didn't, but I do remember your father telling me about your friend called Jake and he mentioned where he lived, so I figured I'd drive by and see if I saw your car."

"And what if I wasn't here?" he asked. Surprised that she cared at all where he was and with whom. No, actually he was more shocked that she'd paid any attention to what his father had said.

"I don't know, I didn't think that far ahead. Does it really matter?"

"I guess not. So what did you need to talk to me about?"

"I think you know, but you also need to get to school. So promise me you'll come straight home afterwards. We need to talk about everything that's happened."

"Yeah, sure, okay."

"Promise me."

"Okay, okay. I promise."

"I'm going into work to let them know I'll be taking a few days off, so I'll be home when you get back?" her voice raised slightly in a question, almost pleading.

No smile surfaced, which told her either he didn't believe her or that he didn't care what she did. Her heart ached, knowing she had chosen work over her own son in the past. She'd made herself a promise before leaving the house—from now on Colton would come first, before anything else in her life.

"I gotta go. I'll see you after school."

She reached out to hug him, but he took a few steps back, turned, and climbed into his car. He didn't know what to think about a hug from his normally stand-offish mother.

Alexis watched as Colton drove off down the road, turning left at the corner. She stood beside her car a few more minutes after he drove away. Her heart pulsated; she could feel herself changing inside. Something she hadn't felt in a long time— sadness.

For so long, she'd done nothing but work, accomplishing her goals and dreams of being a mother and an astronaut. Somewhere along the line, she'd stopped being the mother she once was and focused only on her job, her career.

When Alexis first met Jay, she was happy and in love. When she'd become a mother, she was filled with happiness, but she'd sensed there was something missing inside her. That's when she'd realized what she'd given up.

The year Alexis got pregnant, she had just finished getting her Bachelors of Science Degree, majoring in engineering, biological science, and minoring in physical science and mathematics. It wasn't until Colton was five that she'd started putting in her 1,000 hours of pilot-in-command.

Years flew by, waiting patiently to be chosen for the space shuttle launch. Five weeks ago, she had completed her physical for NASA, and was told she had passed with flying colors. It was just to test basic eyesight, blood pressure, height, and weight. The doctors at NASA never checked her blood for any chance of cancer or some other disease. *Did they?* If they did, then the doctor would've told her. Wouldn't they? She wasn't sure.

Nine

Twenty minutes later, Alexis arrived at NASA and was heading down the long corridor to her boss's office, which was just a few doors down from hers. The door was closed. She knocked, waiting for Fred Simon to answer.

"Come in."

Alexis took in a deep breath, exhaled, and turned the knob. She didn't plan to tell Fred the real reason for taking a few days off and prayed he wouldn't ask. She stepped inside, closing the door behind her.

"Hello, Alexis. What brings you in to see me?"

Alexis had only been in Fred's office a few times and nothing seemed any different from before. The same old diplomas and plaques were scattered on the wall, along with a portrait of a space shuttle, directly behind him.

As she walked forward, her body became stiff—she was dreading the conversation she was about to have with her boss. She could turn around now, say it wasn't anything important, and walk out the door, but she knew she had to take some time off work. This was something she had no control over. Fred would want to know what was wrong if she called into work and said she was going to be out for a while, so she saw no other choice than to use her vacation days. He didn't need to know about the cancer or the surgery. She'd be back to work in no time.

With a sudden burst of confidence, she quickened her step and took a seat in front of the desk, setting her purse in her lap. Her eyes rose from the desk to his face. The beard he'd once had was now a goatee, and his hair was a salt-and-pepper blend. Fred smiled at her, his eyes a grayish blue.

"Hello, Fred. I came in to talk to you about taking a few days off work." Alexis knew he would probably ask questions. She never missed work or asked for vacation time.

A dazed look surfaced. "Is everything okay?"

"I have some personal things I need to take care of."

"Well, sure, I understand, just surprised. You've been working for me for ten years and the only time you have taken off was..." Fred's voice trailed off.

Alexis nodded. "I just need to take a few days off. That is, of course, if you agree?"

"Certainly." He opened a drawer to his right, took out a sheet of paper, and started to write. "I'm assuming you would like to start today?"

"Yes."

"Just a few days are all you'll need?"

"Yes, a few days should be plenty." Music came from inside her purse; Alexis reached in, pulled out her phone, and pressed the side button. The room fell silent. It was a number she hadn't seen before and dropped the phone back in her purse. "Sorry about that."

"No problem." He tapped the keys on his keyboard and spoke, "I see here you have nine weeks' worth of vacation you haven't taken."

"Oh, I wasn't aware." Alexis thought for a moment then replied, "Could I take a full week off instead?"

"Sure, sure. The way I see it, you haven't missed hardly any work since the day you started here, so for you to come in and ask for time off, there must be something important to take care of."

"Thanks, and yes there is."

"Well, then it's settled. You go and take care of whatever you need to, and I'll see you in a week." Fred Simon looked down, signed his name, and handed her the paper. Alexis read over the form and signed her name on the line indicated, then handed the sheet back.

She said, "Thank you," and left his office.

Alexis walked down the hall and opened the door to her office, shutting it behind her. She took a seat behind her desk and turned on the computer. She checked over her emails, and then typed in a forwarding email address that she used at home. When she'd finished, Alexis reached in her purse and took out her phone.

The person who had called had left a voicemail. She listened to the message and then hit delete. Alexis hadn't spoken to her friend Carla Michaels, since Jay's funeral seven months ago. She'd been so busy with work that she hadn't kept in contact with her. Alexis felt ashamed of herself for neglecting the people who cared and loved her the most. She hated to admit it, but if it weren't for the breast cancer diagnosis, she would have continued pushing everyone who loved her…away.

Alexis thought to herself, *"And I'll be going into outer space, or will I?"* She felt as if her world had turned upside down and yet at the same time, maybe the universe was showing her what she was missing.

Alexis didn't want to think about the conversation she might need to have with Fred when she returned to work. Hell, she didn't want to think about not going into space—period! She needed to stay positive and hope things went smoothly so there would still be a chance she could fulfill her dream.

Alexis scrolled through the contacts on her phone. When she found Carla's name, she tapped the number, but it went straight to voicemail.

"That's weird," Alexis mumbled. She left a short message, hung up, and then decided to call the number she hadn't recognized on the recent call list. Two rings later, a voice came on the other end.

"Hello, Silver Cross Hospital, how may I direct your call?" a woman with a perky voice answered.

Hospital? Why would she...

"Hello," the voice said again."

"Hi, I received a call from this number a few minutes ago. By chance is there a Carla Michaels at this hospital?"

"Let me check for you. Can you please hold?"

"Yes, I can hold." *I hope nothing has happened to her,* Alexis thought.

The perky woman came back on the line. "Yes, we have a Carla Michaels; she's in room 303. Do you want me to transfer the call to her room?"

"Yes, that would be wonderful, thank you."

"Just one moment." Music played in her ear as she waited for Carla to pick up.

"Hello."

"Carla?"

"Yes, this is Carla. May I ask who's calling?"

"It's Alexis."

"Alexis, oh my God, it's so nice to hear from you. I take it you got my message?"

"Yes, yes I did. Is everything okay?"

"I'm fine, now."

"What's wrong? Why are you in the hospital?"

"Well, it's a long story, but to get you up to speed since… what, seven months ago?"

"Yeah, sorry it's been so long."

"Well, I was pregnant and had a daughter."

"I didn't know you were pregnant. You didn't say anything at the funeral."

"That's because I wasn't pregnant yet."

"What do you mean? It's only been seven months, not nine."

"She was early. I was only six months pregnant when I went into labor, if you want to call it that."

"Oh, dear. How is the baby doing?"

"She's in Neonatal Intensive Care Unit, NICU, right now. They're doing everything they can for her. All we can do is pray she will survive and get stronger."

The sound of Carla's sniffles filled the line between them. Alexis was speechless from what her friend had told her. She'd been so preoccupied by work she hadn't made the time to call and see how Carla was doing. *And now…now I've found out my best friend in the whole world had a premature baby and didn't know if she would survive.* Alexis thought how her life had turned upside down in a day and now this news about her friend Carla. *Is God trying to say something to me? Tell me that life is too short and I should start changing my ways before everything in my life disappears and left totally alone?"*

"Are you still there?"

"Yes, sorry. I just… I don't know what to say."

"You know I call you every few weeks, even if you don't return my calls."

"I know and I'm sorry for that. I have no excuse for not calling you back. It surprises me that you still call me."

"Are you kidding? You're my best friend and I know you work all the time, but you'll always be my friend no matter what happens. Besides, I knew you were going through a tough time when Jay died and all, but I figured once time passed you would reach out to me."

Alexis sat at her desk thinking about the words Carla had just spoken. *"How could I have been so selfish not to keep in contact with her? How many other things have I missed out on?"*

"Carla, I'm so sorry about not being a good friend to you."

"You are a good friend. What would make you say that? Look, it's not important. What matters now is that you called, and we're talking?"

"I guess you're right."

"Yeah, I am." They both laughed. "So, when do you think you can take time off work and come for a visit?"

Alexis gasped. How could she tell her friend what was going on with her? That right now was not a good time. "I have to go through my schedule first and see what I can do," Alexis responded, hoping Carla wouldn't question her.

"Okay, I guess. I do hope you can make time to see me. I mean us."

"I promise to come visit you soon. I just have a few things going on at the moment."

"I'll hold you to that promise."

"I know you will. Well, I'd better go. I have some things to take care of, but I'll call you soon."

"Alexis?"

"Yes."

"Is everything okay with you? You sound like there's something wrong. Something you're not telling me."

"I'm fine, really I am. No need to worry about me. Look, I'll call you soon okay? We'll talk then."

"Sure, I'll talk to you soon."

Alexis tapped the end button before Carla could say another word and stared at her phone. She wasn't ready to tell anyone about the breast cancer, especially her friend Carla. Carla Michaels was going through enough with the baby being in NICU; she didn't need to worry about anything else.

Alexis would tell Carla eventually, but now was not a good time.

Alexis's mind wandered back to the first time they'd met in college. Carla was sitting by herself in the library when Alexis walked up to her and asked if she could sit at the table with her. After a few awkward moments, they started chatting and became friends.

Carla had told Alexis that she'd moved from Ohio to Florida after she graduated high school to attend the University of Tallahassee. Of course, finding that odd, Alexis had asked why Carla moved down here when they had great schools up north. Carla had replied, "The warmer weather, of course." They both had laughed at her response and began an inseparable friendship.

In college, they'd hang out every day and did many things together, even though they were in different classes; they met up at the library and worked on their homework together. After Carla met Tim, who would become her husband, they continued to hang out. That's how Alexis met Jay Finley. Jay was Tim's best friend. Tim and Jay were both studying to be lawyers, except Jay changed classes and decided to take business and accounting, a year later.

Alexis felt guilty inside for not keeping in contact with Carla after she started her career at NASA. Even though Carla continued to reach out to her, Alexis pushed Carla aside and made work her life. She knew she'd done that with Jay and Colton as well.

With everything going on lately, she wished her son would stop the feud and acknowledge her as his mother. Even though now she knew why her son was so distant—hell, she'd be the same way if someone she loved chose their job over family! Alexis hoped one day Colton would forgive her, and they'd be a real family. She had to admit, Jay and Colton had more of a relationship than she'd ever had with Colton since he'd started school.

Alexis didn't know what else to do, but to keep trying to talk with Colton. Right now, what she needed most was to call Dr. Ramsey and set up another appointment. She wasn't going to be able to deal with anything else until she knew how this cancer was going to affect her life.

Ten

At the local high school, Colton slammed his locker door and headed to his first class. Luckily, after reading through his father's autopsy report, he had decided to do his algebra homework. He knew he needed to bring his grades back up if he was going to be allowed to continue playing basketball for the season. This had nothing to do with Alexis's rules. She probably didn't even know he played basketball! How embarrassing would that be? *The math geek getting kicked off the team for bad grades.*

Besides, they had a few more games left, and he was one of the best players on the team. Not that he was bragging or anything. But he didn't think his teammates would be too happy if they lost him before the team made it to the finals, which was almost a *slam-dunk* this late in the season, they'd been doing so well and who knew? They had a good chance of taking it all the way and winning the district championship this year!

That hadn't happened at his high school in many years. Now that the district had replaced the gym coach with Coach Martin, the basketball team was *unstoppable.* Colton couldn't help remembering with a *pang of pain* how proud *Dad would be over this. He couldn't let Dad down. There was a part of Colton that believed his father watched him from heaven or some place in the hereafter, even though he wasn't sure how he felt about that religious stuff.*

Colton took his seat and pulled out his algebra notebook. Jake sat down next to him and asked Colton if he'd finished his homework. As always, Colton placed his homework paper on the side of the desk so Jake could copy down the answers. Colton knew it was wrong, but he also—like all the other players on the team—needed Jake to play on Saturday.

"Okay, students, quiet down. If you did your homework last night then you shouldn't have a problem with the pop quiz I'm about to hand out," Mrs. McNickle said, shouting over the students who were still chatting among themselves.

Jake mumbled, "Crap."

Colton chuckled, "Guess you should've done your own homework."

"How hard can it be anyway?" Jake replied.

As Mrs. McNickel walked around the class setting quizzes on each of the student's desks, she picked up their homework assignment at the same time. Colton smiled after reading the first problem on the quiz. "Dude," Colton whispered. "It's the exact same problems from the homework assignment we had last night."

Jake frowned as if knowing he would fail.

Most of the class was still taking the quiz when Colton stood up and handed his in. The teacher smiled at him and nodded.

"Can I see you after class, Colton?" she whispered.

"Yeah, sure." Colton sat back down, took out his biology book and started on the homework assignment he'd never even looked through. If he planned to leave home right after high school, he needed to bring his grades back up to graduate and get into a good college. That's if he even wanted to bother with going to college, but what else could he do? Work at McDonalds the rest of his life? He wasn't too keen on that. He had one particular college in mind, Jacksonville University, so he could play college basketball. It was the only sport in which he truly excelled.

When class ended, he waited until everyone left and approached Mrs. McNickel.

"So, what do you need to see me about?"

"I know you're having a hard time since your father passed away. You've been neglecting your homework assignments, and the scores on your quizzes and tests are just passable. When I noticed you'd finished your quiz so quickly, I might add, I assumed you would receive a low grade." She slid a sheet of paper across the desk. He glanced down and looked back up at her.

"An A+?"

"Yes, shocking I know. You got an A+ on your homework assignment as well. So, my reasons for having you stay after class were to see if you needed help with tutoring or something, but I guess you've decided to apply yourself."

"Basketball," Colton blurted out.

"I figured as much. If you ever need someone to talk to, Mr. Shoebe, the guidance counselor, is available for all the students."

Colton nodded, ducking his head to hide his blush.

"Here's a pass to your next class, Colton. Oh, and great job on the quiz and homework assignment."

"Thank you." Colton grabbed the slip and went out the door, never making eye contact with one of his favorite teachers.

In each class Colton went to, he was able to work on the homework for the next class he'd failed to do the night before by rushing through his in-class work. By the end of the school day, Colton's spirits had lifted and he'd forgot all about promising Alexis to go straight home after school. He was on a mental high, knowing he could catch up with his schoolwork and not let down his team, or his father. It wasn't even a conscious decision to meet up with Jake and a few other guys from the team and play basketball.

After they'd finished playing basketball, Colton and his teammates went to Moe's Pizzeria. Hours later, he glanced at his phone and it dawned on him he'd forgotten about going home right after school to talk to Alexis. He felt a little guilty because he usually kept his promises to everyone.

Colton stood up and shoved the phone back in his pocket. *"Oh well, too late now. Look at how many times she's let me down!"*

"I'll see you guys tomorrow," Colton said as he turned and walked out of the restaurant and to his car. Time to go home and face the music, but he wasn't really worried about it. Anger had crept back into his feelings concerning his *absentee* mother. She'd probably forgotten all about it anyway and was working late, too. *Story of his life!*

Eleven

Earlier that morning, only an hour after Alexis left NASA, she sat in the parking lot at the medical center, trying to persuade herself to go forward with the surgery. When she'd called for an appointment, she'd been pleased that Dr. Ramsey could see her immediately, but now she was reluctant to take the next step. *I've been through all this! I need to do this!*

She knew she had to think of Colton and have the surgery for him, though she needed to do this for herself as well. She wasn't ready to give up on her life—there was still too much she wanted to do. "Okay, here goes nothing," she softly said out loud.

She exited the car, made her way inside, and headed to the elevators. Once outside Dr. Sarah Ramsey's door, she took in a deep breath and knocked.

"It's open."

Sarah Ramsey was perched behind her desk, talking to a man who sat in one of the leather chairs in front of her.

"Please, sit down, Alexis."

Alexis made her way to the empty chair and glanced apprehensively at the man who was now seated right next to her.

"This is Dr. Brownski, he's the Oncologist over at the Anderson Cancer Center I told you about. He will be the doctor performing your surgery. I called him as soon as we hung up, and he told me he was available to come and see you today."

Alexis smiled and nodded at him; he did the same.

"We were just going over your test results, and Dr. Brownski wants to set you up for the lumpectomy on Friday." There was a warm smile on Sarah's face, but Alexis could sense her firmness as well.

"This Friday?" Alexis questioned with a surprised look on her face.

"Yes, will that be a problem for you?" Dr. Brownski replied.

"No, I just thought… Well, I thought it would be a while before the surgery."

"No, breast cancer is very serious, and we like to start as soon as the results show any tumors. The cancer tends to spread quite fast, so the sooner we start the better the outcome," Dr. Brownski said. He smiled encouragingly at Alexis, but his tone was firm as well.

Alexis nodded. "Friday, it is then. What time should I be there?"

"I have an opening at ten in the morning. You should be there at least one hour prior to the surgery. No food or liquids after midnight the evening before. Unless, of course, you have any medications that need to be taken, but Dr. Ramsey has already confirmed that you are not on any prescriptions. Is that correct?"

"Yes, that's right."

"You will need someone to bring you and pick you up, or they can stay at the hospital during the lumpectomy procedure."

Alexis thought about what Dr. Brownski had said—someone *else* to drive to and from the Anderson Cancer Center. She could only think of Colton, but she hadn't told him about the cancer. She wanted to, but she couldn't find it in herself to tell him, not yet. There were too many other issues between them right now. She wasn't feeling too happy about having him there while she went through the surgery anyway; besides, he had to go to school. *But, there was no one else!*

Alexis didn't have any close friends or family in the area. Nearly everyone she knew lived up north, and Carla wouldn't be able to come down. Carla had enough going on in her life. Alexis had a few so-called friends at work, but no one she felt close to; anyway, she wasn't ready for her boss to find out about her medical condition.

"Alexis, are you feeling okay?" Sarah asked.

"What? Yeah, I'm fine. Was just thinking who I can ask to go with me on Friday."

"Alexis, if you don't want your son to go, I have the day off on Friday. I can take you to the hospital and home?" Sarah suggested.

"Oh, well, I don't want to bother you. I'm sure I can find someone."

"It's no problem, really. I wouldn't mind helping you out with this. I know there's been a lot for you to digest, but you're doing the right thing. I would love to help you out." Again, that warm, caring smile.

"All right, thank you," Alexis nodded, humbled by Sarah's offer…of support and, well, friendship, but it was frightening, too, that the doctor thought it was so serious she'd spend her day off work, taking her to the hospital.

It dawned on Alexis in a flash that Dr. Brownski had said "tumors"—more than one? A breath caught in her throat; a panic attack was threating.

"When you show up on Friday, the nurse and I will go over everything we'll be doing in surgery, so you'll be aware of the procedure. Do you have any questions for me at this moment?" Dr. Brownski asked.

"No, not at this time," Alexis managed to stammer.

"Good, I will see you Friday morning. I have to head back to the hospital now. I have some afternoon patients coming in."

Dr. Ramsey stood and walked Brownski out, then returned to her chair. "You'll probably need to take some time off work for a while. Maybe a week or so, depending on how you feel after the surgery."

"I just talked to my boss this morning, but I'm sure he'll extend my leave if I ask him to," Alexis practically whispered.

"Great, it would be good for you to spend some time with your son, and for yourself as well. I suggest after the first couple of treatments, it would be a good idea for you to join a talk group called *Blossom Buddies*. It's a support group for breast cancer patients. It will help you to talk to other women who are going through the same thing you are. I'm not sure what's going through your mind as we speak, but the women in the group have lived to talk about their cancer, and some may still be fighting the disease. You're not alone, Alexis. Here's a pamphlet about the talk group. Read over it and maybe sit in for a session or two. See how you like it." Sarah handed Alexis the pamphlet and without looking at it, she stuck the brochure in her purse.

Sarah was concerned that Alexis had nothing to say, so different from the angry denial of yesterday. Ramsey continued to fill the silence. "I'll pick you up at your place Friday morning; let's say around eight-fifteen. It would probably be best if you wear something simple to get in and out of, like sweats or something."

Alexis sat in the chair with her head down, not speaking a word. She couldn't find it in herself to even look at Dr. Ramsey. She knew this wasn't *her*. She never froze up like this. This whole cancer thing was changing her into a person she wasn't familiar with. *But all in all*, change *wasn't always a bad thing, was it?*

Alexis couldn't even comprehend that now. She felt broadsided. *Treatments—how many treatments? How sick am I?* Yet, she couldn't find her voice to ask.

Sarah Ramsey realized that Alexis had finally accepted the seriousness of the situation, which was good, but it was so hard to watch this active, vivacious woman crumble before her very eyes.

Alexis agreed she needed to spend more time with Colton and less time working. The cancer had shown up when she'd least expected it. Maybe it was a sign. A sign to start living her life with friends and family and not working every damn second of the day. Alexis rolled her shoulders back, feeling the tension ball up in her shoulders and neck. She lifted her head and finally looked at Sarah.

"Yes, I'll see you on Friday morning." Alexis forced herself to speak as she stood up and walked out of the office. The door clicked shut behind her. She leaned against the wall and took in deep breaths. In just two days, her life would change completely.

Twelve

Alexis left the Medical Center, stopped at the grocery store, and then headed home. It was going on eleven, and she already felt exhausted from the stress she'd endured this morning. In a few hours, Colton would be home from school, and they would need to talk.

Alexis thought about laying down for an hour or so, but decided against the idea. She had too many things to do before Friday. Laundry, preparing meals for her and Colton, she knew he'd have to eat while she was recuperating, and cleaning up around the house. She put the groceries away and went into her room. Gathering up her laundry and putting it in the basket, she felt a little better now that she was doing something constructive.

Next, she headed to Colton's room. When Alexis walked in, Colton had clothes scattered all over the floor. She couldn't tell what was clean or what was dirty, so she picked up the clothes off the floor and off the chair, and tossed them in the basket. The drawers to his dresser were half open, so she decided to fold the clothes that were all jumbled up and set them neatly inside. Yes, she felt good doing something for her son.

While she was in his room, she decided to freshen up his sheets, which looked like he hadn't changed them in a long while. Alexis lifted the corner of the mattress to fit the clean sheet when her hands touched something that felt like plastic. She lifted the mattress higher to get a better look and pulled out a bag. Her face went pale as she stared at the contents. She opened the bag to confirm what she'd already known.

Marijuana.

"Where in the hell did he get this?" she mumbled out loud. She sealed the bag and stuffed it in her pocket.

Colton should be grateful he was at school at the moment. Alexis was disappointed and angry with him. She needed to calm down and think things over before he came home. She couldn't get past the thought of her son smoking pot. *What was he thinking? Doesn't he know drugs are bad for him? That drugs can harm you or kill you if you abuse them?* She thought to herself, *"Colton should know better!"*

Her head was jammed with so many questions, but none would be answered until Colton returned home. She finished making the bed, collected dirty glasses, and emptied his garbage can. She wasn't the kind of mom who snooped through her son's personal belongings, but she couldn't resist after what she had just found. Alexis knew it was wrong, but she needed to search the rest of his room, if only to ease her mind he wasn't hiding anything else from her.

She found nothing.

She threw a load in the washer and headed to the kitchen to occupy her time. By three, Alexis had a pan of lasagna and a chicken potpie. Colton's favorite meals prepared and cooked. She placed the containers in the refrigerator and returned to the stove to stir the beef stew that was simmering for dinner tonight.

By the time the stew was ready, and she'd finished drying and putting the dishes away, Colton hadn't come home. He had promised to be here after school, but he'd lied to her. Minutes ticked by and still no Colton. Alexis tried calling his cellphone, but it went straight to voicemail.

The time was going on six and he still wasn't home. She turned off the stove and went over to the sofa in the family room to lie down.

Minutes later, Alexis sprang to a sitting position when the front door squeaked open.

"Hello," she called out.

"Hey, Alexis, I'm home," Colton responded, sounding more cheerful then he had been this morning.

Alexis closed her eyes, breathed in, and then exhaled a deep sigh. *At least he was all right.* She walked to the foyer where Colton stood.

"Where have you been? You were supposed to come home after school."

"Oh, that. Sorry, must've forgot. I stayed after school to shoot hoops with the guys and then went out for pizza."

"Well, you should've called and told me. I was worried, you know, and I called several times." She knew she had to sit down and talk to him about the drugs she'd found in his room.

Colton slipped by her and walked to the table in the kitchen. She followed behind him like a mother watching over her baby walking for the first time.

"Do you have a lot of homework to do?"

A look of surprise surfaced on his face. "You've never asked me that before."

"Oh, I haven't?"

"No, you were always busy with work. Dad was the one who was around and cared about school and stuff."

Her heart sank. "I know and I'm sorry for that. I guess I was always thinking of myself, but now I want to put you first in my life." She watched as he grabbed the chair in front of him as if he were about to faint.

"Wow, Alexis, that's a first," he said sarcastically.

She frowned at his childish display, then pulled a chair out and sat down. "Sit down, we need to talk," Alexis ordered.

They gazed at each other; then Colton did as she asked.

"Before you run off to your room, there are a few things I would like to talk to you about."

"Okay, shoot."

"First, I want you to know how sorry I am that I was always too busy with work to be the mom you needed." She kept her eyes on him. A look of sadness appeared on his face. "Second, I want you to know that there are rules in this house you will need to follow." She tapped her forefinger on the table. "I may have been too busy before to care or notice what you were doing, but I am here now, and you *will* follow the rules I am about to enforce."

His mouth opened then closed, too shocked to speak.

"You will no longer be allowed to sneak out of the house. You will have to tell me where you're going and when you'll be back. I want to know you're safe. I am truly sorry that I have never showed you how much I care, but I do. I know there's no excuse for the way things have been, and I do apologize." She swallowed. "I would like a second chance to make things right again and be the mother I should've been to you a long time ago."

She wasn't sure where all this was coming from—having never shared her feelings openly with anyone. She'd always tried hard to keep herself detached; she let others show and give her love, but she didn't allow herself to give freely to anyone. A thought came barreling into her mind, that maybe, just maybe, Jay couldn't live like that any longer, so the only way out was suicide. Although, that seemed selfish to her. Jay could've talked to her, but maybe he'd tried and she'd been too busy to listen. Well, no more! Alexis was going to change the person she once was and be a better person to everyone, especially her son. She'd realized with a sense of guilt that she didn't like the person she had become in the past. Maybe change could be good?

Colton cleared his throat, bringing her out of her thoughts. "Are we done now?"

"No, we are not finished yet. There's one more thing I need to confront you with."

He looked at her as if she had two heads.

"I was in your room today, cleaning. When I put some clean sheets on your bed, I found this." Not taking her eyes off him, she pulled the plastic bag from her pocket and placed it on the table in front of her.

His eyes widened and his face showed fear, which then abruptly changed to anger.

"What were you doing in my room?" Colton huffed.

"I told you and besides, does it matter why? This is my house, and I'm allowed in any room I choose," she replied, not allowing him to defeat her.

"But…but you never go in there, except to make sure I'm up for school. Why would you start now?"

"Well, things have changed, and I am trying to be different now. I want to get to know my son I've neglected all these years. Colton, aren't you aware of the effects drugs have on people? How bad they are? When pot isn't enough, what will you do next? Start drinking or experimenting with cocaine? The list goes on and on. I want to know why you're doing drugs! What made you turn to them? Was it because I was too busy and not around? You need to talk to me, please!"

Her throat was parched from all the words she'd spoken. She swallowed, but the saliva didn't help much. All the questions she had rolling around in her mind earlier had surfaced. She wished he'd say something. She didn't even care if they yelled at one another as long as they were talking. "Talk to me please. Tell me what you're thinking? What do I need to do or say to have you understand that I want to be the mother you should've had? How often do you smoke this? Colton, I want answers, now!" Alexis demanded. She sat back in the chair trying to relieve some of the tension building up again in her back and shoulders.

"I started smoking marijuana right after Dad died. You were never around, and it helped me cope with the loss. It's not like I smoke it every day, just once or twice a week."

"Where did you get it from? Who sold it to you?"

"I got it from some guy, but I'm not giving you names. I won't be a nark."

"Fine, but just so you know, I don't want you smoking pot anymore. Drugs will not make things better. They will not make the problem go away. You could end up in jail or worse—dead. I know that kids your age do drugs; I wasn't born yesterday. I had friends in school who drank and did drugs, but I opted out and you know what? They still remained my friends. Now, I know you said you did this because of losing your father and I wasn't around, but the longer you do these things the more you'll want them. When one drug doesn't give you the satisfaction you once had, you'll find it in another and so on. You are an extremely smart kid and your grades are outstanding; no one would assume you were doing anything illegal. So, will you promise me you'll stop smoking pot and not do any other drugs? I want you to talk to me if anything is bothering you." Alexis was surprised at herself that she'd been able to get all that out. She was even more surprised that he'd let her finish what she had to say.

"I can't promise, but I guess I'll try," he agreed reluctantly.

"I'm not pleased with your answer, but at least you're being honest, so I guess I'll have to trust that you'll make the right decision."

Alexis stood and motioned for him to follow. She made her way to the washroom in the hall and handed him the bag. She lifted the toilet seat and waited for him to dump the contents. When he did, she pushed the lever on the side and watched it disappear. She turned and embraced him in a hug; he responded with an awkward pat on her back. She frowned, but managed to convince herself that in time he would love her back. She couldn't blame him for being cold towards her, but hoped he'd forgive her someday. He pulled away and walked back into the kitchen, grabbing his books off the table.

"I got some homework to do. I'll be in my room."

She nodded and watched him leave the room. When Alexis heard the door to his room clink shut, she fell to the floor and placed her head in her hands. Tears came as she heard him throwing things across the room and scraping something over the floor. He'd been so quiet, so aloof, she didn't realize until she heard him trashing his room through the ceiling how furious he'd been at her. Things weren't getting better. They were only getting worse!

Thirteen

Colton threw his books on the bed and kicked his chair, which ricocheted off the desk. He was beyond mad and wanted so much to punch something, anything! He looked around his room, finding it too clean for his liking.

"She needs to stay out of my room and out of my life," he mumbled. "What the heck was she even doing, nosing around in my room—it's so unlike her." He wasn't sure if he liked this new person, his mom was becoming. *Why now does she have to start caring and butting into my business? Why can't she just leave well enough alone?* His thoughts were vicious cries in his mind. Had there ever been a time when he'd wanted her to care? *Maybe, but not now!*

Colton opened his closet door and went inside. In the far back corner, he moved a framed picture leaning up against the wall and stuck his hand in the hole. He pulled out a small box and made his way back into his bedroom, where he could see. He opened the small box, but it was empty inside.

"Damn it to hell," he cursed, throwing the box at the bed. He couldn't remember the last time he'd gone into his closet and used up the rest of his pot—the stash his *mother* had found was now flushed down the toilet.

He sat down on the edge of the bed, firmly pressing his fingertips into his scalp and temples as he shook his head back and forth. He was distraught with confusion and rage. His brain was whirling with questions; guilt he didn't want to admit, and *so much anger!*

Maybe she was right and he had become addicted to marijuana, but he didn't think so. The guys he hung out with didn't seem to have any problems with addiction. *"She doesn't know anything about it, so how can she judge me?"* he rationalized in his tangled thoughts.

For now, at least for tonight, he'd just have to do without. But wouldn't she be watching to see if he left the house at night? *Why is she taking time off from work? That doesn't make any sense at all.*

Could he learn to deal with his grief in another way? He wasn't sure how. He had to keep his mind busy and not think about his father. Colton dropped his hands and turned to face the scattered books across his bed. He'd use homework to replace his need, though he wasn't sure if that would work, but it was all he had left.

He gathered his schoolbooks and sat down at his desk. Moving the mouse, the computer came to life. Colton had a book report due on American Government tomorrow about one of the forty-four presidents; the teacher had given him Andrew Johnson. He clicked the keys on his laptop and started reading all the information he could find on President Johnson.

Three hours later, Colton finished writing his report and printed the pages. He opened the bottom drawer on the right of his desk and rummaged through looking for a report cover. After not finding one, he opened several of the other drawers and searched them. He found one in the last drawer at the bottom. He grabbed it and inserted the report.

After setting his assignment aside, as he went to close the drawer, he noticed a stack of photos.

Reaching inside, Colton pulled out the pictures and glanced through them. A few were of his father, but the others he'd never seen before. They weren't relatives of his, he was sure. His parents never had friends over or family reunions. He wasn't sure where these had come from; he didn't remember putting them in there.

A man in one of the photos looked familiar to him. He was tall with broad shoulders and had a buzz cut. The man's arm was around his father. If Colton were to imagine the man with short brown hair and older looking, he would resemble his basketball coach, Coach Martin.

Thinking back eight or nine months ago, he remembered one day coming home from school and hearing his father arguing with someone in the kitchen. When he entered, his father stopped yelling and looked at him, then told Colton to go to his room because he had some business to take care of. Colton grabbed a Coke from the refrigerator—mostly to get a look at whomever his father was yelling at—and left the room. The man in the baseball cap had turned his head away from Colton, like he was looking at something outside the sliding glass door, so he wasn't able to get a good look at him. Colton remembered standing at his bedroom door, trying to listen to what they were talking about. But since they knew he was home, they stopped yelling at each other and talked in low voices so he couldn't hear what they were saying. When the man left, Colton watched from the window of his room, but the man's back was to him so he still couldn't see his face when he got in a car and drove away. The man had been driving a dark blue Honda Accord.

Something clicked in Colton's head, and he went to his nightstand. He reached under a stack of magazines and pulled out his father's police report. His mom hadn't mentioned the file, which could mean she didn't look in the nightstand, or she did and forgot about it when she was busy reading him the riot act over harmless pot and sneaking out of the house. He knew better, though, than to think she'd forgotten about the file. She just didn't check underneath the magazines he had covering the report. *What a relief!*

Thanks to his friend, Jake, whose father worked at the police station, Jake was able to get copies of his father's file for him without anyone knowing about it. He skimmed through the pages until he found what he was looking for. A jogger had stated seeing a vehicle leaving the parking lot where his father's body was found. The description of the car was a dark blue Honda Accord. He read a paragraph stating that the car hadn't been found. Things just weren't adding up.

Maybe it would help if he talked to Detective Bowen again. He reached for his phone and searched his contacts, then hit the call button.

"Hello, Detective Bowen speaking."

"Hey, Detective, this is Colton Finley, I was wondering if I could come in and see you this evening, say in twenty minutes?"

"Colton, I'm not sure why you're calling. We've been over this before. There's nothing new on your father's case. I'm not even sure what else to tell you—no new evidence has surfaced to change the ruling of suicide. We've closed the case. I'm sorry," Bowen stated.

"That's why I'm calling you. I've found some photos, and there's a man that I remember my father meeting with several weeks before he died. The man drove away in a dark blue Accord when he left our house. The same vehicle you have recorded was at the lake where my father was found dead."

"Son, how do you know about that?"

Crap! Colton had forgotten that Jake insisted he tell no one he'd given him the report. He tried to come up with something, a lie of some sort, but he just couldn't think of anything. "Does it matter how? Can I come to the station and see you?"

"I'll be here until seven, but you'd better explain how you got ahold of a police report that we didn't make public."

"Yeah, sure. I'll be there in twenty minutes." Without giving Detective Bowen a chance to respond, he tapped a key, ended the call, and headed for the closed bedroom door.

Once downstairs, he found his mom in the kitchen and told her he had to go out for a little while, and would be back in an hour. Before she could object, he was out the door and behind the wheel of his red Grand Am.

Fourteen

Early Friday morning, Alexis stood inside the Anderson Cancer Center, looking out through the large plate-glass window at the rain pouring down all around her. She couldn't help thinking how the weather matched her gray, dismal mood while she waited patiently for Dr. Ramsey, who was parking the car. She was so glad Sarah was with her, but even this unexpected show of friendship couldn't dispel her apprehension.

Alexis couldn't believe how fast Friday had arrived. She wasn't looking forward to what the day would bring. For the last two days, Colton had come straight home from school, but he spent little time with her. He locked himself in his room, only coming out to eat dinner, where he brooded in silence. Nothing had been discussed or resolved. It weighed heavily on her mind.

What surprised her most and encouraged her somewhat was that for the last two mornings Colton was up before she was and he had breakfast and coffee waiting for her when she came into the kitchen. She hoped this was his way of showing her he was sorry for the things he had said in anger. His silence and aloofness confused her, however, she still hadn't told him about the surgery she was about to undergo. When he left the room, she was so upset she dumped out her coffee and threw her food down the disposal. She'd been so nervous all week that she had no appetite whatsoever. It was all she could do to cook and share dinner with her son, hoping he would break down his barriers and talk to her.

Alexis appreciated what he was doing for her, but she didn't know what to think about the new Colton. She hoped it wasn't just because she'd found and confronted him about the drugs. *Had they turned over a new leaf? Surely, he couldn't keep up the silent treatment for long!*

This glimmer of hope made her smile, and for the first time since their argument, she felt a hint of happiness. In the past two days they had spent together, she had apologized numerous times for not being there for him. He had said it was okay, that he forgave her, and she should just let it go. She didn't know whether he was being honest with her or not. The few scant words he'd said to her hadn't sounded very sincere. He was still calling her Alexis instead of Mom, even though he knew she didn't like it. She knew she had to make up for the past and that it wouldn't happen overnight, but if he was trying to change, then so could she. She had to change the person she once was and be the mother Colton needed in his life before it was too late.

Dr. Ramsey entered through the electronic doors and stood in front of Alexis.

"Are you ready?" Sarah asked.

Alexis blinked. "Yes, I think so."

Sarah touched her arm. "Everything will be all right. You're in good hands. Dr. Brownski will take good care of you."

Alexis exhaled a deep breath and walked up to the receptionist desk.

"I'll need your insurance card and driver's license," the woman said.

She pulled out her wallet and handed over the requested items.

"Here are some forms you need to fill out before they call you to the back for prep."

Alexis took the clipboard, nodded her thanks, and took a seat next to Sarah. When she'd finished, she returned the forms, and the receptionist gave back her cards.

Sitting in the chair, Alexis grabbed a magazine and scanned through the pages, but not really looking at anything in particular. Sarah Ramsey opened her purse and pulled out a book. Alexis glanced at the cover, "The Longest Ride" by Nicholas Sparks. She couldn't recall the last time she had read a book strictly for pleasure. Had it been fifteen or twenty years now? She couldn't remember, but knew it had been a long time—at least seventeen years because it was before Colton was born. She decided when the surgery was over; she would get back into reading again. She would start living the life she needed to live and not focus only on work. In the past few days, she had learned that life wasn't about working all the time, but rather to enjoy life, especially with her son.

"Mrs. Finley," said a woman in a flowered smock, probably a nurse.

Alexis stood and turned towards Sarah.

"I'll be here when you're done."

Alexis nodded, thankfully; no words were needed. She took another deep breath, exhaled and then walked towards the nurse. She couldn't stop her hands from shaking. Her nerves were beyond her control.

Alexis entered through the open door and stood to the side. The nurse walked down the hall with Alexis following behind. The nurse stopped and motioned her to go inside a small room. Once Alexis walked inside, the nurse pulled on the curtain. The metal clips *clinked* along the rail as the nurse zipped the cloth to close it. Every sound and every motion heightened Alexis's anxiety.

Alexis sat on the gurney, trying desperately to remain calm and listened to the nurse.

"I'll need you to change into this gown and then we'll prep you for surgery, Mrs. Finley. You can put your clothes in the bag, and we'll secure it under your bed here, so the bag will go with you."

Alexis nodded and waited for the nurse to leave before undressing. A few minutes later, the nurse asked if she was done. After replying "yes," the nurse entered. Alexis stretched out on the gurney and the nurse put a warm blanket over her. The nurse then checked Alexis's blood pressure and temperature, asked her some general questions about her health and if she'd had anything to eat or drink this morning. When the nurse finished asking all the questions she slipped out of the room and a female technician, in a light blue smock, rolled a machine next to the bed.

"I'll be doing an ultrasound on your breast to locate the tumor," the tech explained pleasantly. Everyone was being so nice with lots of smiling encouragement.

Alexis watched as the young woman applied jelly to the end of a wand. "This might feel a little cold," she warned as she untied the gown from Alexis's shoulder and circled the wand around the breast. She watched the monitor and placed a tiny wire on the location of the tumors. When she had finished, she wiped off the jelly and left the room.

The nurse with the flowered smock re-entered pushing a different cart and set it next to the bed. She put on some latex gloves, swabbed Alexis's hand, and inserted an IV, taping it into place. Alexis was glad that part was over and the nurse had found a vein so easily and painlessly. The nurse punched some numbers into the machine, and Alexis watched as fluid began to drip from a plastic bag hanging above the wheeled gurney.

"This might make you a little groggy, but it shouldn't knock you out," the nurse said with a warm smile. "We'll be using a general anesthetic while you're in surgery. The Anesthesiologist and the doctor will be in to see you soon. Do you have any questions?"

"No, not right now." Alexis noticed her voice sounded strained.

"Okay, if you should, I'll be in and out of here before they take you into surgery," the nurse responded and smiled as she patted Alexis gently on the arm. She lifted up the rail on the side of the gurney before she left.

"Thank you," Alexis replied. Whatever medicine they were giving her was already working. She was feeling more relaxed than she had for a long time. She closed her eyes and waited for Dr. Brownski. Every moment of the last fifteen minutes or so would forever be ingrained in her memory, but for now, she didn't have to worry about it.

Fifteen

Alexis didn't know how long she was there, trying only to think of good things and not what was going to be happening to her. She opened her eyes to the sound of a man's voice; Dr. Brownski stood beside her.

"How are you feeling, Alexis?"

"A little tired."

"Good, that's the medicine working to help you relax. We understand the stress you may be having towards this procedure. Before we take you back, I want to go over the surgery with you."

Alexis parted her lips, but nothing came out, so instead, she nodded for him to continue.

"I'm performing a lumpectomy on you today. The surgery will take approximately two to three hours and you'll be in post-op when you wake up. This surgery is done to remove the cancerous tumor in your breast. Depending on what we find, I would like to start you on IORT—Intraoperative radiation therapy—to help kill any remaining cancer cells. Normally, I like to give my patients chemotherapy before surgery to shrink the tumor, but from your images, the cancer doesn't seem to be too large. Ms. Shelby, our radiologist here, has already done an ultrasound and marked the spots with a small wire directly in the area of the tumors. Dr. Sears, our pathologist, will biopsy the tissues to confirm the type of cancer you have and that all of the cancer is removed before you're taken out of surgery. Sears will do more biopsies on the tissues we remove, and we'll notify you of those results. Are there any questions that you might be concerned with or would like to know more about?"

"How much tissue will you be removing?"

"That all depends on what we find and how far the cancer has spread."

"How long will it take to recover?"

"You should be fine in a few days. I will give you some more instructions after you wake up in post-op."

"Will you be able to remove all of the cancer?"

"I'll certainly do my best. If for any reason we should have to do another lumpectomy, due to the biopsies Dr. Sears will be conducting, then I have no doubt you'll be cancer-free. But..." Brownski paused. "But there are always chances of the cancer returning, so that's why we'll need to carry out radiation therapy and keep you on a treatment plan. I'll know more once you're in surgery, and I'll tell you everything we find in post-op."

Alexis said nothing and let the words soak in. She knew there was no way around this; she was here and was getting ready to go into surgery. There was no changing her mind now. She had to go through with it, if not for her then for her son.

The doctor nodded his head and said, "Everything will be fine, Alexis." He then walked out of the curtained area.

The Anesthesiologist immediately greeted Alexis, but she only vaguely listened as he spoke about the anesthetic. An orderly came in and wheeled her out of the room. She noticed the nurse was back with her with the encouraging, pleasant face. Alexis watched as the lights on the ceiling *zipped* by and then they entered a room that was no bigger than her bedroom. She tried to look around—her eyes feeling heavy—and saw numerous pieces of equipment staggered all around her. Someone grabbed her hand and placed a clip on her index finger then stretched her arm out to the side. There were several people moving around, one was Dr. Brownski, but the only other one she remembered seeing was the Anesthesiologist. She heard a voice to her left and turned, her head groggy. She couldn't quite hear what he was saying, then the man placed a small mask over her nose and mouth, and everything went dark.

Sixteen

As Colton made his way to the next class, he felt a tap on his shoulder and turned to see Jake standing behind him.

"Hey, my dad said you stopped by to see him last night."

"Yeah, I did. Why? What did he tell you?"

"He asked me if I was the one who gave you a copy of your father's report."

"What did you tell him? I didn't say it was you."

"I denied it, of course, but my dad's a smart detective. I'm sure he'll figure it out."

Colton shifted his books from one arm to the other. "I wasn't thinking when I called him last night to meet with him. He asked me how I got the police report, but I avoided the question. I thought he'd forgotten about it because he never asked me again."

"So what did you need to talk to him about?"

He filled Jake in on what he'd found at his house and what was in the report. "Your father said he would check into it and get back to me, but otherwise he thinks it's probably nothing.

I'm going to do more searching on my own. Maybe I can figure things out. They have sites on the web where you can search for public records. Maybe I'll get lucky, find the real owner of that car, and find out what really happened."

"Let me know if you need any help. No matter what my dad says, I'll do what I can to help you. I'm sure if it was the other way around, you'd do the same."

"Yeah, I would." The bell rang and they started down the hall. They split when they reached their classes. Colton went left and Jake went inside a classroom across the hall.

~~~~~

After school, Colton headed over to the library before meeting with the guys to play a game of basketball. He searched the Department of Motor Vehicles website and typed in the model of the car. No name had appeared; only an address was listed as a prior residence. He hit print, walked up to the librarian behind the counter, asked for the copy and sat back down.

He had no clue what the person's name was who was at the house that day. He tried to think back, but nothing came to him because his father never mentioned his name. Therefore, the only thing left for him to do was drive to the address he'd found.

Colton had a tough decision to make—play basketball with his friends or go to this address and, hopefully, find out the truth.

He knew what mattered more, so he texted Jake and told him that something had come up and he couldn't make it. Jake texted back, *"Okay, bro', I'll see you later."*

Once in his car, he tapped the navigation screen and inserted the address. An hour later, he turned onto the road of the address and followed it down until a small house appeared at the end of the street. There were no vehicles in the drive, and all the other houses on the street were spread acres apart. He didn't know whether to park in the driveway or along the side of the road. Parking on the road wasn't much of an option and would definitely give him away, but so would parking in the driveway. He decided to go back one street, park his vehicle and then walk to the house. He wondered if he'd decided too quickly to come here alone. *Could this be dangerous? After all, my father had been killed!*

Colton felt a little more secure since there were no cars in the driveway. He prayed no one was paying any attention to him as he walked down the road. Someone might call the police, thinking he was trying to steal something. He tried to walk as casually as possible. Once in front of the house, he turned and looked around; no one seemed to be watching him so he headed to the front door.

Instead of ringing the doorbell, he peeked in through the window to get a look around. The place had a few bits of furniture inside, but nothing else that gave him the idea that someone lived there. He opened the screen door and turned the knob, it was locked. He closed the screen and jogged around towards the back of the property. He made his way to the back door and twisted the knob, but again it was locked.

"Damn it," he mumbled out loud, "Now what?"

After checking all the windows around back—all locked—he felt he had no other choice but to break a window to get in. He had never broken the law before and didn't want to start now, but he had come this far and didn't want to turn back with no more answers than he'd had before.

He looked around the backyard for something to break a window with and found a rock the size of his palm. He stood in front of the window, lifted his hand, and froze. Was he hearing things, or did he *for sure* hear the sound of gravel crunching?

In agonizing fear, Colton dropped the rock and threw himself against the house. He slinked his way along the wall and peeked around the corner, hoping to see who was in the driveway. The sound of a vehicle on gravel that he'd thought he'd heard was gone, but then a car door slammed; he was sure someone else was here.

Scoping out the landscape for a place to hide, he saw an old Ford pickup, half-covered in moss under a torn-up tarp. He knew his best chance for not being caught would be to wait until dark, unless he was able to cut through the woods beside him.

He wanted to see who was in the house, though. *Was it the man his father had been arguing with?*

The kitchen light flickered on. Colton knelt down to hide, nervous with sweat dripping down his back under his shirt. He knew he had to be visible from the window if he could see in, but there was no one, not a single shadow or figure came into view. Colton knew he should feel relieved to be safe, but he was overwhelmed with disappointment. *I have to find out something, anything! I have to know who killed Dad because he sure didn't commit suicide!*

~~~~~

Colton wasn't sure how much time had passed, but he noticed the sun was going down behind the trees. Night was creeping in, and he was exhausted by fear of discovery and the tension. Reluctantly, he decided to come back another day and scope the place out. He'd come back earlier in the day when whomever was working. He also needed to get home before his mom had a cow!

Colton managed to cut through the woods and started jogging down the road. When he glanced one last time over his shoulder, he caught a glimpse of the vehicle in the driveway. Even in the dark twilight, he could've sworn it was a dark blue Accord.

Seventeen

Alexis's eyelids fluttered open and light poured in, causing her to blink. Her lips were dry and cracked. She moved her tongue and licked her lips to make them moist. Other than feeling a little nauseous, she felt good. Not like she'd thought, she'd feel. Shouldn't there be some kind of pain or even a sick stomach? Vomiting? She'd never had surgery before in her life, so she didn't have anything to compare it with. Besides giving birth to Colton, she'd never been in the hospital before.

A nurse stood to the right of her. She had dark hair that cascaded over her shoulders. "Welcome back, Alexis. Would you like something to drink?"

"Yes, please," she croaked.

The nurse left and returned with a small bottle of apple juice and handed it to her. "You may feel a little groggy, but that will pass once you've eaten."

Alexis was thirsty. She drank all the juice, and handed the empty bottle back to the nurse.

"I'll go see if the doctor is free. He wanted to talk to you once you'd woken up." The nurse slipped out behind the curtain. Alexis tried to sit up, but was unable to get comfortable.

Minutes later, Dr. Brownski entered, "Hello, Alexis. How are you feeling?"

"Good, tired."

"Once all the anesthesia wears off, you'll feel like yourself again."

Alexis nodded and glanced at the manila folder he held in his hands. He opened it and began going over her results.

"As you were told by Dr. Ramsey, you have Stage II breast cancer, which wasn't entirely wrong. The cancer we found is called lobular carcinomas; it sort of looks like it has tentacles. The tumor branches out and attaches itself to whatever is there. We were able to remove the cancer, but I'd like to start you on radiation as soon as possible to keep any cancer from returning. Would Monday be a good day for you? If not, you can stop at the desk, or I can have the nurse here check what times and days are available for treatment. Here's a prescription to start you on chemotherapy. The chemo is in pill form, and you'll have to take it once a day until I tell you otherwise."

"Are there any side effects I should be aware of?"

"Well…" he paused. "The worst would be vomiting. Some people get very sick from the chemotherapy treatment, while others may have other side effects, like losing their hair. I would say it all depends on your body and how well you handle the medication. Of course, if they make you too sick then we will discuss further options."

"How will we know if the cancer is gone?"

"We'll be testing you every few weeks by doing ultrasounds or perhaps an MRI. If the tests come back showing no cancer then we'll have you come in once a month. It all depends on your body and, of course, the cancer itself. Just make sure you take the chemo as directed. Try not to miss a dose as this can affect the treatment. And, of course, if you are having any kind of problems whatsoever, please call the center, and we'll get you on a medication that is right for you. Stop taking the medication if it makes you extremely sick and call us to make an immediate appointment, so we can change or adjust the medicine right away."

"And if the cancer doesn't go away?"

"Then we'll have to make some further decisions. You'll either continue with medication and radiation until the cancer goes into remission, or we can perform another lumpectomy or even a mastectomy, which some women end up doing in the end. We understand that chemo and other medicines can make you very sick, and it would have to be your decision, but in some cases, the doctor will advise surgery that is more aggressive. As doctors, we want our patients to get better and feel better, but sometimes-alternative treatments have to be considered. It will be completely up to you. My suggestion for you is to try the chemo and radiation and see what happens, especially if you don't want to have your breasts removed. Are there any other concerns you may have at this time?"

"No, not right now. I'll take the medication and see what happens."

"Good. I'll have the nurse come in and schedule you for your next appointment."

"Okay, thank you, doctor." He nodded and disappeared behind the curtain.

Alexis stared at the ceiling, taking in deep breaths; her mind racing with all the information Dr. Brownski had given her. She wasn't looking forward to what was ahead of her. She had told Dr. Ramsey about wanting a mastectomy, but did she really want to have her breast removed? She could always get implants, right?

Alexis sighed and shook her head. She didn't know what she wanted to do at this point in time, she'd just have to start the medication and see what happened. Maybe, just maybe, she would feel fine, not get sick, and the cancer would disappear. She was a little unsettled that Dr. Brownski had mentioned radiation before the lumpectomy, but not chemotherapy combined with it. Was the cancer worse than they had anticipated?

When the nurse with the dark hair came back in, they went through the schedule for next week and the weeks that followed. She would have to be here at the same time and day every week for the radiation. She didn't want mornings because it would mean going into work late, so she chose late afternoons.

After they were finished, the nurse helped Alexis to sit up and put on her clothes. She was thankful the nurse was there. Her head was woozy and she almost fell over. She sat in a wheelchair as the nurse handed her all the information she needed for the medication and what to expect from the surgery, then wheeled her out to the lobby.

Sarah stood up when she came out and walked over to her.

"How are you feeling, Alexis?"

"I feel kind of faint, but I think I'll be all right. I think I just need to eat something, is all."

"I'll go get the car, so we can get you home and in bed."

Alexis watched as she made her way out the door and through the parking lot. The nurse hit a button on the wall and the doors opened for them to exit. The rain had finally stopped and the sun was shining with no clouds in sight. Once outside, Alexis closed her eyes letting the warm breeze flow over her face. She opened her eyes just as Dr. Ramsey pulled up alongside the curb. She jumped out of the car, ran around the front to the passenger door, and helped Alexis inside.

~ ~ ~ ~ ~

Dr. Ramsey stopped at a drugstore in Alexis's neighborhood to get the prescription filled. Alexis stayed in the car. She was too tired to go in and wait. Being a doctor had its rewards evidently; Sarah was able to get the medicine dispensed in record time.

Just a few minutes later, Sarah pulled into the driveway and shut off the car. Once inside the house, she helped Alexis to her room and into bed.

"I can't thank you enough for being there with me today."

"It's no problem really. It was my pleasure. You can call me anytime if you need anything."

"Thank you, but I don't want to bother you with this."

"It's not a bother, trust me. Besides, being a doctor, I really don't have a life. I didn't just say that out loud, did I?" They both laughed.

"Yes, but I can relate to you. Before this cancer, I did nothing but work, but I plan to change the working all the time part. These past few days I've spent at home and with my son have good, and I want to continue spending time with him. But you don't need to hear all about my pitiful life. Though, I'm surprised you're not married or even have kids of your own. You're still young and attractive. Why hasn't someone swept you off your feet yet?"

"It's quite a long story, and I really don't want to bore you with my life. Besides you need to get better and spend time with your son."

"Oh, I plan on it."

"That's actually good to hear. I was really worried when I first told you about the cancer. I thought you weren't going to return."

"I'll be completely honest with you; I wasn't sure myself if I wanted to. All I cared about was my work. After my husband died you'd think I would have changed my old ways, but instead I worked harder and longer hours, thinking about nothing but what I wanted."

"You mean flying into outer space?"

Alexis laughed, she hadn't even thought about her job much or the fact that she had been chosen to be one of four to fly the space shuttle. "I still do, but I also realize now that there are more important things than my career, or flying into outer space, as you say." Alexis saw her face cloud over. "I'm sorry, did I say something wrong?"

"What? No. You just got me thinking is all. Well, I'd better let you get some rest."

"Sure and thanks again for taking me today. I do appreciate your kindness." Ramsey waved her hand as if to say it's no big deal and left the room. She felt a closeness to Alexis, almost like a kindred spirit.

Alexis glanced at the clock beside the bed and saw the pill bottle. She reached for it and brought the bottle into view to read the label, and then set it back down. She wasn't sure what to expect, decided she didn't want to think about it, and closed her eyes before falling into a deep sleep.

Eighteen

Alexis jolted up, jumped quickly out of bed, and raced towards the bathroom and lifted the toilet seat as she vomited. When the dry heaves had subsided, she spat a couple more times, flushed, and sat back on her heels. She hadn't started the medication yet, so she figured it was probably the anesthetic she'd been given.

Once she felt better, she used the counter to pull herself up. She glanced in the mirror and saw how pale her complexion was. She used her hand to push down her cheek, as if trying to see into her eye, and brought color to the surface, but it quickly turned pasty white again. She grabbed the cup on the counter, filled it with water, and took a sip. When she finished, she set down the cup and made her way back to the bed. Her legs felt like Jell-O, and her body was weak. She just made it to the bed when her legs went from under her and she fell onto the sheets. Grabbing at the mattress to pull herself back into bed, she covered her body. As she nodded off, the door to her room opened and Colton came in.

"Hey, Alexis, what's wrong? Are you sick or something?"

"Just sick to my stomach. Must have the flu or something. Can you do me a favor and bring the wastebasket to the side of the bed for me?"

"Sure." He padded into the washroom, grabbed the can, and set it down next to the bed.

"Thank you."

"Would you like anything else? Have you eaten today?"

As soon as he'd said the words, she knew that was probably the reason she didn't feel good. She hadn't eaten since yesterday. "No, I haven't."

"Would you like me to bring you some saltine crackers? Dad always fed them to me when I didn't feel good."

She nodded and watched him slip out of the room. She turned her head just enough to catch a glimpse of the pill bottle. She quickly grabbed the bottle and tossed it in the drawer next to the bed. She closed the drawer just as Colton returned with a box of crackers in his hand. He set the box next to her and sat down on the bed. "Here, I'll help you," he said and opened the box, pulling out a plastic bag.

When she tried to grip the cracker, she found her fingers were too weak, so he put the cracker to her mouth and she bit down. The snap of the cracker echoed through the room. Although she was tired, she chewed and swallowed, then opened her mouth for more. After the fifth cracker, she turned her head, telling him no more.

When she looked back at him, he wore a sad expression on his face. She never wanted her son to see her like this. To see her unable to feed herself; it made her heart ache inside. He stood and went into the bathroom, returning with a glass of water.

"Here drink this," he said and helped her to sit up. He held the glass and tipped it, allowing water to flow into her mouth. She choked with the first swallow and then took another sip. She pinched her lips together when she was finished. He set the glass down on the nightstand and stood up, pulling the blanket all around her. "You rest and I'll come back and check on you in a couple of hours."

She nodded and closed her eyes as she felt shivers up and down her body. She was cold and the blankets didn't seem to help warm her body.

Weight hugged her, and she opened her eyes to see her son laying a thicker blanket upon her. She smiled up at him and closed her eyes once more.

Nineteen

Colton went downstairs, made himself something to eat, and sat at the kitchen table. For a couple of minutes he wondered why his mom was so sick...flu, she'd said. *She sure was sick, like I've never seen her before, but she'd be okay in a day or two.*

His mind was much more absorbed with what he'd seen at the house the other day. He just couldn't believe whoever was living in that house was driving the same car that was seen near his father's body. A part of him wished he'd stayed longer until he'd got a good look at the person. He needed to find out what happened seven months ago, and who was behind it.

Colton had never once thought his dad had killed himself, no matter what the report said. He fished his phone out of his pants pocket and saw that there was a message. He tapped the voicemail button and listened. It was Detective Bowen stating that he'd checked the model of the car again, but the DMV's database was still giving him the same results. He ended the message saying that Colton should stop trying to find out what happened because the truth was that his father had committed suicide, end of story.

Irritated, he hit the home key and set his cellphone down on the table. After what he'd seen tonight, there was no way he was going to drop his investigation to find out what really happened. He wanted to call the detective back and tell him what he had seen tonight, but after the message Bowen had left, he was sure the detective would blow him off and say he was imagining the whole thing. The only proof he had of the car was what he'd seen, no photo or real evidence. Wouldn't that be enough for Detective Bowen to check it out? Maybe…maybe not. He didn't have to think too hard about what he was going to do—he'd keep his findings to himself and gather whatever evidence he needed to prove his father had been killed rather than committed suicide.

He thought about going back out to the house, but for some odd reason he wanted to stay home near his mom. What if she needed him, and he wasn't around? This had to be the first time in a while that he'd cared about her needs. He knew she was trying to be a better mother, and cared for him, but it didn't change what she'd done in the past. He'd told her that he'd forgiven her, but that was a lie. Colton couldn't forget how she'd ignored him and Dad for so long.

Right now, he needed to focus on the game tomorrow, not about her or that strange person in the house with the dark Accord in the driveway.

He cleaned up the dishes and headed to his room. Instead of climbing into bed, he stood by the window and peered out. The moon was full and lit up the street. Stars twinkled all around.

He wasn't sure what he was looking for, but an intuitive feeling urged him to look outside. He searched the darkness for clues or some sort of answers to his quest. But before he turned away, he caught a glimpse of a car driving slowly by. He couldn't tell exactly, with the little light he had, the color of the car that drove by at a snail's pace. Was the driver searching for someone or checking the numbers on the houses? He wasn't sure?

Practically holding his breath and taking one step back so his silhouette wouldn't be visible in the window, Colton stood for another minute or so and waited to see what the person in the dark car was going to do. The car kept on going until it was swallowed up by the trees along the street and was gone. He thought about waiting to see if the car came back again, but he shrugged it off, thinking he was just being paranoid—he wasn't even sure if it was the same color, make, and model of the car he was looking for—so he went into the bathroom to get ready for bed.

After a quick shower, Colton towel-dried his hair and tossed the towel on the chair by the desk. He heard his phone ringing, which he'd left in the bathroom, and went back to retrieve it.

"Hello."

"Hey, Colton, a couple of the guys want to get together before the game tomorrow and practice. Are you up for it?" Jake asked.

"Sure, sounds good."

"You sound different, is everything okay?"

"What? Yeah, I'm fine. What time tomorrow do you want to get together?"

"Around two."

"Okay, I'll see you there." Before Jake could ask any more questions, Colton ended the call.

He put on a pair of boxers with shorts over them and went to check on his mom. He cracked opened the door, and saw a heap of blankets on the bed, then a silhouette of his mom's face peeking out of the top. He closed the door and went back to his room, peering out the window one last time.

Colton thought he spotted a shadow near the base of the tree. He rubbed his eyelids and looked closer. He couldn't be certain, but it almost looked like a person standing by the tree, looking up at him. He opened the window and stuck his head out.

Had he wasted so much time trying to get the window open that whoever it was had left? His eyes searched the yard and the trees, but there was nothing. If he had seen someone, they were gone now. *Am I imagining that I saw someone watching my home? Have I conjured up the dark blue Accord at that other house and again on my street because I desperately needed to find answers?*

He knew he was anxious about school and the upcoming game. There was stress in the relationship with his mother, and he missed his father so much, the pain never completely went away. *Maybe my mind is just playing tricks on me?*

Colton pulled his head in and closed the window, never taking his eyes off the ground below. He turned, flopped down on the bed, and climbed under the covers. He flipped on the television, but nothing much caught his attention so he decided on the show 'Cops'.

He'd only been watching a few seconds when he sat upright in bed. The camera on the TV was aimed directly at the car's license plate. Colton realized immediately that he *might* have proof to show Detective Bowen.

Colton reached over and opened the drawer next to him. He quickly scanned through the papers and stopped when he found what he was looking for. He slid out of bed, grabbed his jeans and searched his pockets for the copy he got at the library. Once he found the paper, he searched for the license plate number, but found nothing on the copy from the library. He was no closer to the truth, then he was a minute ago, but no matter what, he wasn't going to stop.

Twenty

Around eleven that same night, Alexis was relieved that she was feeling better. She was able to keep the saltines down and managed to walk around the house. Colton was in his room when she opened the door, fast asleep. She stepped inside, silenced the television, and closed the door before heading back down the hall. She picked up her laptop and climbed back into bed. Reaching over, she opened the drawer of the nightstand and grabbed the prescription bottle. She took out one pill and washed it down with the glass of water Colton had left. She skimmed through her emails, replying to the ones from work and deleting the rest. When she glanced at her alarm clock next to the bed, it was nearly midnight. She closed her laptop, set it beside her on the bed, and slid under the covers.

~~~~~

Light peered through the curtains as she opened her eyes. Noise came from the kitchen so she crawled out of bed and slipped on her robe. By the time she reached the doorway to the kitchen, she was feeling faint. She clasped her hand around the wooden doorframe to steady herself, but she wasn't feeling strong enough and fell to the floor. Colton turned when he heard the noise and rushed to her side.

"Alexis, are you all right?"

"I don't know what happened. I was fine when I got out of bed, but now I don't feel so good."

"Here let me help you to the table, or would you rather go back to bed?"

"Table is fine."

"Would you like some coffee, maybe something to eat? You didn't eat much last night, so that's probably why you don't feel good?"

"Yeah, you're probably right. I'll just have coffee and a banana, please." Colton poured a cup, added two sugars and cream, and then grabbed a banana from the bowl on the counter. He set them both down in front of her and took a seat.

She took a sip from her cup and swallowed. "Oh, that tastes good. How do you know what I like in my coffee?"

"I've seen you do it many times."

She nodded.

"I have a game today, so will you be fine here without me? Should I call someone to stay with you?"

"No, I'm fine. I wish I could go with you, though. I haven't been to any of your basketball games." She looked over at her son, who had a frown on his face. She wondered if he was hurt by her not attending any of his games, and now she wished she had. Why did she feel the need to put work before her son, her family? No more was she going to put work first! She had her health to work on and then she had to put all her focus on a relationship with her son.

"Well, it wouldn't be the first time you've missed one," he said before dunking his spoon in the bowl of cereal.

"I know and I'm sorry, Colton. I was a different person then and I'm trying to change. Believe me when I say this, I'm so sorry about work and not spending time with you. I wish you could see that now. I know I sound like a broken record, but if I have to repeat myself, I will."

Her eyes etched over his face and then fell to the table. When he stood up, his lengthy body towered over hers. She couldn't believe how tall he'd got in the past year. He had to be at least six-foot-three or so, now. She couldn't even remember the last time she took him shopping for clothes. Jay had taken care of that. She had missed so much these past twelve years; how much she wished she'd been there for him! Could they rebuild and start a new relationship? One where they could spend time getting to know each other, again? She hoped so. She wanted to get to know him more than anything.

It seemed to her that every time she started to reach out to him, he would pull away or say something smart to her, hurting her feelings. She knew she deserved it, but wished he'd at least try to be civil toward her. She honestly didn't know what else she could do, but she wasn't going to stop reaching out to him. He was her son, and she loved him with all her heart. Why couldn't he see that?

"What time is your game today?"

"It starts at four. A couple of the guys and I are planning to head to the courts at two for a warm-up game."

"Oh, okay. Is the game here or away?"

"We're playing at home this week. If we win tonight, we'll be in line for the championship game in two weeks. My coach said that if I continue doing as well as I have been I'll probably be offered a scholarship by Jacksonville University to play basketball."

"Oh, Colton, that's wonderful news. How come this is the first I've heard about it?"

"Really, Alexis, do I need to answer that?" he quipped sarcastically.

Alexis looked at her son, and then at the table. "No, I guess not, but I'd like to be involved now."

She was trying so hard to be a part of her son's life, but he kept slamming the door in her face. What did she need to do or say to get him to realize she was here for him? To be the mother he'd always needed. No matter what, she was going to be at his game today. She hoped she'd be feeling better so she could go. Then she thought, *"Does he even want me there?"*

Alexis was determined to go whether he wanted her to or not. She gulped down some more coffee and peeled the banana.

Twenty-One

By the time two o'clock came around, she was feeling sick to her stomach, but she refused to give in. She took a shower and got dressed. As she sat down on the bed to put on her shoes, bile rose to her throat. She grabbed the garbage can just in time to vomit. When she couldn't puke up any more, she went into the bathroom, emptied the can in the toilet, and rinsed it out. She set the can down beside the bed and finished putting on her shoes. Once she was out the door and in her car, she felt a little better. She had to go for her son. She kept repeating the mantra over and over in her head. She was determined that her stubborn personality and willpower would not let her down!

She started the car and drove towards the school. She fiddled with the vent, trying to get the cold air to blow on her face. She couldn't remember sweating like this before; it was as if she was running a fever. Yesterday she was freezing and today she was boiling hot.

She pulled into the parking lot of the school and parked the car. She sat back, waiting for the dizziness to pass. When it did, she climbed out of the car and headed inside. She walked in the direction of voices and entered the gymnasium. There were five boys running up and down the court, so she made her way to the bleachers and sat down in the third row.

She glanced around and saw several other people; they could have been the other boy's parents, watching them play. She looked out onto the court and saw Colton dribbling the ball. She wanted to wave to him, but he wasn't looking her way so she sat and watched.

A man came onto the basketball court dressed in slacks and a blue dress shirt with a tie. He blew a whistle and the boys on the court stopped and walked towards him. She couldn't hear what he was saying, but after the man was done talking, they all headed to a set of doors labeled locker room and went inside.

She sat perched on the bench and glanced around the room. More people started to show up and take their seats in the stands. Her head turned to the sound of doors opening and she saw Colton and his friend, Jake, come walking out. When she thought Colton was looking toward the stands, she waved at him. He said something to Jake, and then walked over to where she was sitting.

"What are you doing here, Alexis?"

"I came to see you play. What, I'm not allowed to see my own son play basketball?"

"What's the point? You never cared before."

"Colton please, I'm trying hard to build a relationship with you. Why can't you accept it and work with me?" Alexis replied, trying to keep her voice at a whisper.

He shrugged his shoulders and took a seat next to her. "How are you feeling?"

"I'm doing okay. Nothing you need to worry about. You focus on the game, and I'll just sit here and watch."

"Believe it or not, Alexis, I do worry about you, and I'm sorry if I come off a little rude sometimes. It's just…just that I'm not used to you being around. You were always away, so I took care of myself—that's all."

Tears stung her eyes, but she was able to hold her composure. She wanted to say more to him, but thought against it. He had a game to focus on, and she didn't want to upset him anymore then she already had. She put her arm around him and squeezed his shoulder. He started to lean into her, but stopped and stood up.

"Go win this game," she said before he strolled away.

He smiled as he turned back and replied, "I will try."

Twenty-Two

Three hours later, she was climbing out of the stands, trying to make her way to her son. He was being carried in the air by his teammates—for making the most points—they headed to the locker room. She turned and went out into the hall looking for the girl's restroom. When she'd found it, she went inside and emerged a few minutes later. While she waited around for her son, she browsed over the trophy case in the hall. She jumped when a voice from behind her spoke.

"Quite a few trophies we have?"

She turned and saw a man in tan slacks and a blue dress shirt. She remembered him, blowing the whistle when she first arrived. He had short brunette hair, which was feathered on the sides, and his face was shaved clean. "Yes, there are."

"Are you Colton's mother?"

She nodded. "Yes, I am."

"I haven't seen you at any of his games before."

"No, this is my first one. Always seemed to be working when he played."

"Well, I'm glad you could finally make it. I'm Troy Martin, known as Coach Martin around here. Colton is a terrific player and is being considered for the basketball scholarship to Jacksonville University."

"I heard about that. Is there anyway he wouldn't be accepted?"

"No, not really, though he needs to keep his grades up. He's one of my best players. I didn't tell him that the coach would be out here to see him play next week and, hopefully, the championship game. If he plays like he did tonight, I don't see us not winning."

"That's wonderful news, he'll be so excited. What's this about his grades? I thought he was an A student?"

"He was, until…until what happened to his father, your husband. Please accept my condolences. Although, I've noticed his grades have been improving lately. I also think it's best if he doesn't know college coaches are here watching. People tend to get nervous and play poorly. If you could keep it between us, I would appreciate it."

"Sure, I won't say a word. Thank you so much for telling me all this, I will try and be here for the rest of his games."

"That will be great, if you can. He seemed to play a more competitive game tonight. Maybe it had something to do with you being here. Don't get me wrong, Colton is a terrific player, but I think knowing you were here made him play even better."

"Oh, well, thank you," Alexis said, smiling.

The doors behind her swooshed open and a few boys from the team appeared—Colton being one of them. She waved at him, and he strolled over to where she was standing with his coach.

"Hey, what are you still doing here?"

"Well, I just thought I'd stick around and at least say goodbye before I left."

His eyes looked over at the coach, nodded, and then looked back at her. "The guys and I are heading out for some cheeseburgers at Mike's Grill, do you want to come?"

"No, no, you go on ahead, and I'll see you at home later."

"Okay. I'll see you later."

She wanted to reach out and give him a hug, but decided against it. She didn't want to embarrass him in front of his friends. Parents weren't supposed to show their love around other people because it was just too icky. Although, she didn't really know what it was like. Her parents had never showed her that kind of love; they were hardly home and didn't have time to come to any of her school events.

She said her goodbyes and drove home. When she'd returned, she made her way to the kitchen and rummaged through the refrigerator for something to eat. When she couldn't decide on anything, she had soup and crackers, instead.

After Alexis had finished, she rinsed out her bowl, placed it in the dishwasher, and climbed the stairs. She changed into her nightclothes and got into bed. Her eyes caught a glimpse of the prescription bottle and remembered what the doctor had said about taking the pill at the same time everyday. Last night she took one around eleven, but she wasn't sure if she would be able to stay awake that long to take her next one. She decided a couple of hours earlier wouldn't hurt her. She'd take one at ten every evening from here on out. She slid out of bed and refilled her glass with water, then hunkered back under the covers. She turned on the TV and flipped through the channels, settling on the movie *The Hobbit*. Every once in a while, she glanced at the clock so she wouldn't be late taking her next pill.

She must have fallen asleep because when she woke, it was past one in the morning. Mad at herself for falling asleep, she popped a pill, washed it down with water, and got out of bed. She opened the bedroom door and heard noises coming from the kitchen. She peeked her head in and saw Colton pulling food out of the fridge.

"What are you doing?"

"Oh, hi, Alexis. Just getting something to eat," he laughed.

She didn't think looking for food was hilarious. As she moved closer to him, she could smell smoke on his clothes. It wasn't stinky like cigarette smoke and then it hit her.

"Please tell me you weren't out smoking pot again?"

He stopped and stared at her, his pupils large. "It was just a few joints, Alexis. Chill out."

"A few joints! Well, let me tell you something. You have your whole life in front of you and if you continue to do drugs, you're not going to get that scholarship or anything else. You'll end up alone and living on the streets! Do you hear me?"

"Whatever." He shut the refrigerator door, walked past her, and up the stairs, slamming his bedroom door. She was too weak and upset to go running after him. She put the food he'd taken out back in the refrigerator and shut off the lights. She'd wait until morning to talk to him.

Twenty-Three

All day Sunday, Alexis was knelt down in front of the toilet. She would make it back to the bed and sleep for a few hours, but then be hovering over the toilet once more. Now it was Monday, and she still didn't feel any better. Her body felt like she'd been hit by a freight train, and the color in her face had turned completely white. She didn't even feel like talking to her son, who had been avoiding her since Saturday night's dispute.

Alexis had taken the pills as directed, but all they did was make her sick. She knew she had an appointment later today, but wasn't sure she could make it there if she tried to drive.

Finally able to make it to her feet, she used the wall to help guide her back towards the bed. Her legs wobbled with each step she took; her muscles felt weaker than the day before. When she reached the bed, she grabbed the phone on the nightstand, and dialed a cellphone number.

"Hello?"

"Hi, Dr. Ramsey, it's Alexis, Alexis Finley."

"Yes, Alexis, is everything okay?"

"That's why I'm calling. I have a radiation appointment later today, but I don't think I'll be able to drive myself there."

"What's wrong? Is the medication making you too sick?"

"I can't seem to keep any food down and my body hurts."

"Is there anyone at the house with you?"

"No, I think my son is at school. I haven't really seen him much the last two days."

"I'm going to clear my schedule for the next few days and come over to help you."

"You don't need to do that. I'm fine, really."

"Well, you don't sound fine to me. I'll finish things here, and come over. Don't try to change my mind, Alexis."

"All right, but it's only because I don't have the energy to argue with you. I'm going to lie here and get some sleep. There is a spare key under a fake rock in the flower bed, next to the front door, so you can let yourself in."

"Okay, I'll be over there as soon as I can."

She tried to respond, but her body went limp. She slid off the bed onto the floor, and everything went black.

Sarah heard a small moan and hoped that Alexis had just forgotten to hang up the phone since the line was still live. But the doctor knew that was probably not the case. *I hope that Alexis had just had a weak moment and went to lie down or rushed to the bathroom, but Alexis could have fallen and hit her head!* Sarah Ramsey thought.

Sarah knew she needed to get to the Finley home as soon as possible.

Twenty-Four

A warm hand caressed her cheek and then someone gently shook her shoulders, making her open her eyes. She was in her bedroom on the floor with Dr. Ramsey hovering over her.

"Alexis, wake up, please. The ambulance is on its way."

She moaned out loud, her throat dry. She licked her lips and spoke softly, her voice as weary as the rest of her, "What happened?"

"I'm not sure. We were talking on the phone, and I thought I heard the phone hit the floor so I dropped everything and got here as soon as I could. I arrived just a few minutes ago, and I've been trying to wake you. I called 911 on my way here, and I'm surprised they haven't arrived yet. Can you try and sit up?"

"I don't know. I feel too weak."

"Here, let me help you." Sarah Ramsey wrapped her arms around Alexis, then lifted and propped her up beside the bed. "Can you tell me how you've been feeling lately?"

"All I've been doing is vomiting. I try and eat, but I can't seem to keep anything down."

"I think you're dehydrated and need to be in the hospital."

"I don't want to go to a hospital. I need to stay here with my son."

"Do you honestly think you're capable of looking after your son in this condition?"

Alexis wanted to reply, but no words came to her.

Dr. Sarah Ramsey reached for the phone on the floor and dialed 911 again. When she spoke to the dispatcher, the woman stated that the ambulance vehicle was involved in an accident on the way to the house and another ambulance had already been sent out.

Dr. Ramsey replied that no one had shown up yet and told the dispatcher that she'd take Alexis to the hospital, instead. Alexis could hear the dispatcher arguing with Sarah, saying it was a bad idea, but Sarah ended the call.

"Come on, I'm taking you." Dr. Ramsey wrapped her arms around Alexis, pulled her up off the floor, and sat her on the edge of the bed. She took Alexis's arm and laid it around her neck, and then helped her to walk out of the bedroom and down the stairs.

"You should have been sleeping in a bedroom downstairs."

"I know, but the last two days I've been way too sick to move my things downstairs."

"Where's Colton?"

"We had another fight last night, wait, maybe it was the night before. I'm not sure, but he's been avoiding me ever since."

"Well, let's not worry about that now. I want to get you to the hospital. I'll have a talk with him after you are well."

Alexis wanted to smile at what she said, but the muscles in her face were as frail as her body. Inside, she was thinking how much she really liked Dr. Sarah Ramsey and was thankful she'd been able to help her. Alexis realized she hadn't had a real friend in quite some time.

Twenty-Five

Once at the hospital, Alexis was taken into the emergency room and then admitted for dehydration. She had an IV filling her with fluids and a light pain medication to ease the discomfort she was having. Sarah was sitting by her side when Dr. Brownski entered the room.

"Hello, Mrs. Finley. Dr. Ramsey here notified the staff in the emergency room to give me a call. Most doctors won't admit their mistakes, but I should have given you a prescription for anti-nausea and vomiting. Some patients have few reactions to the chemotherapy, though, most do. Today, I want to start you on a drug called Serotonin (5-HT3) antagonists along with Dexamethasone (Decadron), which is a steroid. These medicines should resolve any problems you may have had. Please accept my apologies."

"Well, I'm just glad I called Dr. Ramsey, and she was able to come to my house. I owe her a great deal for saving my life."

"Alexis," Sarah replied, blushing slightly, "There's no need for any of that. I was glad to be of help and I told you a few days ago, I'll help you anyway I can. I'm just glad I got to the house when I did."

"I appreciate your kindness. I'm grateful for what you did." Alexis looked away from Dr. Ramsey to Dr. Brownski. "Are there any side effects to the new drugs you're giving me I should be aware of?"

"There are always side effects to any drug you take and to answer your question, yes. You may suffer from a headache, diarrhea, constipation, and/or hiccups. Not everyone has the same side effects and the degree of severity can be very mild or even dissipate as time goes on. Each person is different, so consequently, the side effects are different," he smiled at her for encouragement. "Don't dwell on the side effects as your mind can actually create them or make them worse. It happens with fear and stress, and you are under medical and mental stress right now. It's normal, but you have to let us, Dr. Ramsey and myself, know what's going on," he finished rather firmly.

"Hiccups?"

"Yes, I know that sounds odd, but apparently while the drug was being tested someone experienced having hiccups from using it. Although, it's not uncommon."

"As long as the pills work and I no longer vomit, I'll be happy."

"Good. Like I said, after your surgery, we try to make recovery as comfortable as possible for our patients. You're already going through an ordeal and we don't want to add more discomfort than you may already have. In addition, the biopsies from your lumpectomy came back negative. "

Alexis nodded.

"I will be checking back in later to make sure everything is working out for you and that you're feeling better."

"Thank you doctor," Alexis said. Dr. Brownski turned and left the room.

"You don't have to stay here with me. I'm sure you have better things to do," Alexis said to Sarah.

"No, I had some of my appointments rescheduled for the week and some of the other doctors that work with me at the medical clinic were able to fit my patients into their schedule as well. I'll be staying with you until you feel better and can go home; besides, I want to meet this son of yours and give him a piece of my mind."

"Oh?"

"Oh, is right. I'm not sure what you've told him or what you both have been disagreeing about, but he needs to stand by you and work through these matters. You need someone to help you out during these times."

Alexis didn't know Ramsey as well as she wanted to. How often do doctors and patients bond together? None that she knew of, but there was something about her she wanted to get to know better. Sarah was kind and caring, willing to drop what she was doing to be by Alexis's side. She didn't ask her to—Dr. Ramsey had insisted. Even though Alexis kept her feelings locked away tightly, she was starting to open up and confide in her. Alexis felt a common kinship between them, but she didn't quite know what it was.

"You don't know my son that well," Alexis said in defense of Colton.

"I hope to get to know him better."

Alexis didn't know how to respond to that, so she just nodded.

"I'm going to get some coffee, do you want anything from the cafeteria?"

"No, I'm good. Besides I have these crackers the nurse gave me to help my stomach."

"Okay, I won't be long."

Later that afternoon, Dr. Brownski returned and suggested they get started on the radiation treatment that had been scheduled to start today. Alexis was transferred from her room to radiation on the first floor. Two nurses helped her onto a table and covered her with a sheet. After marking her breast with a marker—for them to see in the monitor in the next room—a petite nurse went over what to expect during and after treatment.

"This will take approximately fifteen minutes, and you will have to lie still. If for any reason you feel sick or think you may pass out, just talk out loud. My assistant and I can hear every word you say. You may hear clicking and whirring, sort of like a vacuum cleaner, this is the sound of the machine aiming the radiation where it needs to go. Do you have any questions?"

"No, not right now."

"If you should, like I said, just speak out loud and I'll answer them the best I can."

"Okay."

The nurse squeezed her arm. "You'll be fine." She then placed headphones over Alexis's ears and left the room.

Twenty-Six

On Sunday before his mother was awake, Colton was up, dressed and had slipped out of the house. He had agreed to meet his buddies for a game and catch a movie afterwards; anything to get out of the house and away from his *so-called* mom.

After Saturday night, he wanted and needed to avoid her in every way, shape, or form. He wasn't in the mood to argue over what had happened. Besides it was just pot; it's not like he was doing cocaine or heroin. She needed to get a life and quit butting into his. Yeah, he knew she was trying to be his mom, but he actually wished she would be her old self again, so he could do what he wanted.

Actually, he wasn't sure what he wanted from her. He did want her around, but then he didn't, especially, not when she picked at the things he did. He knew she was right about the drugs, but they helped him to forget things—they made the nightmares disappear. It seemed to be the same dream every time. He knew it wasn't real and that he hadn't been with his dad when he died, but for some reason he dreamed he was standing in the grass, staring at his father's body by the lake. Then again, he'd been reading the police report way too much lately, so Colton figured it had something to do with that because what else would cause the dreams?

When Colton returned home, part of him wanted to check in on his mom, but another part wanted to leave well enough alone. He was thankful she wasn't in the kitchen because that meant she was in bed. He stepped over the wooden steps that squeaked as he made his way up the stairs and to his room. When he reached his bedroom door, he opened it and went inside, closing it silently behind him. He didn't want Alexis to know he was home.

Twenty-Seven

The next morning, Monday, Colton dressed and headed downstairs to grab something to eat before he left for school. His mother never came out of her room, nor did she venture downstairs. He checked the time, grabbed his books, and headed out the door.

He parked his car on the curb in front of Jake's place, climbed out, and jogged up to the house. The door flew open, and Jake stood off to the side, allowing Colton to enter.

"Are you almost ready?" Colton asked.

"Yeah, just let me grab my things."

Minutes later, they stepped outside. Colton headed towards his car with Jake following a few steps behind him.

"So, how long will your car be in the garage?" asked Colton.

"My dad said a couple days. Should have it back by the end of the week."

"Do they know what's wrong with it?" he asked while starting his car.

"Yeah, I think it's the carburetor or something like that. Not into all that car engine stuff."

"Yeah, I hear ya!"

Colton thought about his friend Jake and wondered how he was able to handle life. They were the same and yet different in many ways. Jake never went out smoking pot with Colton's other so-called friends, if that's what he should call them. No, they weren't friends, not like Jake and a few others from the team.

Colton had met these two guys about a month after his dad's funeral. They were older than him, maybe twenty, or twenty-one. He wasn't sure how old they were and never thought to ask. They were just different from the people Colton had ever been around before. They didn't ask a lot of questions about his feelings or what he did with his life. They didn't know where he lived or where he went to school, hell, why should they care? He gave them his share of the money for the weed and sometimes they smoked with him, but mostly Colton went off on his own. He'd venture out to the lake that his dad used to take him to, sit down under the tree and just mellow out as if nothing in the world even mattered. It made him forget about his mom, but mostly he went there with his pot so he wouldn't have to think about his dad's death.

"Earth to Colton, are you there?" Jake waved his hand in front of his face.

Colton blinked and turned his way. "Sorry was just thinking, is all?"

"Just thought you blacked out there for a minute. Didn't know if I needed to grab the wheel and start driving," Jake replied, like it was a joke or something, but his normal grin and chuckle showed how nervous he was.

"Just had a few things rolling around in my head," Colton said.

"Well, think about them when you're not driving, dude. We have a game to play on Friday, and I'd like to play in it."

Colton nodded and turned the corner to enter the school parking lot.

"I don't want to sound like I'm intruding, but what's up with your mom. She didn't look too hot when I saw her on Saturday?"

Colton's shoulders tensed from his friend's question, but he didn't answer.

Colton parked the car, and they both climbed out. He couldn't wait for this school year to end. Then he could graduate and head off to college, leaving all this behind. He shook his head, throwing the thought to the back of his mind and went inside the school.

By the time eighth period came, Colton had decided to drop Jake off and make a trip out to the house with the dark blue Honda from the other night. He was hoping to get lucky and get some unanswered questions resolved. He thought again about telling Detective Bowen about what he saw, but remembered the message the detective had left the other night and decided against it. He'd have to do this on his own. Get the evidence he needed and then talk to the detective.

Twenty-Eight

By a quarter after three, he had pulled in front of the house. No car was parked in the driveway, which told him one of two things; either the person had parked in the garage or they weren't home yet. He decided to turn the car around and park along the side of the road like before and walk down.

Ten minutes later, he was standing at the front door. He cupped his hands around his eyes and peered through the window. Nothing was different from before. He opened the screen and checked the knob, but it was locked. He jogged down the front steps and went around to the back. He checked the back door, and this time he found it unlocked. He looked over his shoulder to make sure the coast was clear and went inside. Not that he thought someone was watching him, but it eased his conscience knowing no one was there.

He stood in a small kitchen. To his right were a few cabinets that surrounded the sink with a window above it. There were a few more cabinets along the wall and a stove and refrigerator. He walked around the room opening cabinet doors and looking in drawers. He wasn't sure what he was looking for, though it didn't hurt to scope out everything. After he hunted through all the drawers in the kitchen, he made his way to the living room. There wasn't much to the room—a sofa, desk, and one god-awful looking chair. The chair looked as if it had been taken from a dumpster. The chair was a lime green color with brown splotches. Apparently, the person who lived here didn't have a lot of money or they didn't like spending money.

Colton checked out the main living area. No pictures hung on the wall, and there weren't any trinkets on the few pieces of furniture. There was nothing that told Colton this person had any family or friends. He was starting to get nervous and was sweating; he knew he didn't have much time.

He quickly and quietly climbed the stairs and stopped at the first door on the left. The door was closed. He hesitated for a second and then wrapped his hand around the knob and turned it. He stood in the doorway and peered around the room. The bed was in front of him with one single nightstand on the right-hand side. He made his way to the table and opened the drawer. He spotted a book inside, and picked it up. There was no title on the front, which meant it could be a journal of some kind. He flipped open the cover and saw a photograph inside. His fingers eased over the two people in the photo. He didn't understand why or who would have this picture.

He jumped in fright when the sound of a car engine pulling into the drive alerted him. He raced to the window and peered out. The dark blue car was back, and someone was getting out of the car. He quickly slipped the photo in his back pocket and tossed the book back in the drawer before rushing out of the room. He took the steps two at a time, racing through the living room to the kitchen door. As he grabbed the knob and thrust the door open, he heard the front door unlock. He stepped outside, closed the door behind him, and hid on the side of the house.

Colton knew he needed to make a quick run for the woods and pray the person wouldn't see him. Part of him wanted to stay and find out exactly who this person was and what he or she was doing with that photo, but he was scared to death and wasn't sure if he was ready to confront this person. He knew the right thing to do was to make a visit to Detective Bowen and have him come out here. That way they could both get answers about his father's death.

Once he got to his car, he drove to the police department in search of the detective. One of the officers at the station led him to Detective Bowen's office and rapped on the door. When he heard him say, "Come in," Colton slipped inside.

"Colton, what are you doing here?"

"I needed to see you and show you something." He took a seat in a chair right in front of the desk.

"I hope this isn't about your father again, Colton. Didn't you get the message I left you a few days ago?"

"Yes, I got that message and, yes, it does have to do with my father. But before you say anything, I need to tell you something and for you to take a look at what I've found."

Detective Bowen shook his head before saying, "Okay, I'll give you five minutes, but no more." He sat back in his chair and waited.

"First, I want to tell you that I did some searching on my own and found an address on that car. It belongs to a house an hour away from here. I took it upon myself to check the place out. The same car supposedly seen near where my father was killed was sitting in the driveway. Well, I don't know for sure if it's the same car, but it fit the description. Second, I found this while I was in the house searching through their things."

"You did what? You broke into someone's house and started going through their things? What the hell were you thinking, Colton? Don't you know it's against the law to break into someone's house and search through their private things?"

"Well, I didn't actually break in. The door was unlocked."

"Oh, like that matters. It's still breaking and entering. I never thought you would stoop to this nonsense. I've known you since you were five years old, Colton." Detective Bowen shook his head and blew out a breath. "What do I need to do to get you to understand that your father is dead? That he took his own life? I'm sorry that you're not willing to accept that he killed himself, but it's the truth. You need to let go and get on with your life."

Colton looked from the detective to his own hands in his lap. Then his head shot up, and he reached behind him, removing the photo from his back pocket. He placed the picture down on the desk and pushed it forward. "Then explain why I found this in one of the drawers upstairs in that house?"

The detective glanced down and picked up the photo. "This is a picture of you and your dad. You found this in the house?" He looked up at Colton and back down at the photo.

"Yes, I did. Now will you help me find out who this person is so we can get to the bottom of what really happened to my dad?"

"I'm sorry, but I can't do that, son. The case is closed, and there's nothing to indicate your father's death wasn't suicide. Just like you, we went to this house and did a thorough search. We found nothing to indicate that someone lived there, or had anything to do with your father. We checked over all the documents, and even spoke to the owner who used to own the house. She said some middle-aged man bought the house from her. She showed us the paperwork, but the man doesn't exist.

We've checked everything. I don't know, but you're going to have to let this go. As hard as it may seem, you have to go on with your life. Close the book, as some might say or turn the page. There's nothing I can do for you."

Feeling defeated once more, he stood up and grabbed the photo from Detective Bowen's hand, and then turned away and walked out the door. The last thing he was going to do was to let this go. No, he would continue searching and if, by all means, he had to confront this person by himself, then that was what he was going to do.

Twenty-Nine

When he returned home, he went inside and headed to the kitchen for something to eat. He sat at the kitchen table when he heard the front door open. He remembered seeing his mom's car in the driveway, so it couldn't be her coming in the front door.

"Hello," he yelled. The clacking of footsteps came closer. He turned and saw a woman standing in the doorway.

"Who are you?" he asked.

"I didn't mean to frighten you, Colton. I'm Dr. Ramsey, your mom's doctor."

"Oh, well I think she's upstairs, if you want to go see her."

"Actually, I came here to see you."

A confused expression surfaced on his face. "Why do you need to see me?"

"By your reaction, I'm assuming you are unaware that your mother is in the hospital."

"What? Is she okay? Did something happen to her when I was at school?"

"Calm down, I'll explain everything to you." She walked over and took a seat in front of him. "While you were at school, she called me and ended up passing out while we were on the phone. When I got here, she was severely dehydrated, so I took her to the hospital. She's doing much better now and should return home tomorrow or the next day. Your mom informed me that you two had a disagreement and that you've been ignoring her to the point where you weren't talking or even helping her. This is very serious, Colton, she needs you to stand beside her and help her through this cancer. You are her son and the only family she has left. I'm not sure what you two have been fighting about, but you had better figure it out and fix things. Don't wait until it's too late. If she hadn't called me, she might be dead right now."

"What do you mean she has cancer?"

"She didn't tell you?"

"No. She said she had the flu." His eyes searched her face and then he looked down in fear, confusion, and guilt.

"I guess I assumed she had told you."

"What kind of cancer does she have? Is she going to die?"

"She has breast cancer, and last Friday I took her to the Cancer Center to have a lumpectomy. The medicine they gave her made her sick. I was thankful to get here when I did. So, do you want to tell me what you two have been arguing about?"

He wasn't sure if he could confide in her or even trust her, but she was his mother's doctor, so she must be someone he could trust. He didn't want to lose his mom, no matter how mad she made him. He had always loved her. He'd never stopped.

"I was smoking pot, that's what we argued about. It's the only way I know how to cope with my dad's death."

After he spoke the words, he knew that it was all an excuse. He made himself believe that he needed the drug to cope with what life had dished out to him, but he knew better. He wasn't stupid or a druggie. He needed to change and make an effort to hold onto what he had left before he ended up scared and alone.

For now, he would set his priorities aside and focus on his mom and school. He would wait to search for the answers of his father's death, because maybe the detective was right and…. No, he wouldn't and couldn't think about what the detective kept saying. He knew deep down Detective Bowen was wrong.

"Do you want to talk about your feelings? I won't judge you or tell you what you need to do. That will be for you to decide. I can offer you my help, but only if you want it." Sarah's words interrupted Colton's thoughts. It was like she was reading his mind.

He nodded and exhaled the breath he'd been holding. He had already told the doctor why he smoked weed, but he wasn't going to tell her about his father and what he'd been doing. He wouldn't tell anyone—until he had proof.

"I really don't feel like talking about what's been bothering me right now."

"Sure, I understand." Dr. Sarah Ramsey looked past Colton and saw a notepad by the coffee pot. She stood and strolled over to the counter. She scribbled something down, then went back to the table and placed a piece of paper in front of him. "This is the hospital your mom was admitted to and the room number. I won't tell you what to do, but I think it would be nice if you went to see her. She could use your support and know that you're there for her."

He read the note, but didn't respond. After several minutes of silence, Dr. Ramsey said goodbye and walked out the door, leaving Colton sitting alone. He folded the paper in half, stood up, and trotted up the stairs.

Thirty

Dr. Ramsey helped Alexis move her things to the downstairs guestroom, where Alexis would be sleeping from now on. Alexis offered Sarah her bedroom upstairs, if she wanted to stay for a while, but Sarah declined. After they had finished moving Alexis's things, they sat on the deck talking and drinking ice tea.

"I don't mind driving here to check on you every day, it's no problem at all."

"Are you sure?"

"Yes, I'm sure. Besides, after having a talk with Colton a couple of days ago, he seems to be around more. I mentioned to Colton about joining a teen group, you know, to help deal with your cancer, his drug abuse and possibly, even his father's death. All these issues are related to his outburst. Kids and teenagers usually act out because they don't understand what's going on or how to deal with their feelings. It's just a part of growing up; he'll pull through and so will you," Sarah smiled as she reached over and patted Alexis on the arm. It was so good to see Alexis more like herself. Sarah was relieved, but she knew they weren't out of the woods yet.

"You think so?"

"Yes, I do. Give him some time."

"Thank you for talking to Colton, though, I wish I'd been the one to tell him about the cancer."

"I was surprised you didn't tell him. I'm not here to judge you, Alexis, but maybe you shouldn't have kept the cancer from him, then maybe Colton would've been different towards you."

"I know, but after his father's suicide, and then finding out he was smoking marijuana, I didn't want to give him any more excuses to do drugs. I know I sound pessimistic and all, but with his behavior lately, I didn't know how else to feel or act."

"You need to think about your health and take care of yourself, Alexis. Try not to worry about other people right now. Colton will be fine. He's a teenager, and being a teenager they think the world will end if they don't get what they want when they want it. It's normal, natural, and a growing experience. Granted, Colton's had a little more thrown at him than most kids his age. It's a delicate age to start with—he's still a kid in many ways, but he feels like he's an adult. He's just trying to find himself in the world."

"Well, I hope he finds it soon because he has a chance at a great scholarship for college."

"That's wonderful news!"

"Oh, crap. I just remembered he has a game Friday night and the coaches from Jacksonville University will be there to watch him. I need to ask Colton what time the game starts. Would you like to go with me?"

"What sport does he play again?"

"Basketball."

"That happens to be one of my favorite sports besides football."

"Football, really? I never pictured you as a fan of football. You must like their tight jersey's," Alexis laughed.

"You know it," Dr. Ramsey joined in, laughing along with her.

"You know, I forgot what it was like to hang out with another woman, a friend," Alexis admitted.

"We actually have something in common. I usually spend all my time working and going home to my cat, Rufus. I don't go out much, and I can't remember the last time I went on a date with a man. God, it feels like a lifetime ago."

"You and me, both. When Jay was alive, we would try to have a date night a couple times a month, but it always seemed like work got in the way. I would call him and say I couldn't make it for dinner, then once I started doing that and he was so understanding, it was my excuse every time," Alexis stated, looking from her glass to the backyard.

"So, what's happened to the once-in-a-lifetime trip into space? Are you still going to do it?" Sarah felt it was time to change the subject back to safer topics.

"I actually haven't thought about the space mission lately, you know with everything going on. To answer your question, yes, I would still like to go, but if I don't..." she paused, thinking of all the hours she'd put in. "I think I'll be fine with not going. I know I've worked extremely hard to get this opportunity, but I've also learned that there is more to life than work. Besides, now that I have breast cancer with an endless amount of treatments, there won't be a space trip in my future." Alexis inhaled deeply through her nose, trying to hold back the tears that wanted to flow.

"What was it like? You know, being in a space shuttle and practicing a launch?" The doctor's words had become serious and inquisitive. Sarah really found Alexis a fascinating woman.

Alexis looked over at Sarah, "Like nothing you have ever imagined in your life. Have you ever been sky diving before?"

"Actually, yes, I have."

"Well, it's sort of like that. Except you're seat-belted inside a capsule. The adrenaline rushes through your body, and there's this one part in our exercise, if you look out the window, you can see stars as if you're actually in outer space," she replied with a dream-like quality to her voice.

"That sounds awesome."

"It was."

Alexis sat enjoying the warm weather and sipping her tea. It helped her to accept the changes in her life. She'd forgotten what it was like to relax and spend time with a friend. She liked Sarah and hoped she would get to know her better.

"Do you mind if I ask you some personal questions?" Alexis asked.

"No, fire away."

"Tell me about your family, where you grew up, and what things you like to do?"

"Wow, okay. Well, my parents live in Chicago. My mom's a librarian and my dad, he works for the state."

"What kind of work does he do?"

"It's all political work, one that I didn't want to get involved in. I love working with people and helping to heal the sick. When I was eleven, I decided to become a doctor when I grew up. My father sent me to the best schools, and after I finished, I chose to live down here."

"Did you ever think about moving back up north?"

"Yes and no, but I like the weather here. I don't know if I could handle living with cold winters. When you're a kid, it's different. When you're able to drive and the weather is bad, which is what the north is all about, you tend to think differently and get sick of driving in the snow."

"I have a dear friend who lives in Chicago," Alexis confided. "She's a schoolteacher. Carla actually lives in the south suburbs, away from all that hectic city life and traffic." Alexis frowned at the thought of her friend; she'd been so neglectful to Carla all these years and wished she'd kept in touch with her.

"Is everything okay? You look lost," Sarah asked.

"Oh, well, I was just thinking about Carla. We met back in college and after we graduated, she married and moved to Illinois. I stayed here, married Jay, had Colton, and as you know, went to work at NASA. I just miss her, is all."

"Well, maybe we should all take a trip up there and see my family and your friend. I'm sure Colton would like a trip before he heads off to college life."

"It all sounds great, but right now I need to get my health going in the right direction before I can think about a vacation."

"Maybe this summer, we could go. You know, after Colton is done with school?"

"Yeah, maybe? So tell me more about you?" Alexis asked.

"I see you're changing the subject. To be revisited at a later date," Sarah nodded, "when you're feeling better. Besides growing up in Chicago, I love to read, collect art and watch movies. I don't have many friends, if any. So, I don't really go out much and I don't have a boyfriend. In fact, I haven't dated in years."

"Art? What kind of art do you collect? I have a couple of paintings in the family room that you might be interested in seeing."

"I love going to art galleries and admiring the paintings I can't afford, but I have three hanging on my wall at home that I just couldn't help buying. One is a Warhol that I bought for fewer than two thousand dollars, if you can believe that. I happened to come across an article in the paper about priceless art being sold for a lot less than what it's worth at an auction gallery. I thought, what the heck, I have to go there and at least see what they have. I ended up buying the Warhol and two Rembrandt paintings."

"Wow! That sounds like a place I'd like to go to one day."

"Once you're feeling better, we should both go. I can never have too much art," Sarah laughed.

"Deal. And what's this about years since you've dated? How come, you're so beautiful and smart? Any man would be lucky to have you."

"I don't know. I guess like you, I've been too busy with work to enjoy my life."

"Then, I guess it's time we started living our lives and enjoy it every chance we get."

"Yeah, I guess so."

"Well, don't sound so glum. We were able to open up to each other and become friends. Good friends, I might add. Besides, I want to get to know you better, and that trip up north does sound intriguing."

Sarah smiled. "Let's get you better and make some plans."

They chatted for another hour before Colton came home from school and joined them outside.

"Hey, Colton. How was school today?" Alexis asked.

"It was fine. Got some homework to do, like always. Ah, hi, Dr. Ramsey."

Sarah nodded to Colton and silently listened to their interaction.

"Well, just think of it this way. In a couple more months, you'll graduate and the summer will be here for you to enjoy before you head off to college. Maybe we can take a trip this summer and get away?"

"A trip? Mom, we haven't taken a trip together, well, since I was a kid."

Alexis smiled. Oh, how she'd waited patiently for the moment he would call her "Mom" again. She wasn't going to say anymore right now. She didn't want to get his hopes up and disappoint him if she was too ill to take a vacation.

Colton was a little shy around Sarah. He gathered up his books, waved to them both, and went back in the house to do his homework.

Sarah smiled encouragingly at Alexis.

Thirty-One

Early the next morning, Colton climbed out of bed and headed into the bathroom to wash up before school. After getting dressed, he went downstairs and was surprised to see his mom sitting at the kitchen table.

"Good morning," Colton said.

"Good morning to you," Alexis replied.

He noticed his mom had more color in her face today—she wasn't as pale. He was hoping she was feeling better and that the new pills were helping. His mom hadn't been able to keep any food down before, but he saw she was nibbling on a muffin.

"How have you been feeling?"

"Oh, I'm doing better. Just some achiness in my bones, but I guess it's part of the process."

"Can't the doctor give you something for that?"

"I'm not sure; I'll have to ask the next time I see him."

"Him? I thought Dr. Ramsey was your doctor."

"Yeah, she is, but I see a different doctor for my cancer. Dr. Brownski is my Oncologist for the cancer. Dr. Ramsey is my GYN doctor."

"Oh, okay. Guess I should know this stuff, huh?"

"Colton, honey, I'm sorry. I should have talked to you about the cancer first, but I just didn't...I didn't think you could handle it. You know with everything that's been happening lately and all. But I don't want you to be worried. I'll be fine. Nothing's going to happen to me."

"Well, I hope not. I don't want to lose you too."

He walked to the pantry, grabbed a box of cereal and then a bowl from the cabinet beside the stove. He sat down across from his mom and grabbed the milk off the table.

"That's the nicest thing you've said to me in a long time," Alexis smiled. "So, how is school going?"

Colton was shoveling a spoonful of cereal in his mouth when she asked about school. "It's fine," he answered between mouthfuls.

"Do you have a basketball game this Friday?"

"Yeah."

"Is it okay if I come and bring Sarah with me?"

He looked up from his bowl, his forehead crinkled, "Who's Sarah?"

Alexis laughed, "Sorry, Dr. Ramsey's name is Sarah."

He nodded, "It's fine with me if she wants to come to the game. We play at Stallion High this Friday. Do you know where the school is?"

"No, not really."

"I'll write the directions down for you. The game starts at six." He went back to eating his cereal.

"I can't wait to see you play again."

He nodded and chewed at the same time. For several minutes, silence filled the air between them.

"I'm going back to work tomorrow," she said finally.

He stopped eating and stared down at his bowl. His shoulders tensed while sadness filled his heart. Things between them were getting better, but now his mom was heading back to the place that had caused the distance between them. No more bonding, she would fall back into her routine and they would drift apart. He couldn't even look at her; his heart was heavy with grief. He was so stupid to believe she'd give up her job and be a mother. He felt her looking at him, but he couldn't bring himself to look back at her. He lost his appetite and he set his spoon in the bowl, stood and walked towards the sink. Before he reached the doorway to the kitchen to leave, she spoke.

"Colton, I promise you, I will *not* make work my life, again. You are important to me, and I'll prove it to you. I want us to be a family."

His mouth opened, but nothing came out. He turned the corner and practically ran up the stairs to retrieve his books and head out to school.

When he came back down, he said a hurried goodbye and walked out the front door. He wasn't going to give *Alexis* a chance to cram more excuses down his throat. He didn't even notice how soon the endearment of "Mom" had turned back into her impersonal first name.

Colton wanted to give her the benefit of the doubt, though, but she was right—she'd have to prove to him she was willing to work for their relationship. She'd have to not let work get in the way. Plain and simple.

Thirty-Two

Colton drove by Jake's, picked him up, and then headed to school. Colton didn't even try to carry on a conversation with his friend, but Jake didn't ask what was bothering him, so he just drove.

Colton hadn't made any plans to go back out to the mysterious house and snoop around some more, but that would change once his mom went back to work.

"Are you coming to practice tonight after school?" Jake asked.

"Yeah, I'll be there."

"I don't mean to get personal, but you sure have been acting strange this past week. What's up with you?"

"Nothing's up."

"Well, you could've fooled me. Is there something going on with your mom? I know I asked you before, but you didn't really give me much of an answer, dude."

"Look, I don't want to talk about my mom, okay?"

"You don't have to bite my head off, bro'. I just thought maybe something was wrong, and you needed to talk about it."

"I don't want to talk about her or what's bugging me."

"Oh, so there is something bothering you. Fine, I get it. I won't ask again. Sorrrry," Jake replied.

Colton kept his eyes on the road and turned the last corner into the school parking lot. Neither said another word as they walked into the school.

Colton twisted the combination lock and opened his locker. He threw his books in and grabbed his algebra book, slammed the locker door shut and stomped off down the hall. Everyone around him was staring as he walked by. He entered the classroom and slumped down in his chair. When Mrs. McNickel came around the room, he took out his assignment and handed it to her.

By lunchtime, his mood had lifted, and he was feeling his normal self again. When Jake sat down next to him, Colton nudged him with his elbow.

"Sorry for getting so mad at you earlier," Colton said.

"Hey, no problem, but don't take it out on me next time. And just so you know, I'm here if you want to talk," Jake replied.

Colton nodded and changed the subject, "What are you doing after practice tonight?"

"Probably going home and doing homework, why?"

"Just wanted to see if you'd like to take a ride with me somewhere."

"Where?"

Before he could answer, three guys from the team sat down at the table. "I'll tell you later," Colton practically whispered.

Jake nodded and started eating.

The rest of the day flew by quickly, and Colton met up with Jake and went to the gym. After a couple of hours of running up and down the court and shooting hoops, the team headed into the locker room.

Jake was waiting outside by Colton's car when Colton came out.

"So, where exactly are we going?"

"You know I've been looking through my dad's case, right?"

"Yeah."

"I've found some things out and have been doing my own investigation. I went and talked to your dad, and just like before he told me to stop searching for answers; but I can't. I think Detective Bowen is hiding something from me. Something I'm not supposed to find out."

"Okay, I'm listening."

"There's this house I found on the Internet."

"You've lost me already."

Colton started from the beginning, telling Jake how he came across the house and what he had found, his conversation with Jake's dad, and the photo. Jake seemed to be listening to his every word and didn't interrupt. When he finished telling the story, Jake stood up while staring at the ground.

"So, what do you think? Do you want to go with me?"

"My Dad's a detective, man. What if we get caught and the police come? I don't need a police record before I head off to college."

"We won't get caught."

"You sound so sure of yourself."

"I've been there twice already and nothing's happened."

"First time for everything," Jake quipped.

"Well, are you coming with me or not?" Colton was starting to get irritated.

"Count me out. I'm not into all that cops-and-robber crap."

"I didn't say we were robbing the place. I just want to do some more checking around, is all!" Colton really wanted someone to go with him, and he'd thought Jake would help him.

"You can go if you want, but from what you've told me, wouldn't it be better if you go early? The person seems to be home after three. You need to get there in the morning. Just saying, not that I know what I'm talking about or anything."

"Actually, I think you do. I never thought about the time of day I was going there. I just went when I could, but you may be right," Colton said, immediately calming down and seeing Jake's point.

"At least I'm good for something," Jake laughed.

Colton punched Jake in the arm with his fist—not hard, more playful than anything—Jake grabbed his arm as if it hurt. They both turned and climbed in the car.

Colton dropped Jake off and decided to head home, instead of driving out to the house he found. Thoughts of his mom popped into his head—he had forgotten about their conversation that morning. He sighed heavily as he replayed it in his head. He would have to think more positively and concentrate on the good times they'd been having together. He knew there was no point in continuing to drag up the past. They needed to start fresh and go from there.

Thirty-Three

His mom wasn't in the kitchen when Colton got home, so he headed back to the guest room where she was now sleeping. He tapped lightly on the door as he turned the knob with his other hand and pushed the door open. He saw her sitting up in bed looking at her laptop.

"Hey, you're home," Alexis said looking up with a surprised grin.

"Yeah, I had practice today after school. How are you feeling?"

"Better. Just going through my emails from work so I'm not bombarded when I get there tomorrow."

He nodded and sat down on the edge of the bed, as far away from her as he could get.

"Is there something bothering you? Do you want to talk about it?" Alexis asked as her smile faded to a worried frown.

He shrugged his shoulders and looked at the floor. "Not really."

"I know I haven't been much of a mother for some time, but I still know when something is bothering you."

"It's nothing you need to be concerned about. I'm fine, really." He stood up, towering over her. "I'm going to get something to eat. Do you want anything?"

"I had some soup earlier, but thanks for asking."

He nodded, "I got some homework to do so I'll check in on you later, okay?"

"Sure," she replied.

He walked out the door, closing it behind him, as he'd found it. Colton didn't want to bother her while she was working. He felt like she'd shut a door between their relationship again. Well, he should have expected it when she was wrapped up in her job.

Once in the kitchen, he rummaged through the freezer and decided on lasagna. After he heated his food, he grabbed his books and went to his room. He set his books and plate down on his desk and plopped in the chair. He needed to think about something else besides his mom's obsession with NASA.

His eyes settled on the photo he'd found at that other house and picked it up. He held it in his hand and thought back to when the picture was taken.

It was one of many trips to the lake where they went fishing. His dad had brought the camera with them that day, mostly to take pictures of the fish they caught, and stopped a person walking by, to take a photo of them. He studied the photo of the lake and saw something in the background. Far off in the distance there sat a dark-colored car. How had he not noticed the car before? It wouldn't have meant anything that day, but in the past week with what he'd learned, it sure meant something now.

Colton turned on the light above his computer and held the photo underneath. He wasn't sure if it was dark blue or black, or even the same vehicle? The vehicle was parked at an angle, so the license plate wasn't visible. He tried to make sense of his new findings, but if anything, he was more bewildered than ever.

First, his dad was found dead after a dark blue Accord left the scene. Second, he saw the same car at a house an hour away from here. Nothing made sense!

Suddenly his mom returning to work didn't matter anymore. In fact, for the moment, it didn't even enter Colton's mind. His head was filled with more important questions, and he was going to get answers!

Thirty-Four

Alexis stepped out of the shower and wrapped a towel around her body. With a *zig-zag motion* of her hand, she wiped away the steam on the mirror. Her complexion was still way too pale so she decided to wear makeup and hoped no one would notice she was sick.

After getting dressed and applying color to her face, she blow-dried her hair, letting the soft brunette waves fall over her shoulders. She shut off the light and opened the closet door to stand in front of the full-length mirror. She had lost so much weight this past week and she knew there was no way of hiding it. After she fastened the belt around her waist, she closed the door and left the room, then made her way down the hall and into the kitchen.

She poured herself a cup of coffee and ventured outside. The fresh air hugged her body, making her feel snug. The ocean water from the beach, which was a mile away, made her sneeze. The water let off a salty aroma depending on the time of day.

She lifted the cup and took a couple of sips then turned and went back inside. Colton was entering the kitchen when she came in. They said their 'good mornings' and then she grabbed something to eat.

"Do you have practice tonight?"

"Yep."

"Then I'll make dinner after you get home."

"You know you don't have to cook, right? Besides, you haven't been eating much lately."

"I know, but it feels nice doing things again."

"If that's what you want to do, I won't stop you."

"Are you okay? You seem...I don't know, a little moody this morning."

"Yeah, I'm fine. I guess I didn't sleep as *good* as I would've liked to."

"Oh? Anything I can help you with? Usually when you don't sleep well, there's something eating at you."

She wanted him to open up to her, but he'd locked the door that had opened a little bit between them, and now she couldn't get more than a few words out of him. But no matter what, she would continue to try to unlock the latch he had over his heart. She wasn't about to let this past week slip away and go back to the way it was. She cared for her son and she loved him more than life itself. He *did* understand how she felt about him. Didn't he?

Whether he did or not, she wasn't going to back down and surrender. It had been her choice back then to work all those hours—her boss hadn't made her do it, and he wouldn't start now. She had control of her life, well, except for the cancer part, but she was the one who decided what she was or wasn't going to do.

"Just school stuff," Colton replied, after an awkward pause.

"I'm here if you need me."

He nodded, sat down at the table, and started eating. She refilled her cup, grabbed a banana from a bowl on the counter, and joined him. Like the day before, only the sound of the ticking of the clock filled the room. She looked at her son from the corner of her eye and watched him eat. When he'd finished, he strolled to the sink, rinsed his bowl, and plopped it in the dishwasher. She could feel him behind her and then felt his lips kiss the top of her head. She smiled to herself, warmness hugging her heart. The sound of his footsteps told her he'd left the room and was heading back upstairs.

Thirty-Five

Alexis parked the car in the secure NASA lot and took in a deep breath. "Here goes nothing," she mumbled.

She was a little weak getting out of the car. She leaned against the fender for a moment while her head cleared, then shifted her briefcase from her right hand to the left. As she walked towards the building, willpower allowed her to stand tall with a strong, purposeful gait.

She scanned her card, walked confidently through security, and headed down the hall to her office. Eyes looked her way, but no one said a word to her. By the time she reached her door, she hadn't realized she'd been holding her breath the whole time.

Once inside, she set her briefcase on the desk and took out what she needed. She placed the leather case on the floor next to the desk, and turned on her computer. She grabbed the phone, tapped the key for voicemail, and listened to her messages. She wrote each message down and then rested the phone in its cradle. One thing she enjoyed was the peacefulness of having her own office. The silence made her feel more relaxed.

Tap, tap, tap.

She jumped in her chair, making the wheels *clack* on the wooden floor.

"Come in?"

"Hello, Alexis, glad to have you back," Fred said. "When you have some free time, I'd like to get you up to speed on... Did you lose some weight? I don't remember you looking so...so slim, before."

Alexis nodded, not knowing how to reply. For a second she glanced away and then met his eyes. "I caught the flu while I was off and well...it was hard to eat and keep food down, but I'm feeling better now."

"Are you sure? Because if you're not well, you should take a little more time off. Michael Watts has some exercises for the space shuttle recruits, so it's definitely best for you to hold off if you're not feeling up to par. The exercises are strenuous, as you know."

Alexis had totally forgotten about the program and exercises that needed to be done before anyone could be cleared to take that ride into space. There was no way she could perform in the group. Her immune system was low and her body still hurt. The only thing she felt capable of doing was walking short distances and then sitting down.

A hint of positive energy seeped into her body; maybe this was what she needed to get out of going. Then, maybe they wouldn't have to know she had breast cancer. Her heart sank, though, at the thought of not going on the shuttle—her dream packed away, never to be lived.

Yet, on second thought, she really had nothing to complain about. Look at what she'd already accomplished in her life. How many people could sit here and say, *"I was this close to flying in a space shuttle."* Not many, she was sure.

Alexis knew she needed to be honest with Fred and tell him that she couldn't go; that she had to pass on the once-in-a-lifetime trip into outer space. Inside, she was *okay* about it. No, she was more than okay with the split-second decision she'd made. She wanted a life with her son; one she might not ever get again. She pulled her chair up to the desk and waved her hand for Fred to sit down. Alexis sat up tall and proud, clearing her throat.

"Fred, I haven't been honest with you this past week, or right now either, for that matter," she said, taking in a deep breath. "I took some time off because I was diagnosed with breast cancer."

Alexis stopped abruptly, wanting to take back what she'd said, but this was the right thing to do, so she continued before Fred could respond, "It saddens me to have to tell you that I won't be able to be on the team. You know I've always wanted to go, but I guess sometimes life gets in the way. On my time off, I did some thinking—a lot of thinking—and I know I have to forfeit my position. I'm sorry, but you'll have to replace me with someone else. The crew will have to go without me on this journey." Alexis relaxed her shoulders and sat back, feeling good about getting the truth out, yet, a part of her felt defeated.

She suddenly realized that she'd subconsciously made this decision days ago, but it had just surfaced in her mind. Now, what she needed to say was done and over with. Besides, even if she wanted to go, there was no way her health would allow her.

A look of shock covered Fred's face, as he stared at her, then at the desk in front of him. "Alexis…I…um…" He tried to look up. "I'm so sorry to hear this. I understand your decision and will break the news to the crew and Michael Watts for you, if that's what you want, of course?"

"I'm fine with you telling them. I wish I had some good news to tell you, but unfortunately, I don't. Before you go, I'd like to ask if I could work my hours around the radiation treatments I need to have? I have them scheduled for Mondays, but I can change the day, of course. Also, I won't be able to work more than eight hours anymore. I have to take care of things, you know, like my health and Colton. I want to spend more time with him and less time at work. Maybe, I could do some work from home to make up for not being here?"

"Sure, sure. Whatever is convenient for you. I have no problem with you or how many hours you work. You do what needs to be done. Again, I'm so sorry you have to go through this. You've been through enough this past year. Anything I can do…well, just let me know," Fred finished softly, still having trouble looking Alexis straight in the eye. All of his respect for her, fear of losing a good employee, and so much more was etched on his face.

Alexis nodded, "Thank you for being so understanding about all of this, Fred. I promise to keep you posted on any medical issues that may arise." She was determined to keep the conversation as professional as possible. She couldn't let her guard down because tears were close to the edge. *This is not the time or place, and Fred really is a good man.*

"No problem, like I told you last week, you've worked here ten years, and I've never had any issues with you or your work. You're *top*-notch, and I'm honored to have you on the team. If you need more time off, let me know and I'll approve it for you. I'm sure I'll be speaking for everyone here and they'll agree—you're a hard worker and an asset to this mission." Fred paused for a short breath, then added, "We'll all be praying for you to get better."

"Well, thank you, Fred. I appreciate your kindness and generosity," Alexis said quickly before her eyes could mist over. She hid her fear and loss behind a weak smile.

Fred stood and made his way around the desk to stand beside her. He raised his hand as if to touch her, but let his arm drop to his side. He nodded and turned, then walked through the door. He looked like he was still in shock, and it was obvious he didn't know what to do or say.

Her whole body shivered as if there was a draft in the room. She stood and walked to the door, and removed a sweater from a hook on the back. She slipped her arms through the sleeves and wrapped it close to her chest.

It seemed that life was giving her a second chance, now; it was time to live it!

Part Two

Life

You will never be happy if you continue to search for what happiness consists of.

You will never live if you are looking for the meaning of life.

Albert Camus

Family

I'll never stop dreaming that one day we can be a real family, together, all of us laughing and talking, loving and understanding, not looking at the past but only to the future.

LaToya Jackson

Thirty-Six

Colton set his books inside the locker and changed into shorts and a T-shirt. The rest of the team was ready and waiting in the gym. He was running a little late, due to being preoccupied with other thoughts.

Two hours later, he showered and got dressed. He only had one thing on his mind today and that was to go back out to the house. He dropped Jake off at home, neither of them said much in the car, and then drove towards his destination. He parked his car on the side street again and walked down the road. Every once in a while he glanced at the other homes, but mostly he kept his eyes on the ground. He didn't want anyone to remember him.

As he approached the house, he didn't see a car, so he went around to the back. He tried the door, but this time it was locked. He cupped his hands at the sides of his face and peered through the window beside the door. He saw movement, more like a shadow, near the living room. Without thinking, his knees hit the sandy ground, hoping he hadn't been seen.

Colton at over six-foot-three, was acting like a scared wimp. *How disgusting,* he thought to himself, but this was uncharted territory for him. Except for occasionally smoking pot, he wasn't one to get into any trouble. *But* if he wasn't looking for trouble, then why was he coming out to this house snooping around? Deep inside he knew he needed to find out the truth, but what was the truth? What was he anticipating? Did it matter? He didn't have a clue.

Clunk!

His heart quickened and pulsated fast as he crawled to the side of the house. With his back against the wall, he turned his head just enough to see. Someone had opened the door, but didn't come out. He needed to see their face, but the person, whoever it was, stood out of sight. He took a breath and held it in—waiting. When the door closed, he exhaled and bowed his head. He was this close to seeing the person, but it was as if they knew someone was out there watching, waiting.

He leaned back and slid down the wall until he was on his butt. Knees bent, he rested his hands on the ground. All he could think about was, *what if this person was the one who'd had my dad killed?* They had to have something to do with his death; he was sure of it. They must have parked the car in the garage, as *if* they were waiting for him to arrive. Maybe this person had noticed the photo was missing and figured someone must have taken it, but then why were they hiding it away in a drawer anyway, if it was something of value? So many questions he had no answers to.

He wasn't sure why he was so afraid and hid like a frightened animal. He was tall, strong, and had broad shoulders. Colton knew he looked intimidating, even if he wasn't, but he could probably kick someone's ass if he had to. Although he knew, he wasn't a fighter because he'd never had to be.

All he had to do was go up to the door and knock. If he recognized the person, he would either turn around and run, or start asking questions. He wouldn't run if he didn't know the person. A stranger would have to explain himself. Hell, he didn't even know if it was a 'he' or a 'she' who lived here. He'd just been assuming it was a man. He shook his head; he needed the courage to face this head-on.

Time *ticked* by, and he still wasn't sure what to do.

"Screw it, I'm going up to the door and knock. Whatever happens, happens," he mumbled.

He silently counted down, *three, two, one.*

He stood, walked to the back door, and knocked.

He stared down at the steps, shuffling his feet. Right foot twice, then left foot twice, and started over again.

The dead bolt made a hard *clunk* and the door *squeaked* open.

Colton held his breath, as if that would slow his speeding heart, then looked up.

Thirty-Seven

Alexis dialed Colton's number for the third time but there was no answer. She stood from the table where she'd been sitting in the kitchen and went to the counter. She knew Jay used to keep phone numbers in a book in the drawer by the phone. She opened the drawer and found it immediately. She took it out and flipped through the pages, stopping when she came to Jake's name. She quickly dialed the number. Biting her lip as she waited for someone to answer, after only two rings, she heard a man's voice.

"Hello."

"Hi, this is Colton's mother, Alexis Finley. I...I was wondering if Colton was there, and if I could please speak with him?"

"No, I'm afraid he isn't here, Mrs. Finley."

"Oh, well, did he happen to stop by at all?" She switched the phone in her nervous hands, waiting for a response.

"He dropped Jake off around five. He didn't come in the house, so I'm not sure where he was going after that."

"Could I please speak to Jake; maybe he knows where he went?"

"Sure, hold on."

She heard a *clunk* and figured the man had set the phone down to fetch Jake.

In less than a minute, she heard a different voice say, "Hello?"

"Hi, is this Jake?"

"Yeah, who is this?" Jake asked.

"This is Colton's mother. I was just wondering if you knew where he might have gone after he dropped you off? I thought he'd be home by now from basketball practice and all, but I haven't seen him."

"No, I'm sorry, he didn't say a word to me. Did you try calling his cell?"

"Well, of course. Three times, but it just rings until the voicemail picks up."

Jake didn't reply, only silence filled the line. She thought for a second he had hung up, but then he spoke.

"Well, I'd like to help you, but like I said he didn't say anything to me. I'm sure he'll be home any minute now."

"I'm sure you're right. Thank—"

Click.

She held the phone out in front of her face, her mouth open. "Well, that was rude," she muttered.

Setting down the phone on the counter, she looked at the wall clock. It was past seven. *Where could he have gone?*

Alexis puttered around the kitchen, stirred the meat, and then replaced the lid. Glancing back up at the clock, she saw another twenty minutes had passed. If he didn't come home soon, she was going to wear the coating off the tile floor.

Thirty-Eight

Colton's stomach tightened and then a fluttery, empty feeling appeared. He swallowed and blinked several times. Part of him thought he was dreaming, but he realized that wasn't so.

He had come here right after dropping off Jake and scurried like a *scaredy-cat* to the side of the house. Now he was standing at the back door of a house he'd been to several times. The only difference now was someone was home, and that someone was standing right in front of him. He wiped his palms on the side of his jeans, knowing he couldn't be imaging this. *Am I?*

No. No, he wasn't... This was real. He just couldn't understand how? *The call. The funeral.* Everything that had happened was now right in front of him. The man's voice brought him back to the present time.

"Son, are you coming in, or are you going to stand out there all night?"

"Dad, how?" Was all Colton could muster.

"Come in, and I'll explain what I can to you."

He fumbled up the steps and made his way into the house, but didn't take his eyes off his father. The door shut, and he stood face to face with his dad.

"How are you here? I um…I went to your funeral. They said you were dead. But you're not. You're here." He ran his hand through his hair. Colton was in shock at seeing his father alive and standing in front of him.

Tears filled his eyes as Colton reached out and wrapped his arms around his father. They embraced each other longer than Colton had ever hugged his father before. He took a step back to focus on his dad's face, again.

"Colton, I've missed you so much, and I'm sorry I had to do this to you," Jay Finley said with true sincerity, but hesitate severity as well.

"Why are you living here and not at home with us? Why did you do this to us? To me?" Colton snapped, his dazed shock fading into anger.

"Please, come and sit down, and I'll explain as much as I can to you."

Jay took the lead and walked into the living room, taking the lime green and brown spotted chair. Colton followed behind and sat on the sofa across from him.

Colton couldn't grasp the way he was feeling. Several different emotions were swimming inside him. He just couldn't get over his father sitting right in front of him, alive and well! He prayed that he wasn't dreaming—that this really was happening. But a part of him was furious with his father. He just couldn't understand why Dad would do this to him and to Mom, especially now that she was so sick!

"So, how have you been, son?"

"We haven't seen each other in over seven months and the first thing you ask me is, *'How am I doing?'* I think you should just start by telling me what the hell is going on and why you're here?" he exploded.

"I don't blame you for being upset with me."

"Upset!" Colton gave a hearty laugh. "Dad, I'm a little more than upset. I'm confused and uncertain. I don't know what to think or say. Mom and I were told that you killed yourself and now…now you're sitting here, as if you've merely been away on vacation or something. I love you, Dad. I looked up to you. I did everything you asked of me. I play basketball and get good grades; well, at least I used to. I worshiped the ground you walked on and then what? You faked your death and now you're finally allowing me to know you're alive? Don't you realize how much that hurts me? Do you know what it's going to do to Mom?"

"No, you can't tell your mother."

"And why not?"

"It's complicated."

"You got that right."

"Look, son, it was the only way out. I had to vanish for a while—just until things get cleared up and it's safe for me to come home."

"What do you mean *safe?* What's happened to make you supposedly kill yourself and not let us know?"

"Do you remember the man who was at the house that day when you came home from school? We were arguing, and I asked you to go in the other room?"

Colton nodded.

"Well, I did something I shouldn't have, and he was there to help me out. I can't tell you what because it'll put you in danger. I couldn't live with myself if something happened to you or your mother. Do you understand, son?"

"I'm trying to, but there are so many things I want to know."

"I'll explain what I can, but you have to trust me. You can't let your mother know I'm here. Can you do that for me?"

"Dad, there's something you need to know about Mom," Colton said softly, staring down at his hands.

"Is there something going on with your mother? Is she seeing someone else? What? What is it, Colton?"

"No, she's not involved with anyone. She...she has breast cancer. She needs you, Dad. She's been going to the doctor's and having all kinds of treatments done. She's been really sick and I'm... Well, I'm a little scared something might happen to her. I've already lost you and don't want to lose her too. She's trying to get better."

"She...she has cancer? How bad is it? She's not going to... Oh, God, what have I done? Not my wife. Not your mother." He slumped back in his chair and placed his face in his hands.

"I'm not sure how bad it is or if she will die, but the good that's come out of all this is she's actually been home more and not working like she used to. I think her getting cancer has, I don't know, changed her in some way."

Jay raised his head with a tentative smile surfaced, "She's not working all those hours like she did?" He hesitated, the smile turned to a worried frown. "What was she like after, you know, my death?"

"She took some time off work and stayed in her room most of the time. I don't think I saw her but a couple of times. I blamed her for you killing yourself."

"Colton, why? She isn't to blame, even if I had. Your mother is driven by her dreams. Since the day I met her, she couldn't stop talking about going to work for NASA and one day being able to fly in the space shuttle. She's a hard worker and very determined. That's why I didn't stop her from living her dreams. I wanted her to be happy."

"Yeah, but were you happy? Didn't you miss the woman you met and fell in love with?"

"Yes, yes I did, but when she was happy, I was too. I always prayed that once she got to go to space that she'd come back to us and we'd be a family again."

"She was picked to go," Colton informed him.

"To space?"

Colton nodded.

"That's wonderful news."

"I don't think she can go, unless she doesn't tell them about her cancer."

"Oh."

"Colton, can you promise me something?"

"Yeah, sure."

"One, don't tell her about me. Two, can you please keep me posted on her health? When this is over with, I want to come home. Do you think she'll be okay with that?"

Colton's eyes sparkled and gleamed, "I know I'd be glad to have you home again. And yes, I'll keep you posted. Can you answer a question for me?"

"I'll try."

"I've been doing my own investigation into your *so-called* suicide, and the only thing that puzzles me is the car? In the picture I found here, upstairs, there was a car in the background. Do you know who that car belongs to?"

"I'm not sure I follow," Jay said, shaking his head.

He told him about his last visit and what he'd found. "The dark blue Accord—I've seen it here in the driveway the last two times I've been here."

"It belongs to the guy who is helping me. Have you talked to anyone about this?"

"Only Detective Bowen."

"You talked to him?"

"Well, I went to him a couple of times asking about your suicide and all. The last time I talked to him, he said to quit searching for answers because there weren't any. When I got a copy of the police report, I went on my own and did some investigating. That's what led me to this house."

A grandfather clock tucked in a shadowed corner chimed, making Jay look at the time. "Son, you'd better head home before it gets any later. I wouldn't want your mother to start asking you questions."

"Yeah, I guess so. When can I see you again?"

"I'll find a way to contact you and let you know. For now, you need to go home and remember, don't say a word to your mother. She has enough to worry about."

He nodded.

They both stood and walked through the kitchen to the back door. Jay held out his hand, but Colton didn't take it, instead, he wrapped his arms around his dad and hugged him tight. Jay opened the door and as Colton headed out, he turned and smiled.

"It was good to see you again, Dad. I knew you didn't kill yourself. I just knew it."

"Thank you, son, for having faith in me. I'm sorry it had to turn out this way. There really wasn't any alternative."

Colton didn't know what else to do but nod and lift his hand in a farewell gesture. He turned, walked down the steps, and around the house. The questions he should've asked had slipped to the back of his mind. Why his dad was here and not at home, still remained a secret.

~ ~ ~ ~ ~

By the time Colton pulled into the driveway, it was well past eight-thirty. He got out of the car and locked it. Before he could make it up the walk, the porch light flicked on and his mom came storming out the front door.

"Where have you been, Colton? I thought you were coming home after practice and we'd have dinner together? Do you realize what time it is? I was worried something might have happened to you!"

Colton took two steps back when she came out of the door, ranting. The porch light glowed around her, showing her fragile body in silhouette. He couldn't remember ever seeing her so thin before and wondered how she'd been feeling lately. In fact, though, this had to be the first time she'd showed any kind of affection toward him. She was actually worried about him. He let a slight smile surface as he continued up the brick walk. He climbed the porch steps and took her in his arms—something he hadn't done since he was a child.

Thirty-Nine

Alexis was having difficulty finding the right words and allowed him to embrace her. She couldn't remember the last time they'd hugged. Oh, how she missed her son and wished she'd done things different instead of putting her career first!

No more, she thought and squeezed him tighter, like she never wanted to let him go. He gasped, and she loosened her grip, letting him unfold from her arms.

"Mom, I'm sorry I had you worried, which still shocks me, but I had some things to take care of. I promise not to do it again."

She tilted her head to the side and pursed her lips. Who was this grown boy in front of her? He was being nice to her and showing her affection. She looked at him as though he were someone else and not her son. Her eyes searched him from head to toe. His blond hair was unruly as if he'd been running his hand through it, but everything else seemed to look the same. She glanced down; he touched her hand; she looked back up into his face.

"Are you feeling all right? Should we go inside?" Colton inquired pleasantly.

She was at a loss for words and only nodded. He let go of her hand and placed his hand on her lower back, giving a slight push to go inside.

Alexis could feel him following her as she made her way into the kitchen. She turned around and asked, "Are you hungry? Have you eaten yet?"

"I'm famished," he replied and pulled out a chair.

She walked over to the stove, turning the burner on to reheat the ground beef from earlier. As the meat warmed, she placed lettuce, tomatoes, sour cream, cheddar cheese, and taco shells on the table.

They ate in silence, which didn't surprise her. She picked at her food, not feeling hungry and watched as her tall, handsome son woofed down four tacos and was starting on his fifth. She wasn't sure where he was putting all this food, but he was an active, growing boy.

After they finished eating, Colton insisted on cleaning up and made his mom sit and relax at the table. As he cleared plates and piled them into sudsy hot water, he was comfortable enough with his back to his mom to say, "I think I'm going to take Dr. Ramsey's advice and start going to the group meeting for drug abuse."

Her hand flew to her chest, "Colton, I think that's a wonderful idea. What made you decide to go?"

"Just been doing some thinking, and well, it's time I started acting like an adult and being responsible."

She rose from the chair and turned towards him; her eyes danced and sparkled when she smiled. She could get used to this new Colton, and she decided she wanted to share with him some good news as well. She picked up a towel and started drying the dishes Colton had put in the drainer.

"I decided to talk with my boss today, and I told him that I wouldn't be working long hours anymore. I filled him in on my health. As much as I wanted to and have always dreamed of going in the space shuttle, I had to tell him I couldn't go," she said, her radiant smile turning to a frown. *I wanted this to be good news; why am I still so uncertain?* She thought to herself, surprised by her reaction, especially now that she knew she was doing what was right for Colton. She bowed her head to hide her feelings.

Earlier when she'd told her boss, she'd been okay with the decision, but she guessed it hadn't fully sunk in yet and, *now?* Now, she had to admit, at least to herself, that she felt sad and disappointed.

Her son reached out, stroked her arm, and then lifted her chin to look into her eyes. For a moment, he seemed so much like Jay, so grown up.

"Mom, I know how bad you've been wanting to go, and I'm sorry. I want you to know, no matter what, I'm proud of all the things you've accomplished in your life. You should feel proud of yourself. It makes me want to succeed in your footsteps."

Alexis was taken aback by his words—she wasn't sure how to respond. Two weeks ago, they were jumping down each other's throats and now...now he was a changed person. They both were. Though, tonight, there was something very different about him. Something she wasn't quite sure of. She knew it took time to change and wasn't sure what to think about this sudden maturity or even what questions to ask him so she could understand what had prompted this. She couldn't help but think of Jay, again. He really was acting like his father. It was bittersweet and brought back such vivid memories. *Oh, how I miss him; I need Jay so much right now!*

The questions would come to her when the time was right. She was content just to watch him for now. To her, he seemed happier than he had been since...since Jay died. Maybe he'd finally let go and decided to move on with his life instead of living in the past. *It's possible,* she thought, *anything is possible.*

"Mom, I don't think the plate can get any dryer," he laughed and bumped her shoulder, the teenager surfacing again.

She stopped when he nudged her and laughed along with him. "Guess I was in another world there for a minute."

"Yeah, you could say that again. Well, I got some homework to do; I'll see you in the morning."

"Yeah, okay, see you."

After she heard him bound happily up the steps, she opened the cabinet to her left and placed the plate on the shelf. She hated drying dishes. They usually used the dishwasher, but they'd been talking and getting along so well she hadn't wanted to jinx the moment. Colton had just started washing the dishes by hand, for a change. Or was it a change for him? Did Jay and Colton do this together when she worked late? *Another thought to ponder.*

She hung the dishtowel over the oven handle and turned off the light. She locked the front door on her way to the room. After changing her clothes, she padded into the bathroom and brushed her hair and teeth then climbed into bed. She shook out a pill from each prescription bottle, grabbed the glass of water, and swallowed.

Once under the covers, she stared up at the ceiling, thinking back on their conversation. She still couldn't get a grip on how sweet he was with her tonight and decided not to over-analyze it. A goodnight's sleep was what she needed after her night of worrying, then the affectionate man-child her son had suddenly become, and loving memories of her husband. The tears that glided down her cheeks weren't the sobs she'd had for so long after Jay's suicide—they were a mixture of love and sadness. *No wonder I'm so confused,* she thought, but an endearing smile came to her lips as she drifted off to sleep.

Forty

Sunlight beamed through the slits of the blind and danced across her face. She opened one eye and then the other, feeling as if she hadn't slept. Her body felt weak and tired as though she'd just completed a marathon.

She thought back to yesterday and the day before that. She had felt good; maybe even better, but today she hurt all over. She tossed the blankets to the side and sat up. Her feet touched the cold floor, making her jump. She moved her foot around until she found a slipper and stuck her foot in, doing the same with the other. She stood and made her way to the bathroom and once finished, she proceeded to the kitchen in search of coffee.

The kitchen was vacant. Alexis sighed; she'd been hoping Colton would be up and waiting for her. The coffee pot *sputtered* as it finished brewing. She grabbed a cup and filled it, then went outside.

Every morning since the day they had moved here eighteen years ago, Alexis had her first cup of coffee on the patio. It was like a tradition to her. She loved the feel of the morning air on her face and the warm breeze rippling through her hair. She loved the smell of the ocean air and wished they had bought a house on the beach where she could watch the waves *slap* the sand and the sun poke over the horizon. Maybe one day they'd live by the beach, even though by then Colton will be off to college and Alexis will be left on her own.

She could still do it if she wanted to; she let out another deep weighted sigh. She'd never thought about being alone. She had her work, and Jay had always been here to take care of things at home and Colton. What had she been thinking all those years ago after Colton was born, going to work when he was just a little boy? Did she honestly give up her family and make her job more important?

A few days ago, Alexis had come to the realization that she had neglected her family for all those years. That's why she'd chosen to tell her boss that she couldn't go on the space shuttle and had to cut back her hours. In the end, though, she really didn't have the choice—her health had made the decision for her. Would she have given up her dream if she hadn't gotten sick? *"Probably not,"* she whispered to the ocean breeze.

She let herself reflect on how much more she would have missed of her son's life and Jay—they would never have the time together they'd always planned for after her big dreams were realized—the years afterward that would never be.

Standing against the railing, Alexis thought back to last night. She wouldn't change the relationship she was having with her son, not for anything in the world. Alexis looked up at the sky, straightening her posture and smiled, the feeling of tingling warmth flowed through her body. She raised her cup into the air. "Here's to new beginnings."

Forty-One

Colton stretched his arms over his head and yawned. He couldn't believe two weeks had gone by since he'd seen his father. He'd kept busy with schoolwork and gone to practice every night. The team had won the game that Friday; now tomorrow was the championship. They were to play at home, which he thought was an advantage. He felt more confident and played well when the games were at home, especially when his mom showed up with Dr. Ramsey.

Colton knew his mom and Dr. Ramsey would be coming to watch him play in the championship game on Saturday. Although, he knew his mom had been feeling under the weather lately, she hadn't admitted anything to him. He could tell by the way she walked and eased down to sit at the table. He'd asked her how she was feeling, but she waved her hand in the air as if to say, *"Don't worry about me."* But Colton did worry. Cancer wasn't a friend that came to visit and then left without a trace.

When Dr. Ramsey came over last week, he stopped her outside and asked her questions about breast cancer, and what his mother's chances were. Sarah had filled him in as best she could and ended with, "We'll have to wait and see what happens. Breast cancer can continue to recur, but in some cases with radiation and chemo, it will disappear and not show it's ugly face for many years; every case is different."

The answer comforted him, but deep down inside he continued to worry about his mom. Her body was slimmer than usual, and every time they ate dinner, she picked at her food. The only good thing he saw was that she wasn't working like she used to. Alexis had kept her promise to him and didn't work all those crazy hours. Would he be considered a bad person to think that the cancer that had come into their lives was a good thing? Because now his mom was home and being the mother, he'd longed for?

Colton wanted to believe that things happened for a reason. First, his dad leaving his life and then returning, but only because he wouldn't believe Dad would commit suicide, and he'd gone searching for the truth. Second, Mom got breast cancer and stopped working all the time, but she had to get better—she just had to be completely cured! —For his belief in the universe to be accurate.

He took in a deep breath and exhaled, feeling a heavy weight in his heart. He pulled back the covers and climbed out of bed. Time to start another hopeful, yet challenging, day.

After Colton showered and dressed, he padded down the stairs to the kitchen. He entered the room, but it was deserted. His mom was usually up by now and out on the deck. He glanced outside, but she wasn't there. He turned and made his way down the hall and tapped on the door. No answer.

He turned the knob and went inside. Sunlight lit up the room, giving him a full view. He could see she wasn't in bed and looked towards the door that led to the bathroom. The door was ajar, but no light came out. He strolled over and reached his hand out to knock on the door, just in case she was using the toilet. When she didn't respond, he peeked his head around the corner and saw her silhouette lying on the floor.

Colton rushed inside and flicked on the light, but his mother didn't move. He knelt down and put his hand to the side of her neck. He could just barely feel a shallow pulse. He touched her forehead with his fingers. She was cold and clammy. He turned her chin towards him and noticed dried vomit along her cheek and on the floor. He stood and sprinted to the phone by the bed and called 911.

He bolted for the living room, unlocked the front door, and then ran back to sit by his mother, waiting for the ambulance to arrive. He held her head in his lap and caressed her thinning hair away from her face with a washcloth. From the bathroom, he heard pounding on the door. He laid her head gently back down on the floor and ran to the front door.

Two men stood outside, one was stocky looking and the other slim and lanky; they were carrying a stretcher. He took them down the hall to the bathroom where she was lying.

Colton's heavy footsteps paced the length of the hallway just outside the bedroom where he could still hear what was happening, his hands trembling, as he waited for the EMT's to help his mom. His heart raced and his mouth was dry, but those were the least of his worries. His mom was unresponsive, lying on the bathroom floor.

He couldn't lose her; he didn't want to lose her. They were finally bonding and becoming a family and now…now he felt lost without her.

The two men came out the door carrying his mom on the stretcher. He looked down at her; her eyes remained closed, and she was wearing a neck brace. Her pale face etched in his mind. He moved out of their way as they turned the corner and went out the door to the ambulance. He patted his pocket for his keys and cellphone. He had them both and walked out the door, locking it behind him. He climbed inside the ambulance and sat beside her. He watched the slim, lanky man perform procedures—he had no clue what they were, so he kept his focus on her face. Just as long as they were doing what had to be done to save her life! Colton wanted to cry, but he was *'the-man-of-the-house'* now and needed to be strong.

"*How I wish Dad were here,*" he cried silently to himself.

Forty-Two

They arrived at the hospital twenty minutes later. Colton jumped out and stood to the side, wiping his palms against his jeans. On the ride to the hospital, the man in the back had asked him questions he had no answers to. Why didn't he pay more attention to her? He'd accepted her answers when she'd told him she was feeling fine, even though he'd known it wasn't the truth.

"Stupid, stupid," he mumbled. His body numb as he thought of the worst. *"She can't die. Please, don't let her die,"* he repeated in his head.

He followed the men through the sliding doors. The smell of antiseptic stung his nose when he inhaled. His head swarmed with the sound of cries and moans filling the room around him. The intercom blurted out codes to the working staff. He glanced around the emergency room. A woman with jet-black hair sat with her head down, sniffling and dabbing her nose with a Kleenex. He twirled around when he heard the high-pitch alarm of a machine and then several people in smocks and white jackets came running past him.

Colton had been so distracted by all the activity that he hadn't seen where they'd taken his mom. He saw the nurse's station and took several steps toward the counter. A young woman wearing a red smock with a stethoscope hanging around her neck looked up. She had one of those heart-shaped faces with ocean blue eyes that sparkled when the lights hit them just right. Her lips were thin with just a hint of pink lip-gloss.

She smiled, "Can I help you with something?"

He swallowed the lump in his throat. "My...uh...mom was just brought in," he stuttered.

She nodded. "I'll need a little bit more information than that. We have quite a few people here, as you can see. Can you tell me what she was brought in for?"

"She's been sick and...um... she was brought in by ambulance a few minutes ago."

"Okay, what's her name and I'll check for you."

"Alexis Finley," he told her as his eyes glanced around the lobby and then back at her. He couldn't help feeling some kind of attraction towards this beautiful young girl—an emotion he'd never felt before. He couldn't understand what was happening to him; he should be thinking about his mom and not this girl standing in front of him. Maybe it was because she was trying to help him, and he felt so alone.

School and basketball were his whole life—he'd had no time for dating. Besides, no girl at school had ever made his heart feel all-warm and fuzzy the way she just did. He shook his head to clear his thoughts. *"What's wrong with me?"* he silently chastised himself.

"You can take a seat over there while I find out?"

He nodded and walked over to an empty chair along the wall. The cushion *hissed* as he sat down. He rubbed the back of his neck as his right leg jittered. He glared at the clock on the wall, watching it *tick* by slowly, making him unable to concentrate on anything else.

Finally, he just couldn't listen any more to the seconds of his mother's life ticking away. He picked up a magazine from the table beside him and fanned through the pages, then placed it back down. An elderly man sitting across from him coughed and wheezed into his handkerchief. Colton placed his head in his hands and waited for someone to give him some news.

"Excuse me, sir."

He looked up and saw the same girl from the counter standing next to him.

"I have located your mother. If you want to follow me, I can take you to her."

A slow smile surfaced on his face, and then he stood. He followed with an unsteady gait down a hallway lined with curtains. Machines placed on carts were being shuffled from one area to the next. He didn't remember ever being in a hospital before, or even an emergency room for that matter. He'd never broken a bone or been sick enough to be taken to the hospital before, and he hoped he never had to. *This is chaos!*

The young girl stopped and pulled the curtain back, "You can sit with her and wait for the doctor."

He glanced down at her nametag. "Thank you, Anna," he said with a smile. He stood waiting for a reply, but there wasn't one; she nodded and smiled, then turned and walked back the way they had come.

Colton walked over to the bed and reached down, slipping his hand into his mother's. Alexis moaned, but was otherwise motionless. His tongue glided over his lips, wetting them. He bent down and whispered in her ear. "Mom, if you can hear me, please wake up and open your eyes."

He searched her face, but there was no reaction. He saw a stool on the other side of the bed. He released her hand, walked around, and sat down. He placed one hand in hers, and used the other to smooth the hair back from her face. A couple minutes later, he rested his forehead on the hand holding hers. Fatigue had settled in, making him feel mentally and physically exhausted.

The *clinking* of the curtain rings startled him. A man in a white long jacket with a stethoscope around his neck glided in.

He stopped next to the bed, his eyes moving furiously as he flipped through the pages on the clipboard. When he finished, the hand holding the clipboard fell to his side, and then the doctor cleared his throat. The doctor reached his right hand out, "I'm Dr. Kettle, and I will be examining your mother."

Colton looked the man up and down. He had red hair and a face full of freckles. He still had a baby-face and didn't look much older than twenty, which he knew couldn't be possible. He rose to his feet to extend his arm, shaking the doctor's hand. "Do you know what's wrong with her? Is she going to be okay?"

Colton took a series of deep breaths, but his heart continued to pump hard and fast.

"Let's see here." He held the clipboard up towards Colton. "Your mom was brought in a couple of weeks ago for dehydration, and it also states she has breast cancer. Is that correct?"

"Yes."

"Can you tell me anything else that I should be aware of?"

"She hasn't been eating a lot; I think it's the medication she's been taking."

"I see." Dr. Kettle scanned through the papers using his finger as a guide. He nodded.

"I asked her how she was feeling, but I think now, she wasn't being honest with me," Colton admitted reluctantly.

"I need to do a series of tests on her to confirm what's going on. As you can see, I have her on an I.V. pumping fluids into her to get her immune system back up. She's extremely dehydrated, but my biggest concern right now is to see what the cancer is doing and how far it may have spread. I will give both Dr. Sarah Ramsey and Dr. Brownski a call and notify them of this crisis. Is there anyone else we should call?"

The thought of his father came to mind, but he knew he wouldn't come. No, actually, he couldn't come; it would jeopardize everything he worked so hard to hide. The question hung unanswered in his mind, should he go see his dad and tell him what's going on? No, he couldn't; he'd promised to wait for his dad to get ahold of him. He was in charge now. He had to make the decisions for his dying mother.

"No, there's no one else. I'm her only family." His shoulders drooped and his eyes fell to the white sheet covering her.

"I'll go make the calls to her doctors, and then go from there. You're Colton Finley, correct? You live with your mother so we can get in touch with you through Alexis's contact information?"

Colton sat motionless, his eyes a distant stare. With much effort, he nodded to the doctor's statement; then realized Dr. Kettle had asked a question also. Colton gave the doctor his cellphone number, and assured him that he would be staying with her.

Forty-Three

He wasn't sure how much time had gone by when a nurse came in and told him that she was taking his mom for some tests.

"If you want to wait in the lobby you can, or there's a cafeteria one floor down. Most likely, she'll be admitted and will be taken to another room when she's done. Stop at the desk and let a staff member know where you're going so we can notify you when she's done and what room she'll be in."

"Okay," he whispered. He leaned over, kissed his mom on the forehead, and then disappeared behind the curtain.

His head lowered as he stared at the floor, walking back down the hall. More and more emptiness filled his body with each step he took. Once he entered the lobby, he glanced around the room and decided to head outside. The sliding glass doors zipped open, and he stepped out into the morning air.

The sky above was a gray overcast, which fit his mood. He needed to clear his mind, so he strolled down the sidewalk beside the hospital. He hadn't gone twenty feet, when Sarah Ramsey approached him.

"Hey, Colton. How's she doing?"

He shrugged his shoulders.

"It's going to be all right. You did a good thing getting her to the hospital." She opened her arms and embraced him.

His strength was depleted; he had nothing left to stop the tears from falling. His inner child surfaced and he cried uncontrollably. When no more came, Sarah let go, slid one arm around him, and led him to a bench a few feet away. He slumped down and wiped the wetness from his face. A light breeze came and went, brightening his mood. He gathered in deep breaths and exhaled, calming his nerves.

"Do you feel like talking? If not, I can wait until you do," Dr. Ramsey said.

"I woke up just like every other morning. I didn't see her. I even looked outside. So, I thought maybe she slept in this morning. I knocked on her door, no answer. So, I went inside, she wasn't in bed. The door to the bathroom was open. I looked inside and found her on the bathroom floor. I didn't know what else to do, so I called 911 and waited for them to show up and here I am," Colton paused for a couple of seconds; Sarah just nodded so he continued, "I want to understand what's wrong with her, but I don't. Is it the cancer making her sick? The pills? What? I wish someone would tell me and help her."

Dr. Ramsey still had her arm around his shoulders and squeezed his body into hers. A tear slid down her cheek and dropped off her chin, leaving a wet circle on her tan slacks.

"She'll pull through this, I promise."

"Please, don't promise something you can't guarantee. No one knows what's going to happen. One day you're here and the next you're gone. I guess that's just how life rolls, and it sucks, big time."

His shoulders sagged and his hands quivered. For the past two weeks he was beyond happy, knowing his dad was alive and well, but today, right now, it was as if someone had cut his heart out. He knew he could trust Sarah and wanted badly to tell her what he knew. He needed to tell someone and relieve some of the pressure on him; it was just too much for him to bear all alone. *But will Sarah keep the secret to herself or tell his mom?*

He couldn't tell Jake because his father was the detective involved in the case. He had no one to turn to. He'd been the one to investigate and had found out the truth, but now, part of him didn't want to hide it. Colton needed someone to help him accept everything. *It's just too much!*

"I know a good counselor you can talk to. You know, to help with your anxiety? It may help you in the long run," Sarah suggested.

"What's that supposed to mean—*'the long run'*? Like her dying or something? I don't think it will make a difference."

"Sure, it can. You need someone to talk to."

"Why can't I just confide in you and tell you what's bothering me?"

"Well, for one, I'm not a therapist. I'm just a GYN doctor for women. Not really my specialty. You need someone—"

"I don't want to talk to anyone else," he huffed. All the confusion and fear was turning into anger.

"Colton…" she paused. "Okay, if you don't want to go to a counselor or a therapist, then I'm fine with that. Open up and talk to me; tell me what's eating at you; maybe I can help," Sarah agreed.

His father had only told him "not to tell his mother." He hadn't said, "don't tell anyone about him being alive." The thought plagued him. His mouth opened and then shut. He could see from the corner of his eye, Sarah was watching him. He formed the words, parted his lips, and then turned to face her.

"Before I tell you this, you need to swear not to breathe a word to anyone. You have to promise me," he insisted, the anger still very much controlling him.

Sarah's eyes narrowed and she looked him in the eye, "What's this about?"

"You have to promise me. My mom can't know what I'm about to tell you."

Sarah straightened her back and nodded, "Okay, I promise. I won't tell a soul."

Forty-Four

"Did Mom ever tell you about my—"

"Excuse me, Mr. Finley," a familiar voice said.

Colton turned toward the person standing to his left. His eyes dropped and started at her calves and made their way up her long slim legs to the curve of her waist, and then he met her eyes. *Anna, beautiful Anna,* he thought. He looked away, trying to shake the thoughts of attraction out of his head. He cleared his throat, "Yes."

"I thought you might like to know that your mother is in her own room now, if you want to go see her."

"Oh, okay, thanks."

Her radiant smile lit up her face. "She's in room 412. You can follow this sidewalk, go through the front lobby, and take the elevator to the fourth floor, or you can use the elevator in the emergency area."

Warmness flowed through his body, making sweat form around his hairline. "Thank you, Anna," he replied.

She nodded and turned, walking quickly back to the Emergency Room doors.

It was obvious the hospital ER was still very busy, but it was sure nice of *Anna* to come find him outside and let him know where to find his mom. Colton liked her…a lot.

"Are you blushing?" Dr. Ramsey asked with a slight grin.

Her question brought Colton back to reality. He whipped his head around, "What? No, I'm not blushing."

"You like that girl, don't you? She's very pretty. You should ask her out."

"No, I can't; besides, I have enough on my mind." He stood and went down the sidewalk to the front entrance of the hospital.

Colton left Sarah bewildered, but she didn't try to stop him. She knew whatever he'd been about to tell her was really bothering him and that it was important.

~~~~~

The elevator *chimed*, coming to a halt, and the doors opened. Colton stepped aside, allowing the people to exit before he entered. His head down, he walked towards the back of the elevator and leaned against the wall. An arm reached in just as the doors started to close and sprung back open. He looked up to see Sarah making her way inside to stand next to him.

"I'm sorry. I didn't mean to embarrass you outside," Sarah whispered.

He shrugged his shoulders.

"Look, if you like the girl why don't you ask her out or something?"

His lips parted—trying to find the right words to say—and closed.

"By the way you're acting it's as if you've never asked a girl out before."

"I haven't," he whispered.

"What? You've got to be kidding me! You're such a good-looking young man, and you're telling me you've never been out with a girl before?"

"Don't act so shocked. I've just been busy with school and basketball and now my mom."

"Yeah, but…" she paused. "I guess I shouldn't say anything; I haven't been out on a date in more years then I can count."

He turned and looked at her, "Yeah, right."

"No, really. I'm too busy with work. Don't really have time for all that romantic stuff." Sarah batted her hand in the air to demonstrate.

"You're saying that no man has ever picked you up?"

"Well, I guess they might try if I actually went out to places where men *pick-up* women."

230

"Yeah, that would be a start."

"So, I guess we're sort of in the same predicament?"

"I suppose so," Colton stated.

The elevator shook and came to a stop on the fourth floor. Colton waved for Sarah to exit in front of him, a young gentleman. They walked down the hall, following the numbers on the wall until they came to room 412. The door was open, so they went right in. When the bed came into view, Colton saw his mom. Her eyes were closed and he sighed, praying she would be all right. When he stood beside the bed, he reached out and slipped his hand in hers. Pressure hugged his fingers, making him look up. Her eyes were fixed on his face.

"You're awake?" he said, smiling.

"Yes," her voice groggy. "I came to when they were doing tests on me. I scared the nurse because I freaked out when my eyes opened in the machine, and I didn't know where I was. She came running back in the room to calm me down, telling me why I was there. They brought me to this room a little while ago."

"How are you feeling?" Colton asked.

"For the most part, I'm feeling good." Alexis looked from Colton to Sarah.

"I don't know if they got ahold of Dr. Brownski yet or not," Colton said.

"If they did, I'm sure he'll be in some time later. I'm sorry you had to miss school because of me," Alexis answered.

"Mom, really? I came downstairs this morning and you weren't up, so I went into your bedroom and found you lying on the floor unresponsive. I admit you had me worried. I called 911 and waited with you until they showed up. Did they say what caused you to blackout or whatever happened? The doctor in the emergency room said you were dehydrated and that he needed to run some tests."

"He was in to see me right before you both arrived, and said the medication wasn't doing what it was supposed to do. Also, that I was having some severe side effects from it. I've had a few radiation treatments and been taking the chemo pills like prescribed, but he concluded that some patients respond differently. No two patients are the same and that I should've contacted my doctor immediately. I probably wouldn't be here right now, if I'd done so."

"So, what happens now?" Colton inquired.

"Waiting for Dr. Brownski to come, then we'll go from there. Since my file informed them of my breast cancer they did an ultrasound, but I don't know what the results are."

"I'll give Dr. Brownski a call and find out," Sarah replied, reaching into her purse for her cellphone and walked over to the window.

Colton pulled a chair from behind him and sat down.

"I don't think I want to continue taking the chemo pills. They make my bones hurt, and you can see my appetite hasn't been the greatest."

"Let's see what the doctor says before you make that decision, Mom. I want the cancer to go away, but I'm not sure how that happens with pills and radiation. Would you mind if I stuck around and listened to what he has to say?"

She smiled, "Not at all. I would love it if you'd stay."

Alexis felt happy, happier than she'd been in a long while. She loved having Colton by her side. They had become mother and son, something she'd longed for, and she wanted to treasure every minute she could with him. Alexis didn't want to think about the possibility of dying, but she had to. She had to make sure he knew how she felt about him before the cancer took her life.

"I just talked to Dr. Brownski and he's actually on his way here, a few minutes probably," Sarah said.

Alexis nodded.

Just as Colton decided to turn the television on, Dr. Brownski rushed into the room.

"Alexis, how are you feeling?" Dr. Brownski said in greeting. He had Alexis's file in the crook of his arm.

"Could be better."

"Well, I'm most certainly going to try and fix that," he smiled encouragingly at Alexis. "I stopped by and had a brief conversation with Dr. Kettle, and he said that your body isn't responding to the medication. I just looked over the tests results and the ultrasound. I'm glad they did both breasts. It seems the cancer has spread to the left one as well as the right. I'd like to do another lumpectomy to remove the cancer and have you continue the radiation treatments. The lobular carcinomas are spreading. I'm going to recommend a wheelchair for you to get around at home to ease the discomfort you're having."

Colton's head dropped to his chest, once more feeling defeated. He felt his mom squeeze his hand, but he couldn't bring himself to look at her. The words suffocated him, making his chest tighten. He was feeling like he did when his father had died. The last thing he wanted was to give up and assume the worst. For weeks, they'd worked on their relationship, for what? To become a family and have it all taken away? He couldn't deal with the loss of his mother, a woman he'd come to love and look up to. He was so engrossed in his own thoughts he'd tuned out what the doctor was saying. He swallowed hard and realized he was thinking only of himself. It was his mom who needed comforting right now, not him! He directed his attention back to the doctor.

"When you're released from the hospital, have Dr. Ramsey make an appointment for the lumpectomy. As soon as possible, we need to remove the cancer."

"I'll call after you leave and set something up for her," Dr. Ramsey said.

"Good and as for the chemo, stop taking the pills for now. We'll keep you on the radiation only and work from there."

"Wouldn't it be better for me to have a mastectomy?" Alexis asked before Dr. Brownski left.

"In some cases, yes, but let's hold off and see what happens after the lumpectomy. If I can remove all of the cancer and keep you on radiation, then it should disappear, but I can't predict what will happen. I want to try to get you stable without having to remove your breasts. A double-mastectomy is very extensive, invasive surgery. Your general health right now isn't up to it. We'll use it only as a last resort, and hopefully we can get you a little stronger before we have to make that decision."

Alexis nodded.

"We'll keep in touch and I hope to see you soon," Dr. Brownski nodded and walked out of the room.

Alexis glanced towards Sarah. "You said he was the best Oncologist around. I hope you're right," Alexis stated, a single tear rolled down her cheek. "I'm not sure how much more of this I'll be able to take. You can see what it's doing to my son and to me."

"Alexis, I'm sorry. I know this has to be hard and yes, he is the best in his field. The cancer has a mind of its own. I wish I could say or do something to help, but I'm actually at a loss for words. I'll help in any way I can, and we'll work through this to get you better, I promise," Sarah encouraged.

"I would like to be alone for a while, if you both don't mind," Alexis responded, turning her head toward the wall. *They don't need to see my tears…especially Colton.*

Sarah nodded and looked over at Colton. He didn't want to leave his mom, but he did understand that she needed and wanted to be by herself. If anything, Colton knew what it was like to cry in private.

He kissed the back of his mother's hair, felt her quiver from a sob that was trying to escape, then stood and followed Sarah out of the room. Sarah reached out and took Colton's hand.

Forty-Five

Alexis stared out the window on the drive home. She'd spent three days in the hospital and Tuesday, tomorrow, would be her second lumpectomy. She'd been upset that she missed the championship game on Saturday, which they'd won. Alexis was pleased and happy for Colton.

Before leaving the hospital, Alexis listened to a voicemail from her boss, Fred, stating she needed to call him when she had a chance. With the way her body was feeling, she knew she had to make a decision about work. She wasn't able to stand for very long, and Dr. Brownski had committed her to a wheelchair to get around. There was no way she could go to work. One, she couldn't drive herself. Two, she didn't want to depend on her doctor/friend, Sarah, to take her everywhere she needed to go. Three, Colton had school and she didn't want to burden him with her medical issues. Though, he fought her on it, she finally had her way and he'd gone to school this morning. Basketball practice was over, and Colton had promised her that he'd be home after school every day or would call if something came up.

Sarah pulled into the driveway and parked the car. There wasn't any way to get the wheelchair into the house with Alexis in it, so Sarah helped Alexis into the house and got her situated before going out and carrying the chair inside. Sarah moved a couple of chairs away from the kitchen table so Alexis could sit in the wheelchair to eat. Sarah also made sure that the hallway and bedroom were clear of furniture for the wheelchair to be easily maneuvered. Sarah made Alexis some soup for lunch and then helped her into bed before leaving.

Alexis grabbed her phone from the nightstand and dialed a number.

"Hello, Fred O'Brien speaking. How may I help you? "

"Hi, Fred, it's Alexis Finley calling."

"Alexis, it's so good to hear from you. How are you feeling?"

"Could be better, but feeling more myself today."

"Good, that's good. I'm glad you called me back. I know you've been having some medical difficulties, and I wanted to swing something by you to see what you think."

She bit the inside of her lip and waited for him to continue, but he didn't.

"I'm sorry I didn't call in on Friday. I was...um... taken to the hospital," Alexis admitted after an awkward silence.

"Oh, what happened? Is everything all right?" From the sound of his voice, Alexis could tell he was concerned about her well-being.

"I'm fine now. I hadn't been eating well, and the medicine they gave me was making me sick."

"I'm assuming this is as good a time as any to talk about why I called you?"

Her insides tightened, anticipating what he wanted to discuss with her. "Yes, it's why I'm calling." She didn't want to think the worst, but it was too late for that.

"What I've been thinking about, of course that's if you agree, is that it may be better for everyone if you went on a medical leave-of-absence until you're better. I hope you don't get upset with me, but your health is very important to us and we here at NASA just want you to get well."

The phone fell from her hand and hit the blanket. The shock drifted away as fast as it came, and she replaced the phone to her ear.

"I see. Well, I…" The words didn't come to her quick enough. She did agree with what Fred had said, but work had always been her life and now…now what would she do without it? She had never been the type of person to stay home and do nothing. Not saying that stay-at-home people did absolutely nothing. There was plenty of work to be done around the house, but she also knew she wouldn't be able to do those things until her body stopped hurting.

"Alexis, I know this may have shocked you, and I didn't want to have to do this. But this is only a medical leave, not the termination of your job. You have a great work ethic, but I also need someone here to do the work. I'm telling you this because you need to take the time to heal and get well. By all means, your job will still be here once you get through the hard times."

A heavy sigh escaped from her lips as she lowered her head. A sudden onset of nausea stewed in her stomach and heaviness filled her body. She wanted to agree with him; she had to agree with him; what other choice did she have? She'd already been in the hospital twice and would be having another lumpectomy tomorrow. She had no other answer for him, but to say yes and take the leave-of-absence.

"I understand your concern and if you think this is what needs to be done than start the paperwork," Alexis replied.

"I'm sorry to have to do this to you. I really am, Alexis. I'll have it done by the end of the day. Would you be able to come in and sign the forms then?"

"No, I'm sorry, there's no way I can drive to work. Can you mail them to my home address so I can sign them and send them back?"

"Sure, sure. I can do that. Alexis, you will always have a job here at NASA, but life dishes out some harsh stuff every now and then. We needed to make a decision on how to handle things. My prayers are with you and your family. I want you to get better and come back to work; we'll be lost without you here." When she didn't respond he continued, "I'll send the papers out today. You do what you need to do to get well. I hope you start to feel better soon."

What did he think she had—a cold or something? It was freaking cancer, breast cancer of all things, how was one supposed to feel or think? Her body tensed, making her muscles quiver. She needed to—no, she wanted to end this call before Fred really pissed her off!

"Okay, send the paperwork out, and I'll get it back to you before you know it." She took the phone from her ear and pressed the end button.

Forty-Six

She was in the kitchen when Colton returned home from school.

"Hey, Mom, what are you doing?"

"Well, since I won't be returning to work for God knows how long, I thought I'd organize the kitchen."

"What do you mean, not returning to work?" he said, stopping in mid-stride.

"I called my boss back, and he thinks it would be better for me to just take a medical leave-of-absence until I get better."

"That doesn't sound too bad; besides, you don't need the added stress to your body."

She spun the wheelchair around, her half-lidded eyes staring at him. "You're agreeing with him? Well, I guess I've been out-voted then," Alexis stated, the anger surfacing even though she didn't want to take it out on her son. She just couldn't help it!

"Mom, your health is more important; besides, you'll get better and go back to work. It's not like they're firing you, right?"

After a few seconds, she nodded. "Yes, I guess you're right. I'll be your full-time Mom now."

He smiled as he thought about what she'd just said. "About time," he replied, with a hearty laugh.

"Oh, before I forget, there's a package for you on the table in the hall. It didn't have a return address on it, so I'm not sure where it came from."

His heart raced with anticipation, knowing quite well, whom it was from. "I'll take it upstairs when I do my homework. Do you need any help before I go?"

"No, not really, just going through one more drawer in the kitchen and then I'll probably lie down for a nap before dinner."

"You should keep your cellphone on you in case you need me for something, unless I can hear you yelling for me from down here," Colton said.

"That's actually a smart idea," Alexis replied and then turned back to the drawer she was cleaning out. She'd left this drawer for last, knowing it would take her a little longer to organize. It was the proverbial "junk drawer".

Alexis took things out and placed them on the counter until the drawer was empty. One-by-one she looked over each item, deciding whether to keep it or throw it out. Halfway through, she grabbed a thick envelope and opened it. Inside were a few photos and a key. Her eyebrows squished together as she stared at the key. She didn't know, of course, what it was for; most likely Jay had placed the envelope in the drawer and had forgotten about it. It had been shoved to the back and hidden by the rest of the junk in the drawer.

Alexis set the key in her lap and searched through the pictures. Each photo was taken at night, but she was able to make out people in the background. A tall bald man with tattoos covering his arm from the elbow down was handing a short dark-haired man a thick yellow envelope. Each photo was zoomed in on their exchange. There was even one picture of a car, but she couldn't see who was sitting in it.

She shrugged and placed the photos and key back in the envelope, setting it aside on the counter. She finished cleaning the drawer and grabbed the parcel. Once inside her bedroom, she opened the drawer of the nightstand and placed it inside.

Forty-Seven

Once Colton entered his room, he closed the door and sat down on the bed. He prayed he was right about the box being sent from his dad. He tore the tape off and flipped the lid open on both sides. He looked down and took out a small phone. He remembered seeing these phones before at the store and knew it was a throwaway phone. The kind of phones no one could trace. He set the box down on the floor, flipped the phone open, and hit the power button. On the voicemail icon a number one appeared. He hit the button and pressed the phone to his ear:

Son, this will be our way to communicate with each other. This phone is untraceable, so no one will be able to hear or read our conversations. How is your mother doing? It's driving me crazy not being able to talk or see the both of you. I do wish I were there to help take care of her. Soon, I hope. How are you doing? I miss you both more than you know and can't wait for this to be over so I can come home.

That's of course if I'm welcome home after what I have done. I'm extremely sorry that it has led to me faking my own death, but there are some dangerous people involved, and I have to protect my family from them. When you were here last, I forgot to ask you to do something for me. There is an envelope with some photos and a key inside it. I need you to find the envelope and mail it to a P.O Box. Your mother must not know what you are doing. The last place I think I hid it was in the junk drawer in the kitchen. Please find the envelope and send it to me, no questions asked. Text me when you get this, so I know you have received the box. And son, I love you and I hope I can make this all go away soon. I love you, son.

"Crap, Mom was cleaning the kitchen," he mumbled.

He slipped the phone in his pocket and opened the door. Noises came from the kitchen, which told him she was still sorting through the drawers. He'd wait until she went to lie down before venturing downstairs to find what his dad needed. He closed the door and sat on the bed. Removing the phone from his jeans, he flipped it open and called the number.

After several rings, the phone went to voicemail. So, he left a message for his father.

I received the box as you can see. Mom is doing a little better after her stay in the hospital this past weekend. I'd rather talk to you on the phone and tell you what the doctor said and not through a voicemail. I'm doing well. We won the championship game Saturday and the trophy is in the gymnasium case at school. Hope you'll be able to see the trophy one day. I'll go and see if I can find the envelope, but...but Mom decided to go through all the drawers and clean them today. Hopefully she by-passed what you need and put it back in the drawer. I'll let you know what I find. How are you doing? I love and miss you too and of course, you are welcome here. I wouldn't have it any other way. If you're thinking Mom won't, I can talk to her for you when the time is right. Call me when you can. Love you too, Dad

He pressed end and closed the phone. Every few minutes he'd stop working on his homework and stare at the phone, willing it to ring or vibrate; anything to communicate with his father. Hours had passed and still no reply. He finished his schoolwork and decided to see if his mom was still in the kitchen. He poked his head out the door and listened.

No sound.

He climbed down the stairs and peeked into the kitchen.

She wasn't there.

He started with the first drawer and scanned through it, nothing. After searching all the drawers in the kitchen, a thought sprang into his head and he walked to the wastebasket.

Nothing.

She must have found the envelope and put it somewhere else, or his father had been wrong about where he'd placed the parcel. Though he didn't think, that was the case. Dad was too concerned about this envelope and key. He would have remembered where he'd hid it.

Crap, where would she have put the envelope? His mind juggled every possible place in the house and the one room that stuck in his head was her bedroom. That's the only place she went besides the kitchen since she was stuck on the ground floor.

He knew he couldn't go in there snooping with her in the room. He'd have to come-up with a plan, but even if he did, how would he go into her room when she wasn't working any longer? Then he recalled her surgery scheduled for tomorrow. He'd have to wait until he came home from school and search her room before Dr. Ramsey brought her home after the procedure. Would he have enough time?

Forty-Eight

Alexis knew what to expect from the surgery and tried to prepare herself. Though, it wasn't the surgery itself, but the after-effect that worried her. Who in their right mind would enjoy vomiting? The wastebasket remained beside the bed, so she didn't have to put one there. She'd refused to use the wheelchair in her room and held the wall when she needed to use the bathroom.

She clasped her hand onto the doorframe to undress, slipping into comfortable clothes. When she finished, she positioned herself in the wheelchair and made her way to the kitchen. The clock on the wall read seven-ten, which gave her plenty of time before Dr. Ramsey was to show up and take her to the cancer center.

She maneuvered the wheelchair in front of the sink, filling her glass with water. Then remembered she wasn't allowed to have any food or drink before the surgery. She dumped the glass and set it in the sink.

She wheeled her way back to her room and grabbed her cell from the nightstand. She sent a quick text to Colton to see if he was up for school. She knew better then to climb the stairs. He replied that he would be downstairs in ten minutes. The second she entered the kitchen and sat by the table, there was a knock on the front door.

"Be there in a minute," Alexis called out.

Alexis opened the door and moved the wheelchair aside for Sarah to make her way inside.

"I know I'm a little early, but better early then late, they say," Sarah greeted Alexis cheerfully.

"It's no problem. I've been up for a while now. Do you want a cup of coffee or something to eat?"

"Nothing to eat, thank you, but coffee sounds great."

Dr. Ramsey followed behind as Alexis wheeled herself to the counter. Alexis reached for the cabinet door, but wasn't able to grasp the handle. She hadn't thought to have the coffee cups placed on the counter for easy access.

"I'll get the cup for you," Sarah said as she stood a few feet behind Alexis, watching her struggle to reach the cabinet.

"Thank you, I guess I forgot to have Colton put the coffee cups on the counter for me."

Alexis moved back for Sarah to fill her cup. The smell of coffee made Alexis's mouth water. Alexis swallowed as she made her way to the table; a few seconds later Sarah joined her.

"What book did you bring this time to read while you wait?"

"*Winter's Destiny,*" by Nancy Allan. I'm actually surprised I haven't finished the book yet."

"That good, huh?"

"Very. Quite hard to put down—a lot of action and suspense."

"Well, since I'm off work for a while, I'll have to borrow the book when you're done."

"What do you mean, *off of work*, what happened?"

"My boss, Fred, thought it was a good idea I take medical leave and come back when I'm all better."

"I guess I can see his point. How are you handling it?"

"Finally, someone who knows me," Alexis chuckled. "I don't like it, but what can I do? I'm in no shape to try to work, but it's all I know how to do."

"I can understand that. I would be the same way without my job to keep me busy. I will be happy to lend you the books I've already read."

"Thanks, I'd like that. God knows there isn't enough around the house to keep me from losing my mind; that's if I can even do anything."

"You have me and Colton here to help you. I've taken a few vacation days to help you out, and the other doctor's at the clinic have offered to assist with a few of my patients as well."

"Oh, well, I appreciate everything you both have been doing for me. As much as I hate being dependent on others, it does feel nice."

"Do you have any questions about today's procedure?"

"No, I know what to expect, though it doesn't make it easier. I'll be fine," Alexis said, pasting a smile on her face.

Sarah nodded and lifted the cup to her lips and took a sip. Alexis turned her head to the sound of heavy shoes pounding down the stairs and watched Colton as he joined them.

"Good morning," Alexis said.

"Hey, Mom. Hi, Sarah."

"Morning, Colton. I heard you won the game on Saturday. Great job!" Sarah smiled at Colton.

"Yeah, my coach can't stop bragging about how great the team did. Coach Martin says it was our best game ever. He's having a celebration party for the team and our parents before school is out."

"Oh?" Alexis replied.

Colton placed his bowl on the table and grabbed the milk from the fridge. "Mom, if you can't make it, I'm okay with that."

"I know, but it would be nice if I could go."

"Let's just see how you feel. The party could be a few weeks or a month away. You could be better by then," Sarah interjected.

Alexis nodded. She needed to stay positive about the outcome and pray this time around she wouldn't be as sick.

"Are you ready to go?" Sarah asked.

"Sure." Alexis backed out from the table and wheeled her way to the doorway. Sarah helped her stand and opened the door, helping her to the car. Colton walked past them and opened the passenger door. Once Alexis was inside, he reached in and gave her a quick hug and a kiss on the cheek.

Alexis gave him a dazed look when he stood up. She loved him more than anything and hoped he knew how she felt. She wasn't one to flaunt affection towards anyone and hoped she'd get better at showing how she felt. She needed to say three simple words, *"I love you,"* but she couldn't. Maybe if he'd say those words first, it'd be easier for her.

She didn't understand why she couldn't tell her own son how much he meant to her, that she loved him. *Maybe he's waiting for me to say the words to him first,* she thought.

Alexis parted her lips and smiled. If they were to have a second chance at being a family, she needed to overcome this fear she had of expressing her feelings and just tell him, before it was too late. She didn't want to think about the possibility of dying, that was one thing Alexis refused to believe, but...but she needed to at least accept that it could happen.

She shook her head, erasing the image in her head. *Not going to happen!* She was too driven to think about her life ending, and she wasn't going to start dwelling on the consequences if it did. If she'd made work so important in the past, then she could change her focus and make their relationship and kicking the cancer a top priority now. She knew she would fight to the end!

Forty-Nine

Once at the cancer center, Sarah dropped her off at the entrance and parked the car. Alexis went through the same procedures as the last time.

She changed into a gown and reclined on the bed. The same two nurses prepped her for surgery. Her eyes felt heavy as lead as the medicine worked its way through her body.

They wheeled her out of the room and down the hall. Lights flickered by, causing her to blink. In the operating room, she heard someone counting and then darkness took over.

~~~~~

When she woke several hours later, her mouth was dry and her lips felt crusty. She swallowed, trying to moisten her throat, but it made her cough instead.

"Would you like something to drink?" a petite woman asked. Her hair was pulled back in a bun and worn neatly on her head.

Alexis nodded.

The nurse left the room and entered minutes later, holding a small bottle of apple juice. The nurse grabbed the remote on the side of the bed, making the bed rise. The nurse placed the bottle to Alexis's lips and tilted. The juice skimmed Alexis's lips and entered her mouth; she swallowed several times before raising her hand for the woman to stop. The nurse set the bottle down and left the room. A couple minutes later Dr. Brownski entered.

"The lumpectomy went well. I removed some lymph nodes from under your arm, and I'm having them tested for cancer cells."

"I thought you did that the first time?"

"I did and they were negative. It doesn't hurt to retest and make sure things haven't changed since then. The tumor measured 3 centimeters in the right breast, which I removed, and I'm having an Excisional biopsy done. Once I get the results back for the lymph nodes, I can determine what needs to be done. *IF*...and I mean *IF* the tests show positive, you'll have to come back in for another surgery for me to remove more lymph nodes; otherwise, the cancer will continue to spread. Right now, the cancer is *Local*, meaning it's confined to the breasts only. Your breast cancer is between Stages I and II. The tumors are large enough to be considered Stage II, but it will all depend on the results. If the lymph nodes are positive this time, then it becomes *Regional,* and we want to stop it before it turns into *Distant.*"

"And what does that mean for me?"

"If the cancer becomes *Regional* that means it's starting to spread to other parts of your body."

The color drained from Alexis's face, and she closed her eyes. Her heart raced, nearly exploding through her chest. The words were lost inside her—she had no idea what to think or say. This wasn't what she'd prayed for. Hope was seeping out of her little by little. She'd tried hard not to think negatively, but what else could Alexis feel knowing this cancer was something she may not be able to fight?

Her weakness outweighed her strength, and all she wanted to do right now was lock herself inside a room and let no one in. Alexis knew this would destroy what was left of her son; first Jay and now her. *How will Colton deal with this? He'll be an orphan!*

Some miracle had to happen to save Alexis from deteriorating away. How was she supposed to find the strength to fight this cancer? The past month, she was able to realize the love she felt for her son and how sorry she was for not being in his life. She couldn't give up, but was it her decision to make? If she fought as hard as she could, wouldn't it depend on her body? Her head was spinning in circles with more questions then answers.

"Alexis. Are you okay?" The man's deep voice was faint and distant.

She saw a flash in front of her eyes, making her blink. Her name echoed in her ear.

"Alexis."

A *clack* of two fingers hitting each other echoed throughout the room. She turned her head and saw Dr. Brownski snapping his fingers in front of her face.

"Alexis, are you with me?" It was definitely Dr. Brownski talking to her.

"What?" she asked weakly. She felt lost and disoriented. *What had happened? What had gone wrong?*

"You were passed out for a few seconds. It's normal after surgery. I'm sure you have many questions going through your mind, and I'll try to answer them as best I can. I want to repeat this because I don't think you were able to hear me. I'm testing you for hormone receptors. This is important because the results will help you and me decide whether the cancer is likely to respond to hormonal therapy or other treatments. Do you have any questions I can answer for you right now?"

She shook her head.

"Later, if you should have a question, my staff or I will be here. Sometimes it helps to write them down for your next visit. My staff will call you when the results are in, but I'd like to see you in here on Friday for radiation therapy. I should have the results back from today's surgery by then, and we can talk more on Friday."

"Oh, okay," Alexis responded.

The doctor patted her arm and then turned, walking out of the room.

Fifty

Twenty minutes later, Alexis was dressed and being wheeled out to the lobby. As Sarah stood and walked toward Alexis, her eyes gleamed as she portrayed a dazzling smile.

Sarah reached her hand out, lifted Alexis's chin and nodded, "I'll go get the car." It was as if Dr. Ramsey realized what Alexis was going through.

Once in the car, Alexis sat quietly and stared out the window, sighing every few seconds. Sarah showed no indication of hearing the weighted sighs.

"So, while I was in the lobby," Sarah said to try and start a conversation, "I scanned through some new breast cancer group pamphlets and stuck them in my purse. If you're too nervous to go on your own, I'm willing to join you. Besides, I think I'd like to hear what other women have gone through. It could benefit me and my patients."

"Yeah, sure. We could do that," Alexis whispered.

"Do you want to talk to me about what Dr. Brownski said?"

Alexis shrugged her shoulders.

"I want you to know I'm here to listen. Besides, I'd rather hear it from you first."

Alexis tried to be calm when she filled Sarah in on what the doctor had said, but she couldn't stop the tears flowing down her cheeks. She couldn't recall the last time she'd cried this much. Alexis was strong-willed and never let defeat overwhelm her, but she couldn't hold in the sadness she felt any longer. Alexis was emotionally drained.

Sarah touched her lightly on the shoulder; no words passed between them. What could Sarah possibly say that would make Alexis feel any better? Alexis would just have to find it in herself to fight the cancer, like some kind of goal she needed to accomplish.

Sarah finally realized that it was no wonder Alexis had hidden her feelings for so long, facing them hurt too much. Her doctor and friend also wondered what else Alexis had been hiding for so long. Alexis had probably never worked through her husband's death only seven months before, but were there more issues her friend and patient had never faced?

~~~~~

When they arrived at the house, Alexis allowed Sarah to embrace her in her arms while she cried. They sat outside on the deck under the umbrella. The sun was scorching hot, but felt good on Alexis's skin after the cold, sterile operating room.

Alexis couldn't believe she'd gone so long without having a girlfriend to talk to. She thought about her friend Carla, who had been calling every few weeks and leaving a message. She'd promised herself she'd call her back, but time had somehow escaped her.

In the past month, she'd learned to love again, to live a full life and not work every minute of the day. Alexis didn't know what the outcome would be with her cancer, but she refused to give up and let everything she now felt just disappear. This was a fight she'd win, and a goal she'd work hard to achieve. Alexis needed her family and friends in her life and wished so much that Jay were here to see it all.

Fifty-One

When Colton turned onto the street he lived on, his heart sank. Sarah's car was in the drive; they were home from the hospital. He slammed his palm on the steering wheel.

"Damn it," he cursed.

He'd been hoping they'd be awhile so he could do some searching, but now he had to come up with a different plan.

Colton pulled alongside Sarah's car and got out. When he opened the front door, he could hear the two of them out on the patio. This was his chance to sneak in and rummage through his mom's room. He eased the door shut silently and looked toward the sliding glass door. Sarah looked right at him. *Busted!*

He swore under his breath.

Sarah waved, he acknowledged it and then she turned back to his mom. He would have to go see them and make up an excuse to leave. When he opened the sliding door, the two of them stopped talking and looked at him.

"Hey, Mom. Hi, Sarah," he said, paused briefly, and then added with a smile, "Don't stop on my account. For once it's nice to come home and see my mom here and actually talking to someone."

"So, how was school today?" Alexis asked.

"Same as always. How was the surgery?"

"It went okay, I guess. We'll talk about it later."

"Oh, okay." He grabbed the handle of the patio door. "Well, I've got homework to do, so I'll leave you two to talk, and I'll get busy."

He turned and headed back in before either one had a chance to respond. He grabbed a Coke from the fridge and glanced over his shoulder before exiting the kitchen. Colton was relieved that the stairs were several feet away from the entrance, and he wouldn't be seen from the doorway. Strolling down the hallway, he listened for any sound of them coming in the house.

The door to his mom's room was ajar. He reached out his hand and gave it a little push. The blinds in the room were opened halfway, allowing some light to come in. He could see to the right of him stood an oak dresser. He scanned over the few family pictures on top, his eyes stopped when he saw a photo of him and his dad. The picture that was taken at the lake last spring. The same picture he had wondered about weeks ago. His mom had had the photo the whole time. He felt a warm fluttery feeling in his heart, which made him smile.

Colton opened the top drawer, feeling guilty for going through his mom's personal belongings; he quickly stuck his hand under the garments and felt around. Finding nothing, he moved on to the next drawer. He didn't find any envelopes in the dresser.

Looking around the room, his eyes stopped when he saw the nightstand next to the bed. It was the most obvious place to him because that was where he placed his personal memorabilia. Walking over to the nightstand, he opened the drawer; an envelope was right in front. Taking the envelope in his hand, he glanced inside to make sure it was what he was looking for—it was. He closed the drawer and hurried quietly out of the room. He'd been so lucky!

Once upstairs, he sat down on his bed and pulled out the pictures and key from the envelope. He scanned through the photos one by one. The two men looked to be exchanging something. *What?* He wasn't sure.

He put everything back inside, but then decided he should take pictures with his phone just in case he needed them for something. *What if they got lost in the mail?* He knew this was really important to his dad.

Once he finished, he sealed the envelope and texted his dad to see where to send the package. A few minutes later, an address with a P.O. Box came back.

He decided to wait an hour before heading back downstairs to drive to the post office. He'd told his mom and Sarah that he had homework, which he didn't have for the first time in weeks. Opening the phone, he texted his dad, asking when he could see him.

A minute later, Dad responded. *"It would be best not to."*

Not accepting his answer, he texted back, *"Why?"*

Minutes passed and there was no reply so he sent the message again.

Immediately, Dad answered, *"After the last time you were here, I relocated to another safe house. It's best we don't see each other until after this is over."*

"When will that be?" Colton texted.

"A month or two at the most."

"Can I tell Mom about you?"

"No, not yet. How is she doing anyway?"

"Not too good. She just went in for another surgery, and I don't know yet how it went."

"Please tell me when you find out. I'm worried about her."

"Then let me tell her that you're alive." No reply. A few minutes passed before his phone finally vibrated.

"She has enough to worry about and doesn't need the stress of what I did on her shoulders," Jay replied.

"Why don't you let her make that decision? Please, she needs to know; it may help her fight."

"Colton, not yet. Let this be over first, and then we can do it together."

"All right, I'll wait, but still think she should know."

"Believe me, son, I would love for her to know, but mostly I would love to be home with the two of you."

"Okay, I'll wait. Two months at the most, right?"

"Yes, that's what I said."

"Okay, love you Dad."

"Love you too, Colton."

He glanced at the alarm clock sitting on the nightstand and stood. He grabbed the envelope, placed it in his back pocket, and opened the door. He jogged down the stairs and into the kitchen. He looked out onto the patio; they were no longer there.

"Mom, are you here?" Colton called out.

"I'm in my room," Alexis hollered back.

He hurried down the hall and entered her room.

"I'm going to run out; I should be home in an hour."

"Where you off to?"

Thinking fast, he responded, "Just need to head over to Jake's for a little while and then I'll be home."

"Sure, I'll be taking a nap. Feeling exhausted from the surgery today."

"How did that go anyway?"

He felt his mom's eyes study him. He'd never come right out and asked her those kinds of questions before. Colton wasn't sure what he would say if she asked him why he was asking now.

"If you have a minute, come sit and I'll tell you."

He let go of the doorknob still gripped in his hand and shuffled over to the bed. Somehow, he knew it wasn't going to be good news. He'd suspected that was why Sarah had stayed so long with his mother—the realization just finally sinking in.

"I don't want to beat around the bush, so I'll just come right out and tell you."

He hoped his mom couldn't see the emotions running through his body as she went over the results of her latest surgery.

"So…" he cleared his throat. "They don't know if they can cure you?"

"I don't think *cure me* is the right way to phrase it, but if you meant to say *remove all the cancer?* Then I'd say, they're doing the best they can. It seems to be spreading faster than they thought. I'll be having more radiation therapy, but I refuse to take the chemo pills anymore. They were making me too sick, and I just can't live like that."

"But was it helping you?"

"I honestly don't think so. The cancer is now in both breasts."

Colton blushed when his mom said *breasts*. He knew she had to talk about it, but it just seemed weird coming from his mom, and he shook the thought from his mind.

"What do you need me to do for you?"

Alexis smiled. "Just help me out when you can, and I guess what I need the most is… you."

He nodded and an idea came to mind. What if he asked her some questions about his dad, but not come right out and tell her the truth? He tossed the thought around and swallowed, then spoke. "Do you think things would be different if Dad was still with us?"

His heart pounded in his chest as he saw her eyes widen. Maybe he shouldn't have asked the question, but there was nothing he could do about it now. As he watched her eyes go from his to the blanket, he was sorry he'd asked her, but then Colton heard her voice, more like a whisper, fill the air.

"Colton, if your dad was here with us, I think he'd be doing whatever he could to fix me. I like to believe he's with us now, you know… in our hearts."

"But would things be different?"

"If you're asking if we'd be more like a family? Then, I would have to say I'd hope so. Like I told you before, I'm not going to be that woman any longer who worked all the time and was never there for you. I'm going to be the mother you should've had years ago. I just wish it didn't take cancer for me to see what I've been missing."

Those three words, *I love you*, bounced around in Alexis's head. More than anything, she wanted to tell him how she felt. She needed to tell him, but she couldn't.

"Colton, I'll prove to you that I am a better person."

He shook his head. "Mom, you don't have to prove anything. All I want is for you to get better and live a long healthy life."

He could see wetness form in her eyes and then a tear slide down her cheek. Colton reached out and wiped the tear away with his thumb. A quaint smirk appeared on her face; he smiled back. He stood, bent over, and hugged her; then kissed her on her forehead and left the room.

He'd wanted to tell her the truth, but stopped himself by leaving. His dad had said not to tell her, and he obeyed. Though, her answer warmed his heart, he prayed for his father to come home soon.

Fifty-Two

Every week for the past five weeks, Alexis had gone to the cancer center. She'd have her dose of radiation and then come home and sleep. For the first few days after the treatment, she hugged the wastebasket next to the bed. She tried to eat some soup when she could, but mostly she nibbled on saltines.

Colton put a nightlight in the bathroom for her, so she wouldn't have to look at herself in the mirror. She didn't have to see herself, though, to know her hair was falling out. She woke in the morning to find clumps of hair on her pillow. She was actually afraid to brush her hair, knowing the rest would eventually come out.

Her body was weak and fragile most of the time, and she used the wheelchair to get around. Besides napping, she sat out on the deck and absorbed the warmth of the sun, which made her bones not ache as much. She was only forty, but felt like eighty.

On her good days, she was able to walk without the wheelchair, but not far. Sarah and Colton watched over her as if she was a newborn baby. She didn't mind on the days after the radiation, but on the days she was feeling well, she wanted to do things herself. Her independence was sitting on a shelf waiting patiently to be used again.

This morning Alexis was sitting in her wheelchair, looking out the sliding glass door. She tried to concentrate on the world outside and not her reflection staring back at her. A knock on the door pulled her away from her thoughts. She didn't need to look at the clock to know who it was. Every day at ten in the morning, Sarah would show up to see how she was doing. Alexis didn't move from her spot in the kitchen by the patio door, knowing Sarah would come to her.

"How are you feeling today, Alexis?"

Alexis took in a deep breath and exhaled. "Same, I suppose. No better, no worse."

She could tell little by little she was losing herself. Where was the Alexis Finley who was once full of life, dreams, and determination? She'd been replaced by this depressed, haggard woman, who just didn't seem to care anymore.

Alexis stared at the same four walls day-in and day-out, driving her slowly insane. She wanted to get out of the house. Go for a walk, though Alexis knew that wasn't going to happen. Her friend's soft voice pulled her back to reality.

"I have something for you," Sarah said, with a hint of excitement in her voice. Alexis turned the wheelchair around to face her and saw a box in her hand. It wasn't a fancy box, like you would get at Christmas time or on your birthday, but a box no less.

"What's that for?"

"Well, I was out shopping and when I saw this, I thought it would be perfect for you."

"You don't have to get me anything. I'm not a child," she grumbled.

A faint bitter smile appeared on Sarah's face, and she shook her head. "I wasn't implying you're a child, though sometimes you act like one. I wanted to do something nice for you. Here, open it." Sarah held out the box.

Alexis motioned for her to place the box on the table and then rolled the wheelchair to the dinette. She lifted the lid, setting it aside and removed the tissue paper. Her mouth fell open as she peered into the box. She reached her hand in and pulled out a wig. Long brunette waves fell around her arm as she held it high.

"What do you think?" Sarah asked, smiling.

For the first time, she had nothing to say. She turned her head, looking up at Sarah. A single tear ran down her face.

"Oh, sweetie, don't cry. Do you want me to help you put it on?"

Alexis nodded, handing the wig to Sarah, and turned the wheelchair to face her friend as Sarah eased the beautiful wig over her own scraggly, uncombed mess. Alexis closed her eyes, feeling the weight on her semi-bald head. The hair skimmed the skin on her face and she smiled. Alexis could feel Sarah's long fingers smoothing the tresses and the warmth of human touch on her forehead. She opened her eyes and looked up sheepishly.

"I'll be right back."

Sarah scampered down the hall and returned holding a small mirror. Sarah cautiously placed the plastic handle in Alexis's trembling hand. Alexis gazed at the image looking back at her. She touched her new hair from the top of her head to the curl that sat upon her shoulder. A soft expression filled her face. It wasn't exactly her hair, but only the people close to her would know the difference.

"Thank you," Alexis whispered.

"It's my pleasure. I was afraid you might hate it. Some women find it hard to deal with, you know, losing their hair and all. Now, how about we go for a stroll?"

"I don't know if I can walk for very long."

"I wasn't expecting you to walk—we'll take the wheelchair, and I'll push you. Great exercise for both of us! I don't know about you, but I'd get a little stir crazy being coped-up in these walls for weeks at a time."

Alexis smiled, "Before you showed up, I was thinking the same thing. I'd love to get out of the house."

"Let's go get you changed and enjoy the weather, shall we? Then, I can give you my other surprise."

A puzzled look appeared on Alexis's face, "What could you have for me that would top this?" Alexis pointed at her head.

"You'll see at noon, when the surprise arrives."

Alexis giggled like a child on Christmas morning, "You're spoiling me, Sarah. What will I do when I don't need you to take care of me anymore?"

"I hope we can remain close friends, whether I take care of you or not."

"I wouldn't have it any other way."

They reached Alexis's bedroom and searched through the closet for something casual. She'd lost so much weight lately nothing seemed to fit her. A long, full peasant skirt with a drawstring waist was just the thing with a loose T-shirt.

Once Alexis was dressed, Sarah placed a soft blanket upon her lap, and they headed to the door. When Sarah opened the door, Alexis saw a small wooden ramp covering the steps.

"When did someone install a ramp here?"

"I ordered the ramp online and had Colton pick it up for me a couple of days ago."

"How did I not know about this?"

"Colton came up with the idea. I just placed the order."

"Oh?" She questioned and then smiled. "Well, thank you for doing that. I'll have to thank my son when he gets home from school."

Sarah pushed Alexis out the door, closing it behind her. Sarah held tight to the wheelchair as they made their way down the ramp and to the sidewalk.

"We'll have to go shopping and get some new clothes for you," Sarah said.

"I'd be happy with leggings and a few T-shirts. I hope to put the weight back on someday. I hate to part with the clothes I have."

"Yeah, I would feel the same way. Once you get used to something, change can be hard," Sarah replied.

"You could say that again. I am definitely not one for change. I've tried hard to keep my life stable and stress free."

"True, but sometimes the things that change can also be better for you. We became better friends, didn't we?"

"Yes, we did, and I'm glad for having you as my doctor and my friend. I guess I was too busy at work to know people like you existed."

"So, you consider us friends, right?" Sarah asked.

"Yes, of course. I just said that."

"Friends talk to friends about personal stuff?"

Alexis tilted her head to the side and looked back at Sarah. "I haven't had a lot of friends, but I guess they do share things with each other. What is it you want to know?"

"Well…" she paused. "You never talk about your husband."

Alexis sucked in a quick breath. No, she hadn't brought up Jay. Not to her son or to Sarah. She didn't even know where to start, or what she'd say to anyone. Alexis had closed the door to that part of her life. Pain and memories weren't something she dwelled upon. The feelings she'd once felt for her husband had been locked away…safe. What would happen if she allowed herself to feel them? To acknowledge she had a heart and that she cared deeply about the things she'd once taken for granted.

"I'm not sure what you're asking?" Alexis questioned.

"What was he like? What kind of things did you two do together?"

Alexis's mind flashed back to the day she'd first met Jay in college. "Jay was the most caring man I'd ever met. He was kind, loving, and thought about others before himself. He allowed me to live my dreams and not once did he make me feel guilty about working all the hours I used to work. He worked as a…" She stopped speaking abruptly and gazed at the ground. "I feel so ashamed," she practically whispered.

"Why? What makes you feel that way?"

"It's too hard to admit."

"Try me," Sarah said.

"I don't know actually what Jay's job was. I think he worked in finance, but I was too busy with my own life. By the time I came home, I was too exhausted to sit and talk with him about his day." She shook her head as it fell to her chest.

"Don't be so hard on yourself."

"Easy for you to say, you've never been married." Alexis gasped, "I didn't mean it like that. I'm sorry."

"Don't be. You're right. I think what's happened to you and us becoming friends has made me realize what I've been missing too. In fact, I have my first date on Friday."

"Really, that's wonderful! Who is he? Do I know him?" Alexis threw out questions.

"His name is Dr. Kurt Giel. He works at the same medical center as I do. He's been asking me to go on a date for quite some time, and I kept turning him down. Last week, I ran into him in the hall. We started talking and he asked what I was doing the following Friday and I replied, *Going on a date with you!*" Sarah giggled.

"No, you didn't?"

"I swear, I'm not kidding."

"What did he say?"

"He didn't say anything at first. The look on his face was priceless, though. Then he said, *'Are you asking me out?'* And I nodded. So, we're going out this Friday for dinner, and I guess whatever else we decide to do."

"You should go to the beach after dinner. You know when it gets dark."

"Okay, does sound intriguing."

"Jay used to take me to the beach on date night. He always carried a blanket in the car, and we'd sit in the sand and listen to the waves crashing in front of us. It was so romantic and calming."

"Sounds amazing! I just might do that."

Sarah brought the wheelchair to a halt at the crosswalk and looked both ways. Besides the few cars parked along each side of the street, no traffic was coming. She pushed the wheelchair down the incline and onto the road, making their way across.

Tires *screeched* to a halt three feet away from them.

Sarah's heart raced as she gripped the handles. Sarah looked up, saw a dark-haired man make sweeping hand gestures at her, and then flick her the finger. The man stared at Sarah with his cold, hard, and flinty eyes. She mouthed *sorry*, as she pushed the wheelchair to the sidewalk.

"Where the hell did he come from?" Alexis shouted.

"I don't know. I looked both ways, but the next thing I knew he was just there and almost ran us over."

The beating of Sarah's heart began to slow its pace as she breathed a few long breaths. They made their way to the next intersection, but instead of crossing the street, Sarah turned the corner. By the time they made it around the block and back to the house, it was eleven-thirty.

Sarah pushed Alexis up the ramp and turned her around. Sarah looked up just as she was positioning the chair and saw the same dark-haired man drive by the house at a snail's pace. His protruding eyes glared back at her and then the van picked up speed and drove away. Sarah thought it could've been a coincidence, but it gave her an uneasy feeling. Sarah pulled back on the metal chair, making their way inside, and locked the door behind them. She didn't think Alexis had seen the man's face either time, and it was just as well. He gave Sarah the *creeps*!

Fifty-Three

Alexis warmed up the leftover chicken soup in the microwave, and Sarah poured the container into two bowls. After they finished eating, the doorbell rang.

"I'll get it," Sarah sang. She looked out the peephole and then unlocked the door.

"Hi, I'm so glad you could make it," Sarah said.

"The directions you gave me were easy to follow."

Sarah stepped back and waved her arm, "Come in and I'll show you around."

"Sarah, who is this girl?" Alexis said, seated in the doorway of the kitchen.

"Alexis, I want to introduce you to Anna Collins. She'll be coming here to help around the house a few days during the week, while I'm at work."

"Why?"

"Well, I need to get back to work during the day, so I can have my evenings free. Anna here is more than qualified to help and get you whatever you need."

Alexis eyed the girl from head to toe. She stood tall with slim long legs and sandy blonde hair. Her ocean blue eyes smiled back at Alexis.

"What gave you the idea I needed someone here during the day? I need to start taking care of things myself," Alexis said in a wavering voice.

"I'm aware you think you can take care of things here, but you have to be realistic. You're tired all the time and with the treatments every week, your body just can't keep up with the everyday chores. Like doing the laundry or changing the sheets on your bed. Anna can also help with some cooking."

Alexis shook her head and gave a long, low sigh. "I wish you wouldn't treat me like a child."

"Alexis, please. I am not treating you like a kid. I'm just trying to make your life easier."

"I didn't ask you to hire someone to take care of me," Alexis replied, raising her voice.

"This isn't up for discussion. Anna will be here Monday, Wednesday, and Friday from eight in the morning until three in the afternoon," Sarah stood with her chin held high. "Anna goes to school in the evenings and works at the hospital on Tuesdays and Thursdays. I'm going to show her around the house while you sit and think about this." Sarah walked to Alexis and knelt down. "I'm doing this because I care about you. It's not permanent, just until you get better."

Alexis gave a hard, disgruntled smile as Sarah stood and placed her hand on Anna's lower back; then they turned and walked down the hall.

Alexis sat alone in the kitchen doorway, contemplating. She did need the help around the house when Colton wasn't home, but it still made her feel less of a person. The cancer made her see what she'd lost with her son, but it also took away her ability to be whom she once was. Each passing day she became less and less of a woman. Alexis knew deep down that Sarah was right, but it didn't change how she felt about it—alone and helpless.

Fifty-Four

Prom was just a few weeks away, and Colton wasn't sure if he wanted to go or not. It had never bothered him before to miss school dances. After all, he wasn't dating anyone. He'd drop by the after-game parties, but he usually hung out with his friends from the team, laughing, joking, and talking about basketball.

Jake had told him last week that he asked a girl to the prom and wanted to know if he was going with anyone. Colton shook his head and kept walking down the hall to his next class.

Colton knew that if he went to prom, he wanted to ask the girl from the hospital. Anna had been on his mind for the past five weeks. He could still make out the sound of her voice that seemed to whisper in his ear. Everything about her was beautiful, especially her eyes.

Besides the small talk they'd shared at the hospital, he didn't really know anything about her. A few days after the first time he'd seen her, he wanted to go back to the hospital to see her again. The thing was he didn't know what to say to her. He had never been with a girl before.

It had nothing to do with being popular in school; Colton could've had any girl he wanted. But that was the thing, he didn't want any of those girls or any girl at all; at least not until the day he saw Anna. He wished he had the courage to ask her out. What's the worst she would say? He wasn't sure if could handle her saying *"no"*.

Colton had been thinking about this on the way home from school. He pulled into the driveway, parked, and climbed out. He wasn't surprised that Sarah's car was here; it was the red Saturn parked at the curb. He hadn't seen that car before and wondered who it belonged to. He opened the back door of his car and grabbed his books, then went inside.

Colton saw Sarah sitting on the deck and headed in that direction. He slid open the sliding glass door and stepped out. He looked from Sarah to his mom and then he saw her. Anna was here at his house, but why? Was she here to see him? He smiled at the thought, his cheeks heating up.

"Hi, how was school today?" Alexis asked.

"F...f...fine," he stuttered.

"Colton, you remember, Anna?" Sarah asked.

He nodded, rubbing the back of his neck, which he was sure was as red as his face.

"She's going to be helping out around the house and taking care of your mom."

Did he hear her right? Anna was going to be here helping his mom? This had to be a dream, a really good dream. Colton had a fluttery feeling in his stomach, like he'd had at the hospital the first time he laid eyes on her. From the corner of his eye he could see her sitting there with her head down, twisting her fingers.

"Is she just as nervous as I am? Could she be feeling the same butterflies in her stomach as me?" he wondered to himself.

"Earth to Colton, did you hear what I said?" Sarah asked.

He blinked several times. "What? Yeah, that's great. We could use the help around here."

"What the hell am I saying? Was I implying that we're slobs? Crap, she's looking my way. I got to get outta here! Quick doofus, think of something..."

"Um...I gotta get started on my homework."

"What was that—Forrest Gump talking? What's wrong with me? It's not like I haven't been around girls before." Maybe Sarah had a point; he did like this girl more than he thought he did.

Colton looked at Sarah, who was glancing from him to Anna and back to him. Sarah smiled. He grabbed the handle and pulled the door open.

"Colton, don't be rude, use your manners," his mom said.

"Sorry, it's nice to see you again, Anna; bye Sarah."

He closed the glass door behind him and leaned against it. He didn't understand why he'd acted so stupid out there. He ran a hand through his hair, then grabbed his books from the table and mounted the stairs.

He closed the door to his bedroom and fell face-first on his bed. "What the hell was that all about? I'm not sure I can show my face around her again. This must be what love feels like, but I hardly know her. *Ugh!* This is so frustrating," he mumbled in the empty room.

His phone vibrated on his leg, and he flipped over and reached inside his pocket. It was the phone his dad had sent him.

"Hello."

"Hey, Colton. Are you able to sneak away tonight and meet me at the lake, say around nine tonight?"

"Yeah, sure. What's up?"

"I'll explain everything when I see you. Make sure no one is following you. If you see headlights close behind you, turn off somewhere. Don't come to the lake."

"Okay. Is everything all right?"

"Things are fine; I just need to talk to you in person."

"Sure, I'll be there at nine."

"Park by the big willow tree in the far back."

"The same one we always parked by?"

"Yes, I'll see you then."

Click.

He held the phone out in front of him. Was his dad in some kind of danger? His dad had sounded frantic on the phone. *"Make sure no one is following you,"* Dad had said. Why would his father assume someone would be following him there?

His father had mentioned before that he was hiding from some dangerous people. His dad had also said it would be over in two months. Two months were coming to an end. Why would he take the chance of going out and being caught now? Colton was thinking, *"There must be something important Dad needs to tell me."*

Colton closed the phone and glanced at the clock. He had over six hours before he had to leave. The waiting alone would drive him crazy. He had term papers to work on for American English and American History, both not due for two weeks. He couldn't figure out why the teachers had to give everything at once and not space them out.

In less than two months, he would graduate and head off to college in the fall. *But* now that he knew his dad was alive, he wasn't so sure he wanted to leave like he'd planned. He was getting along better with his mom, actually, things were great between them. They'd become so close these past few months, and he wasn't ready to move away. With his dad calling and the thoughts of school and his mom, Anna had slipped to the back of his mind, but only for a minute.

The wall shook from the door closing downstairs. Colton stood and made his way to the window.

Anna walked down the stone path and stopped. She felt as if someone was watching her. She turned her head and looked up at the window, Colton's window. Colton smiled and raised his hand to wave. Anna waved back and then continued walking to her car.

Colton watched as she drove away, knowing he could look at her forever.

Fifty-Five

When Colton had finally sat down at his desk, he didn't move until he completed the first draft of his American History paper. He hit save and closed the laptop. Peering at the clock, he saw that it was seven-twenty. He decided to grab a bite to eat, check on his mom, and head to the lake.

When he stepped off the bottom step and strolled into the kitchen, no one was around, which meant Sarah had left and his mom was probably in bed sleeping or reading a book. He walked over to the fridge and stared inside. Every shelf had at least five containers on them. He twisted his lips to the side and decided on a sandwich. He knew the food in the containers was probably outdated anyway, and didn't want to take the chance of getting food- poisoning.

Two minutes later, he'd devoured the sandwich, leaving only a few crumbs behind. He put his plate in the sink, and then proceeded down the hall to his mom's room, and knocked on the door.

"Come in."

Colton opened the door wide and coasted to the bed. Something was different about her. Earlier she had hair and now he could see nothing but a few scattered strands on his mom's head. He hadn't even mentioned anything to her. Never told her she looked pretty. He'd seen Anna and thought of nothing else.

"Hey, Mom, thought I'd come and check on you before I go over to Jake's house."

He hated to keep this a secret from her, but since he couldn't tell her the truth, he had no other choice but to lie.

"Oh, what are you two going to do?"

"Um… he called and asked if I'd help him with our term paper." Well, that part was true, not the help part, of course.

"Okay, well don't be out too late. It's a school night."

"Yeah, I know, but I'm also not a little kid anymore, remember?"

"Sorry, must be the motherly *thing* coming out in me," Alexis laughed. "Do you have a minute to spare? I'd like to talk to you about something," Alexis said, patting the empty spot next to her.

"Sure, what's up?"

"Well, a few weeks ago you asked me about your father and if he was here if things would be different?"

"Yeah, I recall that conversation, but we don't have to talk about it if it makes you, I don't know, uncomfortable."

"No. It doesn't. I just..." Alexis paused, clearing her throat. "When your father died, I had a hard time finding myself, and the only way I knew to get better was to throw myself back into my work. It's all I knew to occupy my mind. Anyway, I've been thinking about what you said, and I want you to know that I wouldn't be who I am today. I guess what I'm trying to say is that you were right."

"About what?"

"When you found out about the cancer, you told me that it happened for a reason. I think you were right. Getting this cancer has made me see what I've been missing. I was only thinking of myself instead of you and your father; it was selfish of me. I know I've always said to go after your dreams, which I still believe, but I also realize now that you should be with and spend time with the ones you care about. No one knows where our lives will lead us, or when it will end..." Alexis swallowed. "I just hope it's not too late for me and that I get to spend more time with you," her voice cracked.

Colton's heart warmed with her words and yet, he was scared at what might happen to her. He had finally gotten his mother back and now—now she was sick and possibly dying. He never had stopped loving her when she made work first on her list, but he did feel bitter towards her decision. He thought about the last three months repeatedly in his head. He was proud and thankful she had come to her senses, if that was the right way to put it.

Colton guessed God had a way of getting people to understand what mattered most. Everyone made wrong choices in their lives, but things seemed to appear before their very eyes to make them realize they needed to change for the better. Heck, he knew no one was perfect. Colton understood that things happened for a reason because the life you were living wasn't what was meant to be.

He shook his head in wonder. *Where was this stuff coming from?* Had he always thought this way? It had to be his dad's influence on him in the past that made him think these things. Though, he did have to step-up to the plate when his dad supposedly died and become a man. He had responsibilities to take care of when his mom was at work, though he did rather miss the free time he'd once had. Colton never had to check-in and tell his mom where he was going and when he'd be back, but he didn't mind it so much now. Colton would actually say he loved the fact she was home and not working anymore; he just hoped it would last. The question seemed to plague him; if or when she got better, would she go back to the life she once lived? He hoped not.

His arm shook, and he looked down to see his mom's hand nudging his.

"Hey, space cadet, are you with me?"

Alexis hadn't called him that since he was little. Whenever he was zoning out, his mom would get his attention by calling him her space cadet. Back then he'd laughed about the name and said he wanted to be just like her when he grew up, but now, not so much. He just wanted his parents back together.

"I'm here, just thinking is all."

"Okay, thought I lost you there for a minute. Did you hear anything I said?"

"Yeah, I heard you, and I'm just glad you're here with me now."

"You asked me what I would do if your dad was still alive? I hope we could be a family and be together, but son, you have to accept the truth. Your dad isn't coming back. He's gone and I wish I could change that, but I can't. I made some terrible mistakes back then and if I knew then what I know now, things would've been different, I promise you. But I can't think that way; I can only focus on us now. Do you understand?"

Colton nodded, wishing he could tell her the truth. Maybe it would help her fight harder and get better, but he couldn't tell her. Colton had to respect his dad's wishes, and when it was over, then and only then could the truth come out. Then, his dad would be home for good.

"Well, I better head over to Jake's. I shouldn't be too long."

"Okay, I'm just going to read for a while and then go to sleep."

He stood and kissed her on the forehead. "By the way, I liked your new hair you had on earlier."

Alexis smiled, "Thank you. Sarah bought it for me. She said it would help me feel better about myself."

"And did it?"

"Yes, but wish I didn't have to sleep without it. Once I'm done with the radiation therapy, my hair will grow back, but who knows when that will be?"

"How many more treatments do you have?"

"Dr. Brownski wants to do two more and then an ultrasound to see if it's helping at all. I'm praying like crazy that it's working. I'm fighting as hard as I can here; I don't know what else to do?"

"I guess that's all we can do, right now. I love you, Mom. I'll be home soon."

Alexis smiled. Colton, for the first time, had told her he loved her. She had waited so long to hear those words and now she would have to say them back. Alexis wanted to and felt warmth surrounding her heart. "I love you too, honey, goodnight."

Colton smiled back at her and waved on his way out the door, closing it behind him. He patted his pocket and realized he'd left the phone upstairs. A quick dash up the steps. Once he'd grabbed the phone, he was out the door and on his way to see his dad. He didn't know what to expect after all this time!

Fifty-Six

B oom-Boom-Boom.

The pounding of a large fist on the wooden door echoed through the house, rattling the walls, loud enough to wake the dead.

Alexis jolted upright to a sitting position. Dizziness and weakness swept through her body, fogging her brain. *"What's going on? Where's that noise coming from?"* She vigorously shook her head to zero-in on reality.

She heard the pounding once more and realized it was coming from the front door and reluctantly slipped out of bed. The room swirled before her eyes, almost dimming to black—she needed her wheelchair, but whoever this impatient person was, however, wasn't going to allow her enough time to get to it. She held the wall as she made her way down the hallway. *Had Colton forgotten his house key? Maybe? But wouldn't he just call her cellphone?*

Alexis flicked on the light in the foyer, turned the deadbolt, and opened the door. A bald and tall brawny man stood with his fist in midair ready to tear into the door, again.

"What the hell!" Alexis yelled. "What could be so important that you need to slam your fist on someone's door in the middle of the night?"

The man stepped back and dropped his hand. "Sorry ma'am," he said, in a deep husky voice. "I thought I saw smoke coming from the side of the house. I figured people were inside. I guess I over-reacted by beating on the door."

"Smoke? Where did you see smoke?"

"Coming out of the window down at that end of the house," he said, pointing in the same direction as her bedroom.

"I just came from there. I didn't notice any smoke. You must be mistaken, sir."

She went to close the door, but his boot intercepted, knocking her off-balance. He grabbed the door with his thick hand and caught her with the other. Releasing the door, he withdrew a white handkerchief from his back pocket and placed it over her face. Alexis's body went limp in his other arm, and he scooped her up, carrying her to a black van parked on the street.

Fifty-Seven

Colton pulled up alongside the willow tree and put the car in park, leaving the motor idling. This was the spot, their favorite Weeping Willow, where dad had always parked when they'd come here together. It looked different in the dark, more mysterious, but calming and familiar just the same.

He scoped out the terrain, but didn't see another vehicle in sight. Had his father changed his mind and not come? But then he would've contacted him, wouldn't he?

Pulling his phone out to look for new messages, double-checking, just in case he hadn't felt the vibration through his jeans—*no, there weren't any*—he raised his head to look around more thoroughly.

Suddenly, a faint light blinked off-and-on in the distance. He moved closer to the windshield to get a better look and saw the light flicker off. Colton turned the ignition key, killing the engine, and climbed out of his car.

"Hello," Colton hollered.

He was standing in front of his car when the light flashed on him and then flicked off again. He stood tall and trudged forward where the light had last shined. Twigs snapped under his shoes as he maneuvered through the woods.

Colton stopped. "Dad, is that you?" he whispered. Something touched his shoulder and he spun his body around. His eyes surveyed every tree near him. "Dad, are you here?"

A shadow moved from behind a tree about four feet away. Colton nervously tightened his posture for flight-or-fight, his eyes focused on the person in front of him. Colton relaxed when his dad's face came into view.

"Why did you do that? You scared the crap out of me!"

"Sorry, son, just wanted to make sure you were alone."

They hugged each other tightly and then released, stepping back to look at each other in the scant light.

"What did you want to see me about? When are you coming home?" Colton asked anxiously.

"Slow down, I'll answer all your questions soon. First, I want to know how your mother is doing?"

"She's doing fine..." he paused and swallowed. "For the most part." Colton's eyes fell from his dad's face to the ground at their feet.

"What do you mean? Is everything all right?"

"Well, the doctor found more cancer a month or so ago, and she's having more radiation. She said she has a couple more treatments and then they're going to check and see if it's working or not. She's been somewhat sick and can't walk much. She's been using a wheelchair to get around the house."

"Oh," Jay replied, as his eyes filled with tears.

Colton observed the muscles in his father's face droop. Jay leaned back against the tree, blowing out a strangled, deep breath and sliding down the trunk to a crouched position as if his legs would no longer hold him.

Colton, still standing, looked away for a moment with one arm stretched out to the tree as if it were his anchor; finally, easing down to sit beside his father.

"Dad, I wish you could come home. When are you coming home? Mom could really use you right now."

"I realize that, son, but I just can't come out of hiding yet. It would put you both in danger, and I couldn't live with myself if something awful happened to either one of you. This all will be over soon, and we can be a family again." Jay looked down at the ground in embarrassment.

"Mom's not working anymore. She's too sick to go and… and I guess I just hope she stays the person she has become these last few months. We're really getting to know each other. I talked to her about you before I came here tonight."

Jay's head sprung up, "What? What did you say to her? You didn't tell her I'm alive, did you?"

"No, of course I didn't tell her," Colton turned to face his father defensively. "I kept my promise to you. What I did ask, though, was what would she be like if you were? Would things be like they are now, or would she go back to being her old unconcerned self?"

"Oh, and what..." Jay cleared his throat. "What did she say?"

"She said she hoped things would be like they are now and that the three of us would be a family. But she also insisted that I need to let you go and move on with my life because you're dead and you won't be coming back."

"I don't think this is going to go so well when she finds out the truth. I certainly don't want to add to her troubles," Jay mumbled, almost to himself.

"Dad, don't say that. I think if anything it will help her get better. She'll fight harder to beat the cancer."

"Will you do me a favor?"

"Yeah, anything, what is it?"

"When you see your mother can you tell her how much I loved her?"

"Don't you mean *love her?* You still love her, don't ya?" Colton asked, trying to see the truth in his father's eyes, but dark shadows hid the feelings. Dad seemed like a stranger to him in some ways, but so much the same in others. It confused his son.

"Well, yeah, but I don't think that would sound right, considering I died, what…ah, last summer."

"Has it really been that long? It's spring already…"

"Tell me about it," Jay said sarcastically. "I've been staring at the same four walls for months and can't wait for this to be over."

"Can you let me in on what this is all about? You can trust me, Dad."

"It's not safe. I'm afraid someone will come to the house and harm the both of you before it's over. The less you know the better. These people won't stop until they get what they want. I'm just sorry I got involved in the first place."

"Dad, what did you get yourself mixed up in? It has to be really bad; otherwise, you wouldn't have faked your own death."

"I'm sorry, son. Believe me, I am so sorry I got myself wrapped up in this mess. If I could fix it I would, but once I take care of things it should be over, and we can be a family."

"So, if you didn't call me here to talk about what you did, then why did you need to see me?"

"I need you to get your mother and yourself out of town until this is over, but it doesn't sound like that's going to be too easy with her health the way it is. Is there any place you can take her that no one will know about until this is over?"

"Maybe Sarah's house?"

"Who's Sarah?"

"Mom's doctor. She's the doctor that first found the cancer. They've become close since Mom was diagnosed with breast cancer. She comes over every day to help Mom out, well, she did... until..." Colton paused awkwardly.

"Until what? What happened?"

"Sarah has a girl coming to the house now to help out," Colton smiled; he just couldn't help it.

"Um, son?"

"Yeah."

"By the look on your face, I would have to say you like this girl?" It was almost a question, almost a statement of fact.

Was it obvious to everyone how Colton felt about Anna? He stood up, quiet now; he knew he had the same silly expression on his face and stared over his dad's head, instead of meeting him eye-to-eye.

"Hello? Earth to Colton?" Jay pushed himself to his feet and snapped his fingers in front of his son's face. It felt so good for Jay to have a normal teenage moment with his boy. Jay grinned knowingly to himself.

Colton's body quivered a little as the thought drifted away. "What was it you asked?"

"I said you must like this girl."

"I just met her when Mom was taken back to the hospital just over a month ago. She was one of the—"

Jay interrupted, his voice loud and urgent, "What do you mean she was taken *back* to the hospital?" Then he realized where they were under cover of darkness, hidden from prying eyes, and asked softly yet firmly, "What haven't you told me?"

Colton explained in as much detail as he could what had happened five weeks ago. He concluded with, "That's how they found out her cancer had spread to the other breast."

"Oh, no!" Jay dropped his face into his hands, shaking his head side to side.

Colton touched his dad's shoulder as if that would make everything go away. Colton hadn't allowed himself to mourn over the cancer, but here his dad sat, weeping in his hands. Colton pulled Jay into his chest and held him. Colton towered over him by at least six inches.

At first, Colton felt weird holding his father while he cried. His dad was never one to show any weakness and now...now, he was different—more sensitive. Maybe these long months had softened him in some way, making his dad want to come home. He didn't know for sure how his father really felt, but his actions spoke louder than any words ever could.

"Dad, she'll pull through this; I know she will! Don't worry about her. I'll take care of her until you can come home. Finish what you need to do and come home to us."

Jay stepped back, wiping the tears from his eyes. "Sorry, son."

"Hey, don't be sorry. We all have moments that get us down—just do what you have to do."

"I will, but you have to promise me you'll get her out of the house and some place safe."

Colton nodded. "You can count on me."

They hugged one last time and then parted, walking in separate directions. Colton turned around to say something to his dad, but Jay was already gone. Colton had wanted to know where his dad had parked his car, but Colton knew these woods led to another opening and had figured it was best they weren't seen together.

~~~~~

On the drive home, Colton replayed their conversation in his mind and decided he'd have a talk with Sarah to see if they could stay at her place for a while. He'd have to come up with some good solid reason to tell her, so she wouldn't ask any questions. He'd lie if he had to—*of course, he had to*—but he was getting exhausted with everything he'd been hiding from his Mom, Sarah, and even his friend, Jake. He wanted the whole world to know his dad was alive and well. That they could start over as a family.

The phone in his pocket vibrated. He dug in his jeans pocket and flipped his cellphone open, taking his eyes off the road for just a second. It was a one-word text, "Thanks," from Dad.

Honk, honk!

Colton's head jolted up, and he yanked the steering wheel hard to the right, stomping on the brakes.

"Shit," he mumbled.

He watched as a black van buzzed by him, not even slowing down. He could see that the windows were tinted, covering all signs of the person inside.

Colton approached his house, which sat dark when he turned into the driveway. The dash read eleven-thirty, and he knew his mom was asleep by now. He tramped up the walk, keys in hand and grabbed the knob.

It was unlocked.

Colton scratched his head, thinking back to earlier when he'd gone to go see his dad. He'd locked the door behind him when he'd left hours ago. He was sure of it. *But,* maybe he was so excited about seeing his dad, he'd probably forgotten. He shrugged his shoulders, pushed the door open, and closed it, turning the deadbolt. He stepped into the kitchen, poured himself a glass of water, and climbed the stairs to his room.

Fifty-Eight

Alexis blinked several times before fully opening her eyes. The room was dark, except for a shred of light coming from under the door. Cold, stale air chilled her skin. She tried to touch her face with her hand, only to find them tethered to the side of the bed. Once her vision cleared, she lifted her head to see where she was.

The room was small—other than the bed she lay on, there was only a ratty chair set off in the corner by the door. Her throat was parched; Alexis tried to swallow, but there was no saliva in her mouth, and all she could do was choke-out a dry cough.

The door opened and a bright light blinded her, then, it was gone, covered by something big and dark. That *something big* moved closer to her.

Alexis could tell by the shadows that it was a large, bulky man. When he stopped right in front of her, a glimmer of light from behind him allowed her to make-out the body, and she recognized the face. The same husky guy had come to the door and told her he saw smoke coming from her house. Things got a little confusing after that, but she vaguely remembered him grabbing her, and everything had gone dark around her.

She didn't know how she'd gotten here in this cold, damp room, but it didn't take her long to figure things out. She stared up at him, trying to recall where she'd seen him before. He was slightly familiar, but she had no idea why.

The envelope with the pictures and the key. It popped in her head suddenly, and she was sure he was one of the men in the photographs.

The photos she'd seen and placed in the nightstand.

Alexis gasped. There were no words to express her terror!

Could her husband have been involved in something dangerous? No. Jay wasn't the kind of person to hang-out with thugs. *But* in all reality, how well did she actually know her husband? Maybe if she'd spent more time at home and asked him about his job, the things he did every day, she'd have had a better sense of who he really was? *Right?*

"Who…who are you? What…what do you want?" Alexis stuttered.

When the burly man just stared at her, Alexis's mind went wild with crazy imaginings. She was having a hard time accepting the realization that Jay had dealt with someone like this! Then another dreaded thought came to her. *Could her husband have been murdered?*

Still, there was no sound in the dark room. Was this man watching her to intensify the fear and agony of captivity soaring through her mind and body?

Murder would definitely explain things. Was Alexis going to be his next victim? How could she possibly cope with any more tragedy than the cancer ravaging her body?

She had never wanted to believe that Jay had killed himself, not for one minute. Maybe that's why she had forced his death to the back of her mind, not wanting to dwell on it. Now, she had to face all of this while a strange man was quietly, maliciously glaring at her!

Alexis wanted to scream, but was too traumatized, knowing she was completely at the mercy of this huge, fierce-looking individual. She struggled for a moment against the restraints that held her down. It was useless; she couldn't budge an inch. *Why is he just looking at me in the dark?*

His bulk shifted to the right, and a trickle of light fell across his face, revealing an amused sneer. Alexis had never known who her husband was or what he did. Their conversations had always been about her and what she'd accomplished that day. She was paying for her selfishness in a cruel and inhuman way.

Finally, after a course chuckle, the man spoke, "Mrs. Finley, I'm frankly appalled that you seem to be unaware of who I am. I thought sure, of course, your loving husband had told you something about me. Hard to believe he'd keep such a secret from you. From his own wife," the man finished with a smirk.

"I …I don't know what you're talking about."

"As much as I'd like to believe your story…" He looked down his nose at her, "I don't! Your husband thought he was a clever man," the husky man roared. "But if anything he was a stupid, stupid man! A man who thought he could manipulate me. No, no, no…" his voice rose even further. "I've been in control since the day I met your husband! Let me think, going on three years now!" he screamed at Alexis, and she started to cry in ragged, jolting sobs.

The man hesitated for a moment, leered at her with cold-blooded eyes and an evil grin, but lowered his voice when he continued, "When my people brought him to me, saying he could get us what we wanted and we wouldn't have to worry about anything, did he think I was a complete idiot? That I wouldn't check into his life and make sure he was the person he said he was?"

"I still don't understand what you're saying," Alexis swallowed, her heart pounding in her throat.

The man laughed hard and then stopped abruptly as he leaned closer to the bed. "Look here, Mrs. Finley," he barked.

His nose was mere inches away from hers—his fowl breath making her insides cringe. She swallowed the bile rising in her throat. With tears streaming down her face, she knew if she'd known anything her husband had done, she would tell this crude, ugly man, but she didn't!

Alexis felt empty and totally defeated. There was no knowledge of her husband's secret life inside her, but this man, this monster, didn't want to hear what she had to say. To have fought so hard to overcome cancer and then to die this way… *What was to become of Colton? Would this animal go after their son next? What could she do to stop this madness?*

"If you want me to do this the hard way, I will!" the man yelled into her face, leaving his spit sprayed across her mouth and chin.

"What… what are you going to do to me? I told you, I don't know anything about what Jay did! We didn't talk about stuff like that! We didn't have that kind of relationship. That kind of marriage," Alexis pleaded hysterically.

As he stood up straight again, more illumination flooded into the room. Alexis noticed when he crossed his arms, there were dark tattoos beneath the short-sleeves of his black T-shirt. His shiny head was accented with a stud earring in his left lobe. She'd never been close to anyone like this before. He looked like a criminal or serial killer from a TV drama. She couldn't believe this was actually going on. Was this a nightmare? Would she wake-up safe in her bed at home? *No, that's not going to happen. This is really happening to me!*

"So you really want me to believe you?" he bellowed!

"Yes. I'm telling the truth. You must have the wrong man, the wrong wife. Jay wouldn't do anything to hurt anyone. He was a good man," Alexis cried out!

"Is that so?"

Alexis nodded, her frightened eyes glued to his, "Besides, why would you wait so long, if it was the same man? Jay's been dead almost ten months, now."

"Ten months, you say? Hey, Boris, are you hearing this?" he turned and called to someone outside the room.

"Yes, sir, I heard every word she said."

"Why don't you come in here and tell Mrs. Finley what you know."

A light *pinged* on and she closed her eyes. Spots danced behind her eyelids. Slowly, she opened her eyes to the harsh light. A second man with dark hair stood beside the stocky bald guy. Another image appeared in her mind. Could he be the same man that almost ran her and Sarah over yesterday? He certainly looked like the same guy.

"Boss, you think she don't know the truth?" the guy named Boris asked.

The big man's broad, bald head whipped around and he stared the dark-haired man dead in the eyes, "No, stupid, I think she knows more than she's telling us."

"I don't know, Boss; I think he sideswiped her."

"So, you think her husband hid this huge secret from her? This other life?"

"I do, Boss," the dark-haired man replied, nodding his head.

"Okay, so let's say she don't know nothing and that her husband kept the truth from her. Then that only means one thing."

"What's that, Boss?"

"That she don't know her husband ain't really dead."

Alexis's eyes grew large as her body shuddered and shook. A high-pitched scream tore through her throat. The world faded to pitch-black as she lost total consciousness.

Fifty-Nine

"Not dead. Not dead..." the gruff voice kept repeating in Alexis's addled brain as she fought her way back to consciousness.

What does this man mean, not dead? Of course, Jay was dead! she thought to herself.

Alexis had gone to his funeral. She'd seen the casket before it was buried in the ground. *But?* Alexis squeezed her eyes tight, her head spinning. She'd been told she didn't need to go to the morgue, that they had enough DNA to prove it was his body. The detective on the case had told her that she should remember Jay the way he was. She'd never seen his body.

Alexis gasped. Did Colton know his father was alive? Was that why he'd asked so many questions about Jay these past few days? How? When? Unanswered questions flooded through her mind. She opened her eyes and glanced at the two men standing with their backs to her, talking. They must not realize she had regained consciousness.

"I don't understand? How could Jay be alive?" she blurted out.

The smaller man, Boris, was startled, and he stammered, "Sh...she don't know, Boss."

"Shut up, you nincompoop! I'm in control of this operation, not you!" The bulky man turned his head back towards Alexis and scanned her face. "Mrs. Finley, you don't know, do you?"

"Know what? What am I supposed to know?"

"Your husband is alive; he's hiding somewhere, and there's only one way to get him to come out of hiding."

"What do you mean? What's that?"

"You," the big man snickered.

"Me?" Alexis squeaked.

"Yes, you! I'll use you to lure him out. It's actually a well thought-out plan I've masterminded," he bragged. "I've been watching you, your son, and that woman doctor who keeps coming to the house every day. I also know you have some kind of cancer because you continue to go to the same cancer center week-after-week. You, of course, won't be any good to me dead and by the looks of ya', I couldn't wait much longer. So I jumped at maybe my only chance when we saw Colton leave the house tonight," he said with a vicious grin.

Alexis couldn't believe she was hearing this! How could someone be this cruel and inhuman? This was beyond her comprehension… These men that her husband had done business with were worse than animals! How could Jay have brought this into their lives?

"I've been observing your son as much as I have you," the boss man chuckled at the alarmed expression on her face. "Part of me wanted to follow him and see where he'd lead us, but then I might have missed the opportunity to kidnap you…since you're not long for this world."

Alexis cried out, "Leave my son alone; he's got nothing to do with this! *And,* you still haven't told me why? What has my husband done to you that caused you to take such drastic action? For God's sake, he works as a Financial Advisor!"

"A Financial Advisor, really? Is that what he told you?" the man-in-charge replied as both men started laughing at her.

Alexis nodded, her throat tightening as she tried to swallow.

"Your *so-called loving husband* has been selling me priceless art—and charging me more than what it was worth," the big boss roared!

Alexis's mind went reeling: *"Jay doesn't know anything about art!"* She couldn't count how many times they'd gone to Art Galleries, and Jay had looked dumb-founded at the artwork. He'd showed no interest whatsoever in what she liked. Jay had always agreed on a painting just because she'd showed an interest in it.

Alexis's thoughts were puzzling, but also making her angry: *"This husky man is accusing Jay of laundering money, which is extremely hard to believe. He'd never done anything illegal in his life. Art? Jay wouldn't know real art if it slapped him in the face!"* This was preposterous! She struggled again, trying to free her hands.

Both thugs watched her discomfort, totally unconcerned, but the broad, bald man answered, "Your husband sold me some Warhol pieces, a Pablo Picasso, and my favorite Vincent Van Gogh. A rare piece, I might add. It wasn't until a year ago I found out the pieces of art weren't worth what I paid for them! Jay thought he was a smart guy and would get away with my money."

Alexis's mind raced back to the envelope with the key in it. Could this man be telling the truth? It was possible, sure, but still hard for her to swallow what the criminal boss was telling her.

"What are you going to do with me? My son and my friend will know I'm missing, and they'll come looking for me."

"Sure, they will, but it's not them I want. Boris, untie her and put her in the chair in the other room. It's time we get this show on the road," he actually rubbed his hands together in anticipation.

"What are you going to do?" Alexis remembered he had called the other man *Boris* before; she needed to remember that name.

"Don't be afraid, Mrs. Finley, I won't hurt you—yet," the big man howled.

The dark-haired man untied both of her hands, picked her up, and carried her out of the room. They entered another small room, where he placed her in a metal chair, and retied her hands behind the chair.

Alexis's eyes scanned the room. The room was much smaller than the other one she'd been in. Gray streaks covered the walls, and there were stains on the floor, possibly blood, but she couldn't be sure. In front of her stood a video camera...nothing else.

"Good, good. That will be fine," the big guy nodded to Boris, who remained silent as he stepped back out-of-the-way.

The *self-proclaimed "Boss"* went and stood behind the camera. "I want you to say what's on these cards that my buddy Boris here will be holding up. If you should say anything else, I'll start with your fingers and cut them off one-by-one. Do you understand?"

"Yesss," she whimpered.

"Good. No harm will come to you if you do what you're told. I am not a killing machine, nor do I get pleasure out of hurting or killing anyone, but I will do what I have to in order to get what I want. Besides that's why I have Boris with us. He does my dirty work for me."

"Boss, why do you keep telling her my name? Now she knows who I am," the smaller man whined.

"Shut up and do your job, moron!" he barked in reply.

Boris grabbed the white poster boards and stood to the left of the camera, holding the cards. Alexis lifted her head and tears streaked down her face. The light turned red, and she glanced over at Boris, who was holding the cards.

A couple minutes later, the red light went off, and Alexis's chin fell to her chest. Boris untied her, placed her back in the bed in the other room, locking the door on his way out. He didn't bother to tie her up this time. She was so frightened and exhausted she couldn't have tried to escape anyway.

Alexis curled up into a fetus position. She reached behind her and pulled up a blanket, covering her body. She thought of her son and hoped that he had come into her room to check on her. Would Colton go to the police or phone his father? Did Colton actually know that Jay was alive? She strongly suspected he did.

Alexis still couldn't believe that Jay had been alive all this time. He had pretended to kill himself and gone into hiding from these men. He'd been someone she knew nothing about. A thought crossed her mind. How much of his life did she really know? How much was true? How much had been fabricated? She didn't know. She didn't want to believe he'd lied to her all these years. That everything he'd shared with her hadn't been real.

She wasn't sure what the two men were going to do with the video. How would they know if Jay watched it? She hoped somehow he would and she'll get to go home, or would they kill her? They didn't want any witnesses, someone who could go to the police.

Alexis gasped and started to cry again. Then, she pulled herself together. Crying didn't fix anything.

Would Boris really kill her? Would Alexis ever see Colton again? She had to find a way out. Alexis couldn't let them get away with this, but what could she do? She was sick, fragile, traumatized and had no clue how to survive a kidnapping.

Alexis refused to just lie here and die! She had too much to live for.

Sixty

Colton woke up early the following morning. He quickly showered, dressed, and then dashed down the stairs to the kitchen. It had become a habit to eat his breakfast and help his mom get up and out of bed. He hustled down the hall to find her door wide open. He poked his head in. His mom wasn't in bed. His heart quickened as his mind flashed back to the morning he'd found her lying on the bathroom floor. He quickly scurried to the bathroom, but his mom wasn't there either.

He took in a deep breath and walked back to the kitchen. Maybe he hadn't noticed his mom outside on the deck. She's been known to go out there almost every morning. Colton opened the sliding glass door and stepped out. He glanced around, but she was nowhere in sight. Then, it hit him that her wheelchair was still in the bedroom. His mom wouldn't have left the house without it. She didn't even leave the bedroom without it anymore!

He went back inside and checked her room once more— nothing. He peeked out the window—no car. Colton ran to the door that led to the garage. Her car was there. Confusion set in;

he had no idea where his mom had gone or who could have picked her up. Mom would have told him last night if Sarah had been taking her somewhere, or if something had happened unexpectedly, Mom or Sarah would have left him a note or a message on his cellphone.

He returned to the kitchen and made his way to the counter, flipped through the address book, and found Sarah's number. He picked up the phone on the wall, dialed, and waited for her to answer.

Five rings later. "Hello."

"Hey, Sarah it's…"

"I can't get to the phone right now. Please leave your name and number, and I'll get back to you as soon as I can. Thank you. Have a nice day!" *Beep!*

Colton was listening to her stupid answering machine. The voice had sounded so real and life-like. He left a quick message, asking her to call him as soon as she could.

Colton paced the room, trying to put things into perspective. Maybe Sarah had come by the house, and they'd gone to run a quick errand? It was possible. Heck, anything was possible. His dad had said to get Mom and him out of the house to someplace safe because there were dangerous men involved that could hurt them. *What if? Could they have taken her?*

No, he didn't want to think the worst. The black van that had almost hit him last night flashed in his mind. It had been too near to his house for comfort, and he'd seen it in front of their home before last night.

"No, no, no," Colton yelled in sheer panic, raising both hands to gouge his fingernails into his scalp.

He was too late! Someone had taken his mother, and God only knew what they were doing to her!

Didn't they care that she was sick, that she had cancer? Why the hell would they? They were using her to get to his dad, and the sad part was, it just might work! Dad had trusted him to take care of her, but did he have to tell his father? No, he had to find her himself and get her home safely, but how was he supposed to do that? He wasn't a cop. He didn't even know where to look for his mom—where to start.

Colton continued to pace the floor, wearing a path in the tiled floor. He jumped when a knock on the door echoed through the room. He bolted to the door and yanked it open.

Anna stood smiling, "Are you going to let me in, or will I have to stand outside all day?"

His mouth hung open as he stared at her. He'd forgotten all about Anna coming to the house today. What would he tell Anna if she asked about Alexis? He needed to stop and take a deep breath and think about things. He coughed in his fist and stepped aside for Anna to enter.

"Sorry about that, just have a few things rolling around in my head, is all."

"Sure, no problem. I was told to be here at 8:00 a.m. So is there anything special you'd like me to start with this morning?"

"It's eight o'clock?"

"Ah, yeah," Anna tilted her head to one side, grinning up at Colton.

"Crap, I'm late for school. To heck with it, another day won't kill me if I stay home," he reasoned to himself. "Too much going on, lost track of time," Colton replied aloud to Anna.

"Does Alexis need help this morning? I mean, like getting dressed or something?"

His eyes fell to the floor and then back up at her. For a split second, he was lost in her ocean blue eyes. "I think Sarah came and picked her up this morning. She might have told me and I forgot, but I'm not sure."

"No problem, I'll just start the laundry and tidy up a bit until she gets home."

Colton nodded and leaped up the stairs two at a time. He rushed like a tornado through his room, throwing dirty clothes in the hamper and making his bed. He didn't want Anna to see what a pig he was. It was the only place in the house he could make his own and do what he wanted, but she didn't need to know that.

By the time he finished, the house phone rang. "Hello," he answered, breathing hard.

"Colton, did I catch you at a bad time? You sound out of breath," Sarah asked.

"What? No, was just cleaning my room. Never mind that. Is my mom with you?"

"No, why would she be with me?"

"I need for you to come to the house. It's time I told you something."

"What's wrong? Why can't you tell me on the phone?"

"I just can't. I need you to get here as quick as you can."

"You're scaring me, Colton. Tell me what's happened to your mom?" she demanded.

"I'll tell you everything when you get here. When can you come?"

"It'll take me at least fifteen minutes or so to get there."

"That's fine; I'll be here."

"I don't think I like this. You're acting crazy."

"Will you come?"

"Yeah, I'm on my way."

Colton hung up the phone and sat down on his bed, placing his head in his hands. He needed to clear his mind and think exactly how he was going to tell Sarah about his dad and that he was in some kind of trouble. He thought back to the day at the hospital, when he'd been about to tell Sarah his dad was alive. Anna had interrupted, but in a good way.

He didn't want to know what Anna thought of him from this morning. The way she caught him off-guard, standing outside the door with her gorgeous blue eyes and pretty smile. It had slipped his mind that she was coming over to take care of his mom. Though, if his mom had been here, then he would've been at school and wouldn't have seen Anna.

For weeks, he hadn't been able to get Anna off his mind and now all this craziness was happening all at once. With his mom sick, finding out his dad was alive, graduation approaching and prom—which was the last thing on his mind right now—he was overwhelmed to the max! One more thing to add to the chaos: His mom was missing!

Colton figured he'd start by telling Sarah about his father and then, fill her in on what he suspected had happened last night. He prayed that Sarah would know what he needed to do to find her.

He heard a car door slam shut. He stood and glanced out the window. Colton ran half way down the stairs and then slowed his pace before he came to the last step. Anna had beaten him to the door and was letting Sarah in.

"Okay, Colton, I'm here. What's going on?"

Colton motioned toward the patio. Sarah took the lead. She slid the door open and stepped out; he followed, making sure the door was shut solidly behind him.

"Spill it," Sarah insisted.

"Let's sit down, and I'll tell you everything."

Colton cleared his throat, started at the beginning, and didn't stop until he finished with what happened this morning, his eyes on his hands the entire time. He looked up and focused on Sarah's face.

Sarah's mouth dropped open, closed, and opened again. She stared out at the backyard as if contemplating what to say.

Colton knew she'd have to digest everything he'd said. He sat back and gave Sarah time to let everything sink in.

"Colton…" Sarah paused, clearing her throat. "I think we should go to the police or that detective you mentioned. You can't do this on your own. You'll get yourself hurt or worse…" Sarah stopped without finishing the sentence.

"I had a feeling you'd say that. I don't know if I want to go to the police. I mean what can they do anyway? I have no proof—nothing but speculation!"

"Well, we know Alexis didn't just leave and walk out of here on her own. So the logical answer is these people, whoever they are, took her. Oh God! Alexis is too weak for this! I don't even want to think about what they might be doing to her." A tear ran down Sarah's cheek and dropped off her chin.

Colton's heart ached, knowing how much his mother meant to her. He'd have to do something to get his mom home and out of harm's way, but what? They sat in silence, each glancing at the other as they tried to figure out what to do.

"I think you should call your father," Sarah finally said. "Jay might be able to help, since he got Alexis involved in this in the first place. Whatever he's done has jeopardized your mom and you too, for that matter. Your father needs to know, Colton, and fast!"

"Yeah, I know you're right, but I don't want my dad to get caught and they might…" Colton didn't want to say… *"kill him."* He'd just found out his father was alive and didn't think he'd be able to handle it if his dad was really dead, not again; not this time.

Colton dug the phone his father had given him out of his pants pocket and tapped a key. He could hear it ringing before he even pressed the phone to his ear.

"Son?"

"Dad, they took Mom!" he blurted out. He just couldn't help it. This had been bottled up inside him all morning.

"What? What are you saying?"

"I got up this morning, and she wasn't in her room. She was nowhere in the house. I called Sarah, thinking she'd picked her up this morning, but she didn't. Sarah's here with me now."

"Oh my God! Not your mother!"

"Dad, what are we going to do?"

"You're not going to do anything. I'll take care of this. I should've taken care of this a long time ago. Damn it, I'm such an ass! I never wanted you or your mother involved in my problems."

"Dad, what did you do? I think it's time you filled me in on what happened…how long has it been? A year ago?"

"It's been a lot longer than a year, son. What I've been doing for the last *four* years, should have ended… Hell, it shouldn't have ever been done at all, but I got so… so greedy and well, I did some awful things. Some illegal things."

"Dad, do the police know about what you did?"

"No, nothing. And if they found out, I could go to prison for the rest of my life. You must *not* get the police involved in this. Promise me, son. Don't get them in the middle of this!"

"Okay, okay, I promise, but let me help you. I'll do whatever you say; I just want Mom back."

"Meet me at this address in an hour," Jay's voice lowered considerably, "241 Olden Road. I'll text you the directions in a few minutes. This is *for-your-eyes-only!* I don't want you to map quest it. We'll go over things and figure out what to do when you get here."

"All right, I'll see you then."

Colton closed the phone and filled Sarah in on what his dad had said.

"I'll go with you."

"No, you can't. You should stay here in case we're wrong and Mom comes home. I'll keep in touch with you, and you do the same. Does that sound good to you?"

"Colton, I'm just scared is all. Whatever your father has gotten himself into he shouldn't involve you. Good or bad, he should do this on his own."

"No, I'm going, and there's nothing you can say that will change my mind. My mom is in danger and whatever my dad did; I can forgive him as long as my mom's okay."

Sarah touched his arm and nodded, "Let me know what's going on, okay?"

"Yeah, I will," Colton stood and headed back inside.

He went to his room to read the incoming text in private and returned a few minutes later. He had one hand on the doorknob, when he heard his name.

"Colton, be safe," Sarah said, with a hard smile.

"I will. I promise."

Colton opened the door and walked out, closing and locking it behind him. He needed to keep Sarah and Anna safe too; they could unlock the door from the inside if there was an emergency. He prayed there would be no more chaos!

Sixty-One

Forty-five minutes later, Colton parked in a back alley and walked two narrow streets deeper into a dilapidated neighborhood. It was a little closer to their home, situated in a downtown slum.

When he saw the house number, 241, he climbed a few rickety steps. *This would be the first time he entered Dad's new safe-house,* he thought; *this was sounding more and more like a TV drama, and this dump wasn't any better than the last one. In fact, if he didn't know better, he'd have thought the place was deserted. Maybe it was better that way.*

He tapped very lightly on the crooked, wooden door. His dad cracked the door open, allowing Colton to enter.

Colton stood in front of his father, neither one speaking. Colton turned and sat down on a lumpy sofa. It was different from the sofa at the other house that was further out in the country. Jay hesitated and then took a seat in the chair across from him.

"Dad, it's time you told me your story, and I mean all of it."

Jay sat quiet and then spoke, "Well, you know I work in Business Finance."

Colton nodded.

"Things were fine; heck, they were better than fine—they were great. What I did has nothing to do with work. Son, I have a gambling problem, and I got in way over my head. At first, I had won big. I wanted to surprise your mother and had bought her a few expensive paintings. Then, I guess, I got selfish, and my luck had run out. I didn't want to have to sell the paintings I had bought for your mother, so I had to come up with a different plan. A better plan. I owed more money than your mother and I put together could come up with, so I started working in the art industry."

"Art?" Colton queried, looking at Dad with a puzzled expression.

Jay nodded and shifted uncomfortably in the ratty chair. "I met this person named Sergei Leonti. He came to me looking for some priceless art after I let it be known I knew where I could get my hands on some really nice pieces that were inexpensive, and after a while, things were going great again. Anyway, I, of course, had raised the price when I sold them to this Sergei guy. You know for my time. I was making money under the table, so to speak. I paid back what I owed. It wasn't until much later, when I found out that some of the money Sergei gave me in exchange for artwork was counterfeit."

"But," Colton interrupted, "where did you get the artwork from? I haven't noticed anything missing from the house…not that Mom has that much…"

"There's this auction they have where priceless art is sold for only a few thousand dollars. Normally, you'd think hundreds of thousands to millions of dollars it would cost, and probably at one time, it did."

"I can't believe you're telling me this. I never thought you could do something so… so stupid!" Colton shouted. He got up off the sofa and walked a few steps around the small, drab room. There was nowhere to go, nothing to do—he had to hear the rest of this. "Okay, go on," he mumbled to the father he had always respected so highly.

"Son, I'm sorry. I know it was a stupid thing to do, but I just couldn't tell your mother what I'd done. All our hard work, putting money aside for college for you and our retirement. I couldn't just go to the bank and withdraw all our money and her not know. Besides, it wouldn't have been enough to cover the debt I got us in."

"What did you do with the paintings you got for Mom?"

"I keep them in a storage unit a couple of hours away from here."

"Is that what the key is for?"

"No. The key goes to a safety deposit box. There's something else," Jay said.

"What's that?"

"I used some of the money Sergei gave me to buy the art and to pay back my gambling debts."

"So, let me see if I got this straight. Sergei is coming after you for cheating him out of the money for the art? And, how many other people, for paying them in counterfeit money?"

"I don't know, one, maybe two other people."

"So, what do you think we should do?"

"I don't know, Colton. This man Sergei..." Jay swallowed. "He's not one to be messed with. He's part of the coterie of Russian gangsters."

"Oh my God, Dad! What were you thinking?" Colton was on his feet again; Jay rose from the chair and tried to pull his son into his arms. "No, not now!" Colton yelled as he turned his back on his dad.

"I... I don't know. I guess I wasn't thinking." Sweat rolled down Jay's forehead and he wiped it away with the back of his hand.

"Are you going to give me some excuse, like Mom was working all the time and you were bored? I mean, what the hell, Dad? You've put our lives in danger. This is unbelievable what you've done! All this time I blamed Mom for working all those hours and now she has cancer. Then, I find out you're alive; Mom gets kidnapped and you're a thief." Colton's head was spinning in circles. He had looked up to his father his whole life and to learn he was dealing with the Russian mob was just too much!

Colton sat down and fell back against the sofa, looking up at the ceiling. He closed his eyes and shook his head. He wasn't sure what he could do to help, but first things first—they had to come up with a plan to get his mom back—unharmed. Maybe they should go to the police, but Colton didn't want to take the chance of his dad going to prison for the rest of his life, even if his father probably did deserve it. No, they couldn't go to the police. Colton wouldn't be able to live with himself if the cops sent his dad away.

"You've got mail," a computer voice squeaked out. Jay stood and shuffled his feet to a small wooden table in the corner of the room. Jay sat down in front of a small laptop and clicked on the small envelope icon. A video popped up; he clicked on the play arrow. Alexis's face appeared and her voice filled the room. Colton stood and walked over to his dad.

"Jay, if you don't give Sergei *what he wants, he will kill me. Please, do what he*

says," Alexis sniffled. *"And bring the money to 1435 Paddock Street. There is an abandoned warehouse at the end of the street. You have until 9:00 p.m. tonight. If you don't..."* Alexis gasped. *"They will deliver my body to you in separate bags. Please, don't call the police. Come alone and bring all of the money with you."*

Colton's face turned ashen. He had been right; they did have his mom. From the video, she didn't look like she'd been beaten or anything, just her tired, fragile self. He noticed her eyes were looking at something off to the side. She must have been reading the words they wanted her to say.

Jay hadn't seen his wife since she'd been sick. He wasn't prepared for how thin and pale she was. Her beautiful hair was gone. He started to sob, but this time Colton couldn't reach out to him.

It took less than a minute for his dad to pull himself together, and he replayed the video one more time, jotting down the address on a sheet of paper. Jay knew he couldn't allow himself to fall apart. It was time to take action.

"What are we going to do, Dad? They said not to involve the police, but if we go there they could take the money and kill all of us."

"We're not going to involve the police," Jay replied.

"Then what are we going to do?" Colton asked, now pacing the room.

Jay stood up from the computer, stopping Colton in his tracks. He put his hands on his son's shoulders. This time Colton didn't pull away. "We're going to the storage unit and load up the art I bought for your mom. They're worth more than I owe him. Then, we'll go to the address and get your mom home safe."

"You honestly think it will go that smoothly?"

Jay dropped his hands and walked over to a narrow door on the other side of the room. He opened the door and pulled down on a string. Light filled the small closet, and he stepped inside. Seconds later, Jay backed out carrying a gun in both hands.

Colton gasped, shaking his head, "Dad, what are you doing with those?"

"Son, we aren't going in there without some kind of weapon," Jay answered as he placed the two guns on the table and headed back to the closet. He came out with two vests and two oversized jackets.

"Put this on. If anything should happen and they shoot, you'll at least be protected."

Colton looked at his father in a way he never had before. He wondered what had happened to this man he once knew so well. At least he'd thought he'd known him; Colton slipped on the bulletproof vest, covering it with the jacket, while his father did the same. Jay returned to the computer, pulling up and opening some files.

"Are you sure we shouldn't get the cops involved? We can make them a deal that they can have Sergei in exchange for your testimony," Colton suggested.

"I can't do that. There's no way they would take my side in this."

"How do you know?"

"Son, I was embezzling money; why wouldn't they put me in prison?"

"In movies they do that."

"This isn't a movie, Colton. This is real life and since I got the both of you involved in this, it's up to me to fix it."

Colton nodded. There was no sense in trying to argue with his dad. His father was going to do whatever he wanted to anyway. Looking at the clock on the wall, they still had ten hours before the deadline. "What are we going to do between now and then?"

"Let me finish this inventory so we can drive to the storage unit and start loading the car; then... then we'll go from there."

"How much stuff are we talking about?"

"There's at least eight portraits, give or take."

"You are something else, you know that? I would have never guessed my own father would ever be in this kind of mess."

"Son, I... I don't know what to tell you. I don't know what I can say to make it up to you."

"You can start by saying once this is over, you're done with gambling. That mom and I mean more to you than this."

"You and your mother do mean the world to me. I swear I never would have gotten myself into this mess if I'd known the outcome. I wouldn't have put either of your lives in danger. I love you both, more than you know."

"Well, you sure have a funny way of showing it," Colton said as he sat down on the sofa again, suddenly feeling dizzy, and ran his hand through his hair.

It was starting to seem real, but Colton didn't have a clue what to believe. He loved his dad, but he wasn't sure if he knew who his father really was anymore. He would've never guessed in a thousand years Dad would steal and launder money. His dad portrayed himself as a thief, and the trust Colton once had for his father was gone. Could it be rebuilt... in time? He had no way of knowing. It was all so confusing!

All Colton cared about now was getting his mom home safe, and they'd go from there. He wondered what her reaction would be when she found out Jay was alive and well? That he faked his death and lied to the both of them? Did she think Colton knew all about what his father had done?

But, that's right, Colton thought to himself, *she already knows— that Sergei guy must have told her everything before making the video.*

Alexis had probably been just as stunned as Colton was right now. She probably had the same thoughts he was wrestling with. All these years of living with someone and finding out he was someone very different than he'd pretended to be. Had Dad only pretended to love them? His mom was fighting for her life from cancer, and these gangsters were threatening to kill her!

Colton stood up and mumbled to Jay, "Where's the bathroom?"

His dad was concentrating on some lists of numbers on the laptop. He pointed to the back of the run-down shack.

Colton nodded to him and ducked into a dark hallway; he needed to make a call.

Sixty-Two

Alexis opened her eyes to the sound of the door being unbolted. The same big thug entered and stood beside her.

"Okay, get up. We have somewhere to be."

She slid her legs over the edge of the bed and pushed herself to an upright position.

"Where are we going?"

"We're meeting your husband to get back what belongs to me. Come on, we don't have all night," he snapped as he roughly pulled her to her feet and grumbled inaudibly when she fell back on the bed.

"Do you not have any feelings? I've been sick, and it takes me a while."

"Boris, get in here and help her."

"Yes, Boss," Boris hollered from down the hall.

Alexis straightened her T-shirt that was hanging off one shoulder. She was still wearing her nightclothes from when this man had come and taken her. She was thankful she'd worn her cotton pajama bottoms along with the matching top, but she'd been doing that since Jay had died.

She'd never have opened the door in the middle of the night had her brain not been so fuzzy. She had just wanted the loud banging on the door to stop!

She shook her head in disgust. Her husband had lied to her. Well, he didn't lie—he just didn't tell her the truth about what he was doing. Did she even ask him about his job? Only a few times had the subject come up between them. Maybe if she'd put her family first, Jay wouldn't have done anything illegal. She knew she could sit here and blame herself—she was the one working all the time—but he sure as heck wasn't a saint, either.

Boris wrapped his arm around her back and helped her to stand, the two of them maneuvering through the door and down the hall. The hallway was new to her since she'd been unconscious when they brought her here. She moved her eyes around soaking in the layout of the dwelling. She prayed she'd have a chance to use it to escape or tell the police how to catch these criminals.

When they stepped outside into the night, Boris helped her into the back of a black van. She tried to read the license plate number, but a wave of dizziness clouded her vision.

"Boss, should I tie her up, or do you think she's too weak to run?"

"Tie her up, just in case she gets heroic. Don't need her jumping out of the vehicle while it's moving and have her wind up dead or something."

When Boris finished, he slammed the door closed and made his way to the passenger seat.

"What the hell do you think you're doing? Get your ass back there and sit with her."

"Sorry, Boss."

Once Boris was inside the rear of the vehicle, Sergei started the van and drove off.

Her head thick with fog and her stomach queasy, she scooted her butt over and nestled her body on the floor of the van. She listened to the *tha'thunk* of the tires on the road every couple of feet. She had an idea they were on a highway somewhere. The van slowed and turned off, coming to a stop. She held onto the rope—it was not only around her wrists but tied to a bar on the side of the van's wall—as they turned left.

A few moments later, they came to a halt. The engine was turned off and both the rear doors were opened wide. Boris kept the rope around her wrists but untied the rope from the van. Using her feet, she slowly inched her way to the edge of the vehicle.

Boris made his way out and stood alongside her, holding the rope in his hands. She looked at him; he winked and then released the rope from her wrists and held a finger to his lips. She thought he must feel sorry for her and actually cared what happened to her. She kept her hands behind her back so the big guy wouldn't notice.

Her head jolted up when a bright light split through the night. She scanned the area; a dozen or so men were holding guns on them.

"Let the woman go and put your hands on your heads," a man's voice echoed through a bullhorn. The *clack* of guns hit the gravel road and both criminals raised their hands to their head.

"Are you all right, Mrs. Finley?"

She nodded and started to step away from the van. As soon as she took her first step, the big bald man grabbed her by the shirt and yanked her back towards him.

She screamed when he wrapped his arm around her neck. *Sergei*, for that was the crime lord's name Alexis learned when she read the stock-cards in front of the camera, pulled a gun from behind him, holding it to her temple.

"Sergei, you don't want to do this. You can't honestly believe we'll let you out of here alive. I have at least ten men with rifles pointed at your head right now. One false move and they'll shoot and not think twice about it."

"Let me go and she won't get hurt," Sergei demanded.

Detective Bowen stepped forward, "Do you honestly think I believe you? She wouldn't be the first you've killed or the last. We're not leaving here until you are stopped once and for all."

Sergei cocked the gun, pressing the barrel into the side of Alexis's head.

Detective Bowen raised his left hand in the air and made a fist. A gun fired—Boris howled and then dropped to the ground; his kneecap blown clear off. Sergei's arm loosened from around Alexis's neck as he fell backwards with a bullet in his head.

Alexis screamed!

A hand reached out to her and she grabbed onto it, not wanting to turn and see what had happened. Three cops came over to Boris and held him down until the ambulance arrived and took him away.

Alexis buried her head in Detective Bowen's chest, her body shaking. He pulled her along and stopped at one of the police cars next to a warehouse. The backdoor opened and Colton stepped out, wrapping his arms around her. Alexis cried as Colton held her in his arms.

When she pulled herself together, she stepped away from her son and asked him, "Your father..." she paused. "Is it true? Is he really alive?"

Colton turned her around; standing in front of her stood Jay.

She wanted to slap Jay for lying to her and Colton, but with everything that had just happened, she wasn't thinking clearly at the moment. She stood frozen in shock.

"Alexis, I'm so sorry for hiding the truth from you. I...I..." Jay stammered.

She placed her finger on his lips, "We'll talk about everything tomorrow. I want you to take me home."

"I can't go home with you."

"What do you mean you can't come home?" Her eyebrows rose in alarm.

"Jay Finley, you need to come with us," Detective Bowen said.

Jay nodded and placed his hands around her face and kissed her lips. She stood watching as the detective handcuffed Jay and placed him inside a different cruiser. Tears slithered down her face and her body went limp. Colton caught her just before she fell to the ground and held her in his arms.

"Let's go home, Mom."

Colton helped Alexis into the car he'd just exited and slid in next to her, closing the door.

Sixty-Three

The next two days Colton stayed home from school. His mother needed him more now than ever before. By phone, he had filled Sarah in late last night—or rather in the early a.m.—on what had happened at the docks.

Sarah came over early and helped by staying in the upstairs bedroom, not wanting to leave Alexis's side. She had used more of her vacation days to help with Alexis. Sarah couldn't even get Alexis out of bed. She tried to coax her onto the patio, but Alexis wouldn't leave the bed and getting her to eat was even harder. She didn't even talk to Sarah about Jay, and Alexis had told no one about the terror she'd experienced from the hands of Sergei Leonti and Boris Rudolf.

Colton had thought she'd want to talk about his father this morning, but she hadn't said a word. He didn't want to pressure her into talking about him, so he left well enough alone. He'd told Sarah that he was going out for a little while and would be back in an hour or so. Sarah didn't ask why, and Colton didn't say. He needed to find out what was going on with his dad and if he was coming home anytime soon.

Sixty-Four

"Hey, Colton, come on in and take a seat."

"How's my dad doing? How long are you going to keep him here?"

"Don't start hammering me with questions. I'll answer them one at a time. Your father is doing okay; he's resting downstairs in one of our cells. And the second question, we'll have to keep him here until his attorney gets him a bail hearing. Colton, I don't know how else to tell you, but there is a good chance your father will have to serve some time in prison. If they can come up with some kind of agreement, he could do one to two years minimum."

"And if not?"

"Fifteen to twenty-five years in prison."

Colton's mouth fell open. He didn't want his dad to go away for fifteen or more years; he'd just gotten him back. *And his mom*, what would she do? If she stayed in bed, she...she wouldn't fight to get better... he couldn't think about what could happen to her then.

He needed to talk to his father and find out what was going on, but would he tell him the truth? Colton had to at least try to talk to his father.

"Colton, I know you're shocked, but what your father did is a felony, a crime. Not just the laundering of money and all the priceless art, but he also faked his own death. However, there wasn't any crime in his death part—he didn't hurt anyone. You tried to tell me he was alive, but I just wouldn't listen. I guess what I'm trying to say is, you should be proud of yourself that you never gave up hope."

"He faked his death to keep us safe, Detective."

"I'm aware of what he did, but there's just no way of knowing if he'll serve jail time until he talks to his lawyer and they come up with a plea bargain or decide to go to trial. No matter what, he still broke the law."

"But he didn't know the money was counterfeit until after he had paid his gambling debts."

"That's true, but there's still a lot we don't know yet. Besides, I'm not supposed to be talking to you about this. I've told you what I can, for now."

Colton nodded, "Can I visit my dad while I'm here?"

"Sure, I'll take you downstairs, and you can talk to him through a phone."

Colton rolled his eyes. They were treating his dad as if he killed someone.

~~~~~

Colton sat on the other side of the glass, waiting for his father to arrive. Several minutes later, the door in the opposite room opened and his dad entered. His eyes followed him until he pulled out the chair and took a seat. Colton picked up the phone next to him; his dad did the same.

"Hey, son, how's your mom doing?"

"She's um…she's hanging in there." He couldn't find it in himself to tell his dad the truth. "How are you doing?"

"Part of me wishes you wouldn't have made the call yesterday. You know how I felt about getting the police involved. I could've been home with you and your mother right now."

"You don't know what the outcome would've been, and besides Sergei might have killed us all. He would've killed us."

"Yeah, I guess. Probably so," Jay whispered.

"Have you talked to your attorney yet?"

"He's coming here later today. Why?"

"Just wondering what was going to happen to you."

"Son, I'll be fine. I'm sure the lawyer will come up with the best scenario."

Colton nodded. Jay asked once more, how Alexis was doing. Colton couldn't and wouldn't tell him the truth, but he didn't want to lie. That was something his father was good at doing. He wasn't sure why he was feeling so angry inside.

Ten months ago, he'd worshiped his dad, thought the world of him. Heck, he even defended him against his mom when they disagreed. And now...now... he wasn't sure how to feel about the man who was his father.

This whole time his dad had been someone else, someone who was untrustworthy and a criminal. Did he actually think his dad was a bad person, or did his father just get involved in something beyond his grasp? Like being at the wrong place at the wrong time. Colton would have to let his dad handle his own mess; he needed to take care of his mom. If his dad got up to twenty-five years in prison, then what would Colton do? He would have to make sure his mom was taken care of.

"Hey, are you with me, son?"

"Yeah, I'm here. I'll stop in tomorrow and see what's going on. You should know something by then, right?"

Jay nodded, "Sure, sure."

"Okay, well, I'll see you tomorrow then."

"Yeah, see you."

Colton hung up the phone and trotted out of the room, not once looking back over his shoulder.

Sixty-Five

Alexis had spent the last two days in bed; she didn't want to socialize with Colton or Sarah, yet. When she'd seen Jay the other night standing in front of her, it was as if she hadn't known him at all. Her husband had lied to her. He'd made her believe he'd killed himself, but *why?*

While she was recuperating from the shock and rough treatment, Alexis had racked her brain for answers or any tell tale signs she might have missed to explain Jay's actions. She'd come up with nothing—she just didn't know or understand any of this!

Jay wasn't the same man she'd fallen in love with almost twenty years ago. She'd kept herself in bed, reminiscing over nearly a year since *he'd supposedly died.* How could anyone hurt someone that they professed to love this much? The excruciating pain and loss had never dulled in all this time. Had Jay expected his family's grief to subside? And suicide? Didn't he realize the guilt she would feel? Or that Colton would blame her too?

Alexis came up with more questions than answers. How was she to go on? What more could possibly happen to her? She knew she didn't need all this stress from these past two days on top of the cancer she was fighting. She only had one thing to live for—Colton, her incredible son. She had to remain strong for him, but it was even harder now than it had been before.

Sixty-Six

When Colton returned home, he noticed Anna's car sitting at the curb. He wanted so much to talk to her. He was always straightforward when talking to his mom and his friends, but when he was around her—he froze.

The prom was only three weeks from now, and he hadn't found the courage to ask her out. With everything going on in his life, he hadn't been thinking too much about his needs.

He went inside and saw Sarah sitting on the patio. He grabbed a Coke from the fridge and joined her outside. Anna sat across from her and looked up when he stepped out.

"Hi, Colton," Anna said.

He swallowed, "Um…hi."

Sarah stood, "Here take my seat; I need to check on your mom anyway."

"Oh," he replied and plopped down in the chair.

Once Sarah was in the house, Anna spoke, "I hope you don't mind, but Sarah filled me in on what has been going on these past few months. If you need someone to talk to, I'm a good listener. Besides, you look like you could use someone to talk to."

Colton cleared his throat and swallowed. Silence stretched between them. Neither one made eye contact or spoke. He pretended to look into the back yard, but caught himself looking at her from the corner of his eye. Maybe he should open up and talk to her, but would she judge him? Or think he was dumb for sticking up for his dad and keeping the fact that his father was alive a secret from his sick mother? He knew the only way to know for sure was to just say what was on his mind, vent, like she'd suggested.

Before giving the idea another thought, he opened his mouth and let the words flow out, "Well, I just got back from seeing my dad, and the detective said there's a good chance he could spend time in prison."

Anna nodded, so he continued.

"My dad said he was going to see his attorney today and will know more tomorrow."

She still said nothing.

"I don't know how to feel or think about the whole thing. I mean, a few months ago I found out he was alive and now he's in jail, which is probably my doing." The words exploded from his mouth and he couldn't stop—he didn't want to stop. "I'm the one who called the detective and filled him in on what was happening, even after my dad said not to. Am I wrong for calling the cops? I just didn't want things to escalate, and my mom or all of us, for that matter, be killed in the process. My dad did a stupid thing and put us all in danger. The thing is, I don't think what he did is bothering him. I don't think he realizes the danger he brought upon my mom and me. Maybe he should spend some time behind bars and think about what he's done."

His shoulders sagged and he shook his head, "You're so quiet, I suppose you are a good listener. Though, I wish you'd say something. I'm not used to doing all the talking."

"I'm not sure why not. You're good at it," Anna finally replied.

He smiled, "Ah, thanks, I guess."

"Colton, I don't think you made the wrong decision. You did what you had to for your mom and for yourself. I think calling the detective was the right thing to do. I don't know your dad, besides what I've been told, but maybe you're right and he should pay for what he's done."

"My dad just seems different. Not the man I remember. I guess he'd been keeping secrets for a while. My mom, well, she's changed in many ways too, these past few months…with the cancer and not being able to work and all. I don't know if I'll ever tell her, but it's nice having her home."

"You should tell her," Anna smiled. "I think speaking from the heart will cheer her up and hopefully get her out of bed and living her life."

Colton nodded. He liked talking to Anna. She seemed honest and sweet. Her eyes glistened when she looked at him, and the way her lips curled when she smiled made his heart pump fast and his stomach flip-flop. Colton wondered if Anna felt the same chemistry as he did.

"Um…" he swallowed, biting the inside of his lip. He focused on his hands, bending and twisting his fingers. He wanted to find the right words and ask her to prom. Was asking her to go to prom too soon? Would she laugh at him and think he was joking or worse think he was a dweeb? They hadn't even gone out on a date or had a real conversation, until now. If she said no, would he scurry away with his tail between his legs?

Anna could tell he was thinking about something, "What do you want to ask me?"

Colton lifted his head and gazed at her face. "Anna, ah… I know we haven't talked much, but I…" he coughed into his hand. "Would you like to go to prom with me?"

Her eyes widened, but not in a shocked way, more of an excited way, "Yes, I would like to go with you."

"Really?" His mouth unfurled.

"Yes, really. I like you, Colton. You're a nice guy, and I would like to go out with you."

Colton smirked, "I like you too, Anna."

He tuned into her every word as she talked about her job and school. About her family and where she would like to work one day.

When she finished, he told her about the scholarship he might receive for basketball and what University he would go to in the fall, if and only if his mom was better. He revealed his concerns about his father and his mother and that he didn't feel comfortable leaving his mom here with no one to take care of her. *But,* he didn't want to lose the chance he had to play college basketball and hopefully one-day play in the NBA.

~~~~~

A couple of hours later, Colton and Anna entered the kitchen from outside. They worked side-by-side, making lunch for the four of them. Colton was finally able to talk his mom into joining them in the kitchen. She didn't participate in any of the conversations, but he was glad to have her out of bed and trying to be social.

When they all finished eating, Anna helped clean up, and then said goodbye, "I have to head to school now. I'll see you tomorrow morning around eight?"

"Yeah, but tomorrow is Saturday. I thought you only came during the week?" Colton asked.

"Oh, I forgot. Where did the week go? Well, would you like to hang out or something, say around noon?"

"Most definitely, sounds great. Oh, I have this party to go to tomorrow evening; would you like to come with me?"

"I'll have to get back to you on that. I need to see if my dad has any plans first."

"Sure, no problem. I'll see you tomorrow." He held the door ajar and she stepped out. Anna walked to her car, turned, and waved goodbye. When he saw Anna drive away, he closed the door and went back into the kitchen where Sarah and his mom sat staring at him. They both had curious looks on their faces.

"What?" Colton questioned.

"Oh, nothing," Sarah said.

He looked at his mom and for the first time in days, she appeared happy.

"You should take her out on a date," Alexis said.

"I, ah…I asked her to prom."

Alexis's hand flew to her mouth as she giggled like a schoolgirl. "Prom?"

"Yeah, it's in a few weeks and then I graduate."

"Oh my goodness, it's here all ready. Where did the time go? I better get my butt in gear and get well. You'll need a suit and oh, yeah, a corsage. Do you know what color her dress is?"

"Mom, I just asked her a few hours ago."

"Yes, right. What was I thinking?"

"Oh, Colton. I'm so happy for you. I could tell the moment I saw the two of you gawking at each other. You know what they say about love at first sight," Sarah stated.

"No, actually, I don't know," Colton replied.

"You are meant to be together. If you hadn't taken your mom to the hospital at that exact time, you may have never met one another."

"I recall the first time your father and I met. It was love at first sight. I told you that he was caring, sweet, and nice, but it was his intelligence that captured me. He sure knew how to sweep me off my feet in an intellectual conversation, and boy, was he a romantic! I knew right then he would be mine, and we would get married one day. Not once did he ever say to me I couldn't do anything. He, in fact, pushed me toward my dreams and once I started, I couldn't stop myself. Speaking of romance and dates?" Alexis glanced over at Sarah. "How did your date go with Kurt Giel?"

Sarah turned crimson and bowed her head, "It was great. We've been seeing each other steady for weeks now. Every weekend we hang out and see movies together, go for walks on the beach, like you suggested, Alexis. Colton, maybe you and Anna could double-date with us sometime?"

"Sure, maybe after a couple of single dates. We need to get to know each other better first."

Sarah nodded, "Speaking of dates, I have to get ready for mine. Kurt will be at my house at six, and I need to get cleaned up." Sarah stood and hurried out of the room and up the stairs to gather her things. When she returned to the kitchen, she hugged Alexis, said goodbye to Colton, and practically skipped out the door.

"Now let's talk about your father," Alexis demanded.

Sixty-Seven

Alexis wasn't sure if she was ready to hear the answers that she'd just demanded Colton to tell her.

Now after a couple of days rest, she was ready to ask questions. Colton sat across from his mother at the kitchen table, his face lowered to his chest. They had talked vaguely about his father and what had actually happened these past months on the drive home the night she had seen Jay. Alexis had been exhausted and in a lot of pain from being tied up and shoved around.

As soon as Alexis mentioned that she wanted to talk to him about his dad, Colton shut down. He knew there were issues that he still had to admit to his mom about his part in what had gone down.

Alexis had thought they'd worked through their issues only to find out that Colton had been keeping secrets from her as well. Things she should have known, but she could see her son's point in not sharing those secrets. She'd been too ill to move about and be a mother to him after the treatments started. She'd found out that he'd also made a promise to his father not to tell her. *Would she have even believed him?*

The one thing she loved the most about their relationship, was Colton's unconditional love and support. Sure, they struggled at first, both her and Colton butting heads and learning how to be a family. Colton had taken care of her through the good and bad.

She didn't think he was smoking pot any longer, or at least she hoped he wasn't. Should she even ask him? Yes, probably so. She was his mother no matter what, and she needed to open her heart to him. Though, she'd never stopped loving him even when she'd made work her shelter, her life. Alexis needed to tell him this. *Maybe she'd been keeping a few secrets herself?*

It felt like living in a bubble and praying the lining didn't pop. She realized how much she'd missed while her son was growing and wished she'd been able to see more clearly years ago. She couldn't go back and change what had already happened, but she could start over and be the person she was meant to be, Colton's mother.

"Colton, let's talk in detail about what has been going on. I want you to start from the beginning and tell me everything."

Colton lifted his head and searched her face, "You want to know everything?"

Alexis nodded, never taking her eyes from his and listened without one single interruption.

When Colton finished, they both had tears streaking down their faces. Alexis and Colton cried together and laughed together, but mostly, they listened to one another. They built a new relationship and tucked away the old. The two of them, of all people, deserved a new start.

"I want to go with you to see your father." Colton had stiffened at this statement. "I'm not asking you; I'm telling you to take me with you. I feel it's time your father and I talk about everything that has happened and then figure out what comes next."

"I understand, Mom. You don't need to explain why. Come on, I'll help you to your room so you can change into something comfortable and we'll go."

Colton wheeled his mom down the hall and stood outside the room, waiting for her to slip into a new pair of jogging pants and a sweatshirt. With the treatments, her body no longer held the warmth. No matter how warm or hot the temperature was outside, she was cold. Her skin was the only thing covering her bones; all the muscle had faded away from the lack of food. It was just a couple of weeks ago; he had to lay thick foam down on the mattress so she wouldn't hurt from the bones protruding out of her back.

Colton wheeled his mom down the ramp, helped her into the car, and folded the chair, placing it in the trunk. They drove in silence to the station.

Colton pushed his mom up the ramp and entered the police station. Colton talked to Detective Bowen, who led Alexis and Colton downstairs to the holding cell. This time there were no phones or glass between them. They sat in a room no bigger than their kitchen. Colton adjusted her wig that the wind had shifted outside and lifted her chin to meet her son's eyes.

"Try not to be nervous, he won't bite," Colton whispered.

Alexis gave a half smirk and then turned her head when the door swooshed open. The night she saw Jay, it had been dark, and she hadn't noticed the thinning of his blond hair. His face was unshaved, but other than that, he looked like *her* Jay.

Jay pulled a chair out and settled in his seat. He put his hands on the table, but kept his eyes down. She watched everything he did the moment he entered in the room. Jay was not the man she had married—she could tell all this by his appearance. He was quiet and seemed to keep to himself. Now, the rest lay upon his shoulders. If he still cared for her, he needed to show her he was still the same man she once gave her life to.

"Hello, Jay," Alexis whispered.

He looked up, his eyes sad. "Hello, Alexis," he said and no more.

She watched him attentively. "Colton filled me in on what has happened these past few months since he found you. I wish you'd come to me. I thought our love was deeper than keeping secrets. *But,* before you say anything, I have an apology to make. You stood by me when I lived my dreams, not once did you condemn me. You raised our son into the wonderful man he is today. Colton is responsible and caring, just like you. If you hadn't held our family together, God knows what we would be like or where we'd be right now. Although, I don't approve of what you did."

Jay's eyes lit up and he relaxed his shoulders. "You are too forgiving."

"I've been through so much these past few months. Life is too short to be lived in the past or to hold grudges. The cancer has made me see the world in a different way. What I've missed and what I now want in life. I'm not going to sit here and lie to you and say it didn't hurt when I found out you were still alive because it did. I still do. I'm still hurting. Our son here has made me realize what I've been missing all along, and what is most important." Alexis cleared her throat. "Have you met with the attorney?"

"Yes."

"What has he said? What will happen to you?"

"We're going to try for one year probation. If the judge agrees."

"And if he doesn't?"

"We'll fight for one-to-five years in prison."

"What will happen to the art you kept for yourself?"

"The police can't touch some of the art. My breaking the law was mostly in laundering money. The paintings are ours to do with as we wish. Since, I did purchase a few of them with my winning money. The other few paintings will have to be given back because they were paid with Sergei's counterfeit money."

Alexis nodded, "How much are they worth?"

Jay blinked, "You sure you want to know?"

Alexis thought about the question and then nodded.

"There are eight portraits all worth between five hundred thousand and two million dollars each."

Her mouth dropped open; Alexis glanced over at Colton. He too was astonished. "Then it's settled. We'll sell what paintings are ours after you serve your time or whatever happens, and we start over as a family. We'll talk about my job and our life after the judge's decision is made."

"You honestly forgive me for what I've done?"

"Jay, you have no idea what I've been going through these days, weeks, and months. I don't know how else to explain to you. I could have died, and I still may. I'm not willing to give up all too easily. I worked all through our marriage while you raised our son. You should be the one not wanting to give me another chance. You faked your death to keep us safe, correct?"

"Yes."

"And you've learned your lesson?"

"Yes."

"And you still love me?"

"Most definitely. Never stopped."

"And I have always loved you. I was just too into myself to see what mattered most. Assuming you'd be there no matter what. Colton and I are making amends and learning to move forward. Are you with us? Because I need you by my side through sickness and in health, until death do us part."

Jay reached his hand across the table, and she did the same. Jay squeezed her hand and rubbed his thumb across her knuckles.

"With all this said, we need to be open and honest with one another from here on out. No secrets, no lies," Alexis stated. "Besides, I think this family has held enough secrets lately."

Jay nodded, "I promise."

"I want to meet with the lawyer and talk with him. Do you think you can arrange a day and time for me?"

"He'll be here on Monday."

"I have a treatment in the morning. Can we make it for eleven?"

"Here or at the house?"

"I can have Sarah bring me here afterwards. I'm usually quite tired, but I'll manage."

"When will they check you to see if the radiation is working?" Jay asked.

"One more treatment after Monday, then I will have an ultrasound."

Jay squeezed her hand once more, "I hope I can be there with you."

"That would be nice, Jay. I would love for you to be there."

The guard came in and told them their time was up. Jay stepped around the table, hugged Alexis, and kissed her gently on the cheek. They said their goodbyes and left.

Sixty-Eight

"Let's stop off at Men's Warehouse and look at their suits," Alexis said.

"Are you sure? We can wait or I can do it myself."

"Definitely not! I only have one child, and I'm not going to miss his one and only prom. Prom is a special occasion—one I'm glad to be around to see." Alexis looked over at her son, smiling, "I've missed so much, Colton. Please don't let me miss anymore. I want to be in your life. I want to experience things with you. Prom is a big thing. I remember my prom. It wasn't with your father, but he was a special guy." Her smile faded.

"Why so glum, if he was so special?"

"Bryan died two years later from alcohol poisoning. He was at a party making bets with the other guys playing pool. When his friends called a shot and they missed, Bryan had to drink a shot. I heard later that night, Bryan went outside and passed out in the yard. He was found on his back and wasn't breathing. The paramedics said he'd choked on his own vomit, which cut off his air supply."

"Oh, Mom, I'm so sorry. You must have really liked the guy?"

"We weren't dating very long, three months maybe before we went to prom. Two different colleges separated us. We agreed to go our own ways. I found out from a friend I went to school with. She sent me the newspaper clipping. I flew back home to Massachusetts to attend the funeral."

"How did I not know you weren't from Florida?"

"Probably because I was always working and never told you. You know I'm not one to talk about my life."

"How come you never go home to visit?"

"Well, both of my parents died when the Twin Towers were hit. My parents worked in the same building, but different floors. Not many people survived the terrorist attack. I'd turned eighteen and came down here to attend college, ya' know, to one day work at NASA, that's how I met your father. I was twenty-seven when my parents were killed, and you know the rest."

Alexis glanced over at him as she finished talking, his face not showing any sign of emotion. She couldn't tell if he was sad or upset by what she'd said. "Are you mad?"

"What? No, why would I be? That was a long time ago."

"Yes, but didn't you ever wonder about your grandparents?"

"Yes and no. Dad never brought up his family, so I just didn't think about it much."

Alexis nodded, "So, your dad never told you about his parents?"

Colton whipped his head around, "Should I want to know?"

"Not much to say, really. Your dad rather disowned them. Both his parents are alcoholics and drug users. He told me little about them. What Jay did say was, he had been abused, and he left home when he was fifteen. Came down here to live with his Aunt Rose until she died after he left for college."

"How did she die?"

"Car accident. A drunk driver ran a stop sign on her way home from work one night, killing her instantly. Your father doesn't like to talk about what happened. Jay said I was the only one he felt he could confide in."

"I think I did ask Dad about his parents years ago, but he said there was nothing to talk about, so I let it go. I could tell by looking at his face to leave it be."

"How did you become so smart?"

"Look at who my parents are," Colton said, smiling. "Both of you are successful and smart. I guess I inherited your brains."

"Oh, no," Alexis chuckled. "That can't be good."

They both laughed at the remark.

"Just make sure you use your brain and not do anything stupid like I have."

"Yeah, well, you must have done something right—you had me."

Alexis nodded and smiled, "Since we're talking, have you been smoking any pot?"

"No, not after the last time. I guess I didn't think much about it ever since I took you to the hospital."

Alexis nodded. From his answer, she didn't need to ask any more questions. Colton seemed older and wiser since she'd found out about the cancer. His smoking weed days were over. He'd made plans to take Anna to prom and graduate all within a month.

Sixty-Nine

Colton pulled into the parking lot. After retrieving the chair and helping his mom, they entered the store and exited one hour later. Colton placed the suit in the back seat, and they headed towards home.

When they arrived, Alexis asked to be taken to her bed. She was exhausted from the day they'd had. Colton went into the kitchen, returned with two bowls of soup on a tray, and sat with his mom until they finished eating. Colton left the room, and Alexis had just settled down under the covers when the phone rang.

Alexis didn't have the energy to reach for the phone and hoped Colton would answer it. He came back into the room, holding the phone in his hand.

"Mom, a woman named Carla is on the phone. Do you feel like talking to her or should I tell her to call back later?"

"No, I'll talk to her."

Alexis hadn't talked to her friend in Illinois since she found out about the cancer. She was surprised Carla hadn't called her these past few months. Colton propped his mom against two pillows, handed her the phone, and left the room.

"Hey, Carla. How are you doing?" Alexis said, trying to sound chipper.

"I'm doing good and you?"

Alexis needed to tell her friend what had been going on with her. She wasn't sure where to start and decided from the beginning, but left out the part about Jay being alive. She wasn't sure how to tell anyone, at least not yet.

"Oh my God, Alexis. Why didn't you tell me? Is there anything I can do for you?"

"Just talking to you helps."

"I wish I could come down there and see you, but Mya is still in the hospital."

"How is she doing, by the way?"

"She's doing well, actually. Growing stronger by the day. She gained a pound, so things are looking up."

"How are you and Tim doing?" Silence filled the line between them. "Carla, are things okay with you and Tim?"

"They are what they are. We've started going to counseling once a week. Seems to be helping, but…"

"But what?"

"All my thoughts and energy are spent on Mya."

Alexis nodded to the empty room, "I can see you needing to be by her side, but do you still love him?"

"Yeah, I love him. Maybe not like I once did, but I love him."

"You need to decide how important Tim is to you. Are you willing to sacrifice what love you do have for him for the baby?" Once again, silence filled the line between them. "Carla?"

"I'm here. I don't want to lose him if that's what you're asking?"

"Then fight for him. Make Tim see how much you do care for him."

"I wish I were more like you, Alexis. You seem to handle things much better than me. You're so much stronger."

"Carla, you are as strong as I am. You were always the one who gave me advice in the relationship department, remember?"

Carla laughed, "I do recall some of the questions you asked. Like, how do you know if you're in love? How can I be romantic with him?"

"Yes, I was lacking in the love area, wasn't I?"

"I think you did fine. You were able to love and work all at the same time."

"Not really."

"What makes you say that?"

"Carla, there is something else I should tell you. Something that has happened lately, and I could probably use some advice on."

"Okay, shoot."

"Jay is alive."

"What? But you said he...he killed himself."

"Believe me, I was not aware until a few days ago. I was just as shocked as you are."

"Fill me in on the story."

Alexis told Carla everything she knew, and what had happened the past week. Occasionally, she would hear Carla gasp and then silence. By the time Alexis was done telling Carla the story, she thought for sure they had been disconnected.

"Oh, Alexis. With all that has happened with your health and then Jay. I hope the both of you can work through the problems. Your life seems more messed up than mine."

"I don't know about that. Your baby is precious and needs you. She doesn't know how sick she's been or even understands what's going on. Besides, she has doctors and nurses around her 24/7. You need to make things right with you and Tim, especially if Mya doesn't survive."

"I know and I'll try my best. I just don't know where we went wrong or how to make our marriage better?"

"In time you will. Just be open with one another. Don't keep any secrets. As I told Colton and Jay, life is too short to hold onto regrets. Make amends and try to move forward. That little girl of yours deserves the both of you to make things work."

"Yes, she does. Thank you for listening, Alexis; I'm so glad I called you, and we were able to talk."

"Me too. We'll have to talk again soon. I'm feeling quite tired and would like to rest," Alexis said.

"Yes, sure. I'll call you again soon. Please take care of yourself and keep me posted."

"I will. Bye now, Carla."

"Bye, Alexis."

She hit the off button and set the phone on the nightstand.

Alexis thought about the advice she had given her old friend and felt good about it. Maybe she could use her own advice too.

Seventy

The weekend flew by, and Monday crept into another week. Colton had made sure his mom was up and ready for when Anna arrived at eight in the morning. Alexis liked Anna and was glad her son was *into her*, so to speak. Anna had come to the house on Saturday, and Colton had taken her out to lunch and to a movie. Anna was the first girl she'd ever met that Colton had dated.

Had Colton even had a girlfriend over in the past? How would she know if he had? By the way Colton acted around Anna, all nervous, Alexis would have to say Anna was his first real girlfriend. Alexis could tell by watching Colton's hands—how he fidgeted with them when Anna was around. How he stumbled over his words and his rapid speech. Seeing her son happy made Alexis smile and feel warm inside.

Alexis moved around the kitchen and then positioned her wheelchair in front of the sliding glass door. As spring came, so did the rain. It had been drizzling all weekend, and today didn't look like it would be any different. Most days, the rain came in the afternoon, the dark clouds not rolling in until later in the day, letting the bright sun greet the new day, but not this morning. Maybe the raindrops were affecting Alexis's mood, for she was certainly reflective and introspective.

The door creaked open, and the sound of wet shoes came towards her. Alexis spun the wheelchair around, as thoughts of last week ran through her head. She was still frightened by what had happened, even though she was well aware that Sergei was dead—shot in the head right before her very eyes, but a nagging fear remained. Boris had only been wounded, though, but she didn't fear him like she had Sergei. Sergei would have killed her to save his own life.

Anna stopped when she saw Alexis's face; her hand flew to her mouth, "I'm so sorry. I should have knocked. I didn't mean to scare you."

"No, its all right, dear. I should have known it was you."

"Still, I should have let you know I was here."

"Not to worry, my girl. I'll be fine. Just waiting on Sarah to come and take me for my treatment."

"Oh, she didn't call you?"

"No, why would she?"

"Something came up and Sarah asked me to take you to your appointment today."

"Oh, all right then. Is everything okay?"

"Yes, she's fine…just some important work came up."

Alexis nodded and wheeled towards Anna, "Shall we go then?"

"Sure, do you have everything you need?"

"Yes. Afterwards, we'll need to stop at the police station to meet with my husband's lawyer at eleven. Do you mind?"

"No problem."

Anna helped Alexis to the car, folded the wheelchair, and put it in the trunk. Anna then eased behind the steering wheel and drove off down the road.

"I've been praying for you," Anna said.

Alexis's eyes smiled when she heard the words, "Thank you, dear. Have you bought your dress for the prom?"

Anna nodded, "Oh, yes. I can't wait for you to see it."

"What color have you decided on? Colton will need to get a corsage to match."

"I've decided on midnight blue. It's quite elegant. I want the dress to be a surprise when he sees me."

"You sound as if you didn't go to your own prom?" Alexis queried.

Anna remained silent, trying to find the right words. Finally, she admitted, "I didn't get a chance to go to my prom."

"Oh, why?"

Anna shrugged her shoulders.

"You don't have to tell me if you don't want to."

"It's okay. I guess this will be… like my second chance," Anna replied, her heart speeding fast. She wasn't ready to confide in Alexis about her life yet.

"Second chances are usually better than the first-time around," Alexis agreed, putting Anna's mind at ease.

Anna pulled up to the Cancer Center, putting the car in park. A tall lean man wearing a dark-blue uniform opened the passenger door. His long thin fingers circled gently around Alexis's upper arm, helping her out and into a wheelchair.

"I'll be back in an hour," Anna called out. "I have some errands to run. I shouldn't be long."

"No problem, I'll be here for a while. Take your time."

Alexis watched as Anna nodded and then drove away. The young male volunteer turned Alexis around and pushed her inside.

Seventy-One

An hour later, Alexis sat in the lobby, waiting for Anna. The smells of the hospital made her nose wrinkle. The radiation treatments she was having made her smell things she hadn't even noticed before, and they were quite nauseating.

She scanned the room more than once to make sure she hadn't missed seeing Anna. She turned her head when the automatic glass doors zipped opened. Anna strolled in, her posture sagging, reminding Alexis of a lost puppy.

Anna saw her and painted a smile on her face.

Alexis could tell something was wrong, but wasn't sure if she should say anything.

"Hello, Alexis. Are you finished?"

"Yes, I'm ready whenever you are."

Anna grabbed the handles of the wheelchair and pushed Alexis through the sliding doors. Her car was parked along the curb, waiting for them. The same man in the dark-blue uniform opened the car door and helped Alexis stand up.

Alexis caught a glimpse of something small on the backseat, but her attention was distracted when he guided her head down so she wouldn't hit the car frame. Once she was settled inside, she took a quick glance in the back and then faced forward before Anna could see what she was looking at. Alexis could have been mistaken about what she saw, but didn't want to ask any questions. She never was the type to stick her nose into other people's business.

They drove to the police station with little to say. Anna assisted her into the wheelchair and pushed her up the ramp. Inside, Detective Bowen took over as Anna waited in the lobby.

When Alexis entered the visitor's room, a man in a black neatly pressed suit stood when she approached.

"Hello, you must be Mrs. Finley? I'm Attorney Keith McNeal. I'll be representing your husband, Jay."

"Yes, it's a pleasure to meet you," Alexis replied politely, lifting her frail arm to shake hands with the lawyer.

"Jay should be arriving shortly," he said, taking his seat after situating Alexis's wheelchair close to the small table. "I asked him to give me a few minutes with you, so we could go over what I have prepared. You're aware that your husband has a felony charge against him, but I'm positive we can get those charges dropped, and he should only have to do one-year probation."

Alexis nodded, thinking to herself that this was better than she'd hoped for.

"I have a disposition ready for the court hearing. I honestly don't see us not winning this case. I usually win nine-out-of-ten cases that I represent, not that I'm bragging or anything. Those are just the facts. Do you have any questions or concerns?"

"What happens if the judge finds the evidence admissible?"

"Well, then I go to Plan B."

"Which is?"

"Five years in prison for money laundering."

"Oh," Alexis sighed.

"I believe in being totally honest with everyone involved. Honesty is the best policy. The evidence shows your husband gave the owners of the auction counterfeit money in exchange for the art. The way we can win this case is that even though the evidence shows he used counterfeit money to buy the art. Did Jay know that it was counterfeit when he did so? He may have not even known at the time. Then, when he did find out, it was already too late."

Alexis nodded, giving a dazed look. All her hopes dwindling away, but there was still a chance Jay could be found innocent in all this.

"I will help him in any way I can; that is, as long as he's being honest with me. I can't have any surprises. It will only make things worse for him, and the judge will end-up giving him twenty-five years or more. And I don't think you want your husband to go to prison, do you, Mrs. Finley?"

Alexis swallowed, "No."

"Good, then we're on the same page here. Is there anything you know that could help me with his defense? Anything that might help his case?"

The envelope came to mind and she gasped, "I found some pictures of two men. One husky-built man, whom I think was Sergei. Not sure who the other man was," Alexis quickly lied as the picture of the men flashed in her mind. She was staring into the eyes of the other man she recognized from the photos that were in her drawer beside the bed at home.

"Do you still have the envelope?" McNeal asked, looking surprised.

"Ah, yes, I think so," Alexis responded. She wanted to kick herself for not recognizing the other man before she said anything. Now, the attorney knew about the envelope and was looking at her with interest.

His eyes widened, "Can I stop by the house later today and take a look at what you have?"

"Sure, I don't see why not. Do you know where I live?"

"Yes, I have your address in your husband's file here." He tilted his head toward the officer standing by the door and nodded. He raised his wrist to his lips, spoke into the concealed microphone and a few minutes later the door swung open and Jay came shuffling in.

The chains around his ankles made a *jingling* noise as he made his way into the room. He squatted down in the metal chair and placed his cuffed hands on top of the wooden table. His eyes sparkled when he glanced up, looking into Alexis's eyes.

She shook her head, "What's with the chains? Jay wasn't wearing them the last time I saw him? Why are they treating him as if he killed someone?"

"Just procedure when an inmate is hostile towards others," McNeal said with a smirk.

"What do you mean hostile? What has he done?"

"Alexis, it's no big deal. I just got a little crazy?"

Jay stared long and hard at Attorney McNeal and then towards Alexis, shifting in his seat as if he had the *creepy crawlies* in his pants.

Alexis could see Jay was uncomfortable with the attorney present and wondered if something had happened between them. She needed to think of something to get the lawyer to leave so she could talk to Jay alone and find out what had happened.

"Do you mind if I talk to my husband alone for a minute?"

"I don't think there's anything you need to say to him that I shouldn't be aware of." McNeal sneered.

"Look!" Alexis's voice rose sharply. "I want to talk to my husband in private, now!" she demanded.

Alexis was never one to lose her temper, but this man, this attorney, was pushing her to the extreme. She focused on Jay and then on McNeal. The lawyer hadn't budged.

The officer by the door strutted over and asked. "What seems to be the problem?"

"Nothing is—" McNeal started to say before he was interrupted.

"I'll tell you what's wrong. I want to speak to my husband alone, and this man here says I can't."

"Ma'am, please calm down," The officer replied as he studied her face, narrowing in on the dark circles under her eyes that made her already thin face look even more dreadful. "Sir, please step out of the room while she talks to her husband."

Attorney McNeal stared at Alexis then stood, leaving the room.

"Finally, I thought he'd never leave," Alexis huffed.

"What's this about, Alexis? Why are you so upset?"

Alexis leaned forward, mere inches from Jay's face and practically whispered, "I found something awhile back. Something you'd shoved to the back of one of our kitchen drawers. I wasn't sure at first, but after my mind replayed what I saw in those photos—tell me if I'm wrong—is McNeal the man in the photograph with Sergei Leonti?"

Jay swallowed and searched her face, "Yes."

"What does he have to do with the mess you're in? Is he aware you know?"

"I think he suspects that we both do. When I asked for a lawyer, he showed up. We didn't have a lawyer of our own, so they appointed one to me. Anyway, he came in to see me, but it wasn't until his second unannounced visit on Saturday that I recognized his face. He's the man I had to pay all my gambling debts to. Most of the cash was real, but the rest that Sergei gave him was counterfeit. I had told this McNeal person to meet with Sergei, and that he would pay him the rest of what I owed. I hid in the park one night and took pictures of them together as evidence. Since Sergei is dead, I think this guy is coming after me for the rest of the money. This man, McNeal—not sure if it's his real name—found out I was alive somehow and showed up pretending to be a lawyer. I went *berserk* shouting at him, and the guards came in and hauled me away. I guess the guards thought it'd be safer if I was put in chains so nobody would get hurt."

"Crap," Alexis said vehemently in a hushed voice.

"What?"

"He asked me if there was anything I could do to help you, and I remembered the envelope. I told him about the photos inside."

Jay shook his head.

"I'm so sorry. I didn't realize it was him until after…"

"That's not why I'm shaking my head."

"Then why?"

"Colton gave me the envelope."

"I'm not sure I follow."

"I asked him if he could get me something and told him where to find it. He mailed the photos to me months ago."

"But I moved the envelope into my room. How would he know to look there?"

"I guess our son is smarter than he looks," Jay grinned.

"So, now what do I do when he comes to the house to retrieve them?"

"Is there somewhere you can stay for a while? Some place where he won't find you?"

"I can ask Sarah, but I don't want to put her life in danger. She doesn't deserve that."

Jay nodded.

"I might have an idea, but I think it's best if you don't know," Alexis said.

"Oh, okay. You're probably right."

"Jay, I'll take care of this."

"But you're too weak, too sick, to be handling this problem on your own."

"I have Colton. He'll help me."

Jay nodded in agreement, saying no more.

"We're done here," Alexis called out to the officer. "Can you have Detective Bowen come and take me upstairs to the lobby?"

"Yes, ma'am."

"I'll be in touch with you. Just stay out of trouble and keep yourself safe," she said.

Jay reached for her hand and squeezed, "I love you, Alexis. Always have and always will."

"I love you too, Jay." The door swooshed open and in marched Detective Bowen. "Are you ready, Mrs. Finley?"

She nodded and gave Jay a wink.

Back upstairs, Alexis asked Detective Bowen if she could speak with him in private. He propelled the wheelchair towards his office and closed the door behind them.

"What did you need to talk about?"

She told him her side of the story and what happened downstairs. When they finished talking, Bowen pushed her to the lobby and handed her over to Anna.

"We'll be in touch, Mrs. Finley."

The detective left without another word.

Seventy-Two

The sky was a deep shade of blue when Alexis and Anna exited the building. The sun poked from behind a single cloud, drying the remaining puddles the rain had brought. There was no wind, no slight breeze, only the warmth of the sun shining upon them. After they got back into the car, the object Alexis had seen earlier in the backseat was gone.

Alexis didn't want to pry, but she had to ask this one time, if not for herself, for her son. "Anna?"

"Yes?"

"I don't want to come off as being nosy, but I…" Alexis took in a deep breath. "I thought I saw a baby toy on the backseat earlier and now it's gone."

Alexis focused on what she could see of Anna's face. Anna's eyes widened and she visibly swallowed, staring out the windshield as she drove.

"Oh," Anna replied after an awkward pause.

"Is that why you didn't go to prom? I wouldn't be asking if, you know, you weren't dating my son. It's just that neither Sarah nor Colton has said anything about you having a baby."

"I asked Sarah not to say anything. I wanted to tell Colton after we were dating for a while. I like you very much, Alexis. You're a strong woman, and I can see how much you love your son. I look up to you. You're so brave, even after everything you've gone through. My mother wasn't as lucky. I lost her to breast cancer when I was fifteen. I want you to know that I'm not out to hurt Colton. Really, I'm not. He's the first great guy I have been out with since… well, since I had Amanda." Tears slid down Anna's cheek.

"Oh, sweetie, I'm so sorry about your mother. But you can't keep your daughter a secret much longer. Colton will be heading off to college in August. What will you do then? He needs to know the truth. I don't want to tell you what to do, but you can't keep this secret from him."

"Yeah, I know. I just don't want to lose him. He's an amazing guy—sweet, kind, and thoughtful. I could tell the first time we talked at the hospital what kind of person he is. I can see how much he cares about you and is afraid that…that the cancer might take you."

Alexis could see the same things in her son as everyone else did, but she'd ignored the fact about her health. "Is the baby's father still in your life or your daughter's?"

Anna let out a hardy laugh. "You would think so, but when he found out, he bailed on me and on her. Hasn't contacted me in almost four years."

"So, Amanda's three years old?"

"She will be in August."

"So, that's why you go to night school? Who watches her when you're working or at school?"

"My father does. He's a retired firefighter. We live with him, for now at least. I think Amanda has brought life back to my dad since my mom died. He says for us to stay as long as we want to. He loves having us around; he says so all the time. He has his guy nights—you know, playing cards and going bowling on Tuesday nights."

"Your father seems like a great man. I wouldn't mind meeting him sometime and Amanda too."

"He's a wonderful father. I haven't told him yet that I'm dating someone. I don't want him to think I'll screw-up again."

"Anna, I really don't think he feels that way. Like you said, Amanda has given life and love back to him. Besides, I wouldn't call getting pregnant at a young age a screw-up. There are miracles that are just supposed to happen. It's what life is made of. I'll tell you what, after my last radiation treatment and Jay's court hearing, I would love to have your family over for dinner, but I do suggest you tell Colton beforehand."

Anna nodded, "Okay, I will."

Alexis reached out and laid her hand on her shoulder.

"Everything will work out fine, you'll see," Alexis encouraged the young mother, who was still a child herself.

"See, that's what I mean, Mrs. Finley, you're so happy and full of life. You don't seem afraid of the cancer."

"I can't think about that. I have to keep positive and not worry about what might happen. We never know what good things are just around the corner."

Alexis had noticed that Anna called her by her married name, instead of her first name as she usually did. She knew it was a sign of respect, and she smiled at her warmly.

"It's not just the cancer, Alexis. You've been building a new relationship with your son and then finding out almost a year later that your husband had never committed suicide and was still alive... I think I would lose my mind! Especially now, waiting to find out if he'll go to prison or not."

"Yes, I can agree with you there, but I can't let it bring me down. Things happen for a reason and will come together in time."

Seventy-Three

Colton's car was in the driveway when they arrived back at the house. Anna pulled in behind his car and shut off the engine. Before she could get out of the car, the front door opened and Colton jogged down the walk towards them.

"I think I'll have a talk with him now before I change my mind," Anna whispered as Colton pulled opened the passenger-side door to help his mother.

"I think that's a great idea," Alexis mouthed silently.

Colton assisted his mom out of the car, into the wheelchair, and up the ramp to the house, talking rapidly and nervously as he always did in front of Anna about how glad he was to see them both. Anna didn't follow them into Alexis's room, but nodded to Colton and pointed to the patio.

Once Alexis was in the house and settled in her bed, he asked how her day had gone.

Ignoring the question, Alexis immediately asked, "Colton, did you take the envelope I had put in this drawer?" She pointed to the nightstand.

He looked down at his hands, not answering.

"I'm not upset if you did." She went on to tell him what had occurred during her visit at the station earlier.

"Mom, I need to show you something." He pulled his phone from his pocket and showed her the photos he had taken. "Is this the man you saw today?"

She held the cellphone in her hand. She touched two fingers to the screen, zooming in. The picture was taken at night, but she was able to make out some resemblance. "It sure looks like him. How did you get these?"

"Before I sent Dad the photos, I took pictures of them with my phone just in case I needed them for something. They were so important to Dad."

"It seems you were right. Detective Bowen and a few of his men are coming here later. He wants to be here before this McNeal guy shows up. Do you recall ever seeing this man at our house?"

"Not sure. When I saw Sergei last week, I thought he looked familiar, but he had tattoos on his arms. The guy I saw Dad talking to a couple of years ago didn't."

"I'm not sure what we're going to do when McNeal comes here asking for the pictures. I hope the detective will be at the house before he shows up."

"Don't worry yourself; I'll handle him. Get some rest; I'm going to visit with Anna before she leaves."

"Son, before you go, I just want you to keep an open mind about what you and her talk about."

Colton tilted his head and searched his mother's face, "What do you mean?"

"I can't say, but don't jump to conclusions, hear her out before you say anything."

"Is there something wrong?"

"No, not wrong. Just go and talk to her. She'll explain everything."

"All right, I will." Colton reached over, kissed Alexis's cheek, and then pulled the blankets up under her chin. He stood and left the room, closing the door behind him.

Seventy-Four

Anna was in the kitchen, wiping the counter, when Colton breezed into the room.

"Do you still want to sit outside on the patio with me?" Anna jumped when he spoke. "Sorry, didn't mean to scare you," Colton said.

Anna finished, folded the small rag, and placed it by the sink. "Sure," she swallowed.

"Would you like something cold to drink before we head out?"

"Yes, please. That would be nice."

"Soda or water?"

"Soda sounds refreshing."

He yanked the refrigerator door open, grabbed a couple cans of Coke, and walked toward the sliding glass door. Anna slid the door aside, allowing Colton to step out first and then followed him. He didn't notice any water on the chairs from the rain so he plopped down. He waited until Anna sat and handed her the can of soda.

"So, my mom says there's something you need to talk to me about."

Anna bit her bottom lip, looking from the can to his face. She exhaled a breath and then spoke, "There's something I should have told you about me from the start, but first I want you to know that I do have feelings for you."

"I have feelings for you too."

Anna smiled, "When you asked me to prom, I was shocked, but also excited. I never had a chance to go to my prom when I graduated from high school."

Colton nodded, not saying a word.

"I um…" she cleared her throat. "I got pregnant my last year in high school and wasn't able to attend prom. I have a daughter."

Anna studied his face looking for any indication of what he might be thinking. Colton sat still, his jaw twitching. "I'm sorry, I should have told you this before…" she swallowed. "Ya' know, before we started seeing each other."

Colton swallowed and sat up straight, "So, this guy who got you pregnant…is he still in the picture? Are you still involved?"

"No, we're not together. He left after finding out about the pregnancy. Hasn't had anything to do with us since."

"Oh." Colton pulled the tab of his Coke and broke the seal. The can hissed, he waited, and then guzzled half the can.

"I know I should have told you sooner, but I was waiting to see how things worked out with us. I didn't want to introduce you to my daughter, and then you know, we break-up."

He nodded, but didn't speak.

"I hope this doesn't ruin our relationship, but I understand if you're not ready for this and don't want to be with me."

Anna sat quietly, popping the top on the can and sipping her drink as she gave Colton some time to think this through. She couldn't meet his eyes so she watched the clouds moving overhead.

Colton's mind switched into overdrive. He was only seventeen, and this was the first time he'd even had a girlfriend. Anna was wonderful in many ways. Different than any girl he'd ever met. Yes, he had feelings for her. Probably more than he should have in such a short time. Was he going to stop seeing her because she had a child? No, he wasn't ready to be a dad, but she wasn't asking him to be the child's father. He had college in the fall and what about playing in the NBA someday? Would all that change because he was dating a girl with a child? It didn't have to. He could still be with her, go off to school, and see her on the weekends. He wasn't ready to walk away from her, child or no child. He was falling in love with her; something he had never felt before, and he didn't want to turn back now.

He could imagine how hard she'd worked, going to night school and raising a child on her own. He'd be an ass to walk away because she had a child. This had to be what his mom meant by listening to her and keeping an open mind. Would his mom think badly of him if he ran the other way? Did he even care? Yes, he did. He cared what his mom thought. Maybe not so much in the past, but now that she was home and had cancer, he cared what she thought of him.

"I would like to meet her. That's if it's all right with you," Colton suggested.

Anna looked up and smiled, "Yes, of course. Are you sure?"

"Yes, I'm sure." He stood and then knelt down in front of her, taking her hand in his. "Anna, you're the first real girlfriend I've ever had. I know it may seem too soon, but I think I'm falling in love with you. I don't want to lose you. Things happen in everyone's past, sometimes bad, but mostly for the good. I would be a fool to let you go because you have a child. I don't want to stop seeing you once I go off to school either. If I have to find some place closer I will."

"No! I don't want you to choose a school closer because of me. Besides, Jacksonville isn't that far. We can see each other when you come home."

"Or, you can move up there with me?"

"Don't you think it really is too soon for that? We've only gone out a couple of times."

"Yeah, maybe, but I don't want the distance to drive us apart."

"It won't, if we don't let it. I'm willing to work at our relationship, if you are?"

Colton nodded and swallowed, "I am." He leaned forward and kissed her. When they parted, he cupped her face in his hands. "We'll make our relationship work, no matter what."

Anna smiled and rested her forehead on his. They stayed like that for a few minutes and then he kissed her forehead and stood. "What time do you have to leave?" he asked.

Anna flipped her wrist over, glancing at the time on her watch. "It's ten minutes past three; I have to stop at home before I go to school tonight." They walked inside and made their way to the front door.

"I guess I'll see you Wednesday then?"

"Okay. Colton, thank you."

"For what?"

"For being so understanding, sweet, and kind. Guys like you are hard to find."

Colton laughed, "Well, I don't know much about relationships, so you'll have to help me in that category."

"You're doing just fine, Colton. You're the first guy I've ever met who didn't push having sex."

His face turned beet-red. The thought hadn't even crossed his mind. He just loved being around her. His friends always talked about getting into bed with chicks, but it wasn't something he had on his mind. Playing basketball was all he'd ever cared about, until Anna came along.

Colton hoped he wouldn't turn into his mom, how she'd chosen work over family. To him, family and love were more important, but would he have to give up his dreams? He would have to talk to his mom about the things on his mind. She'd said to him that she'd been selfish, but if he juggled school, basketball, and Anna the right way, couldn't he have it all?

Anna nudged his arm, bringing him out of his thoughts. "I gotta go."

"Okay, sure."

Colton kissed Anna one last time and unlatched the door.

Her focus was on Colton when she moved out the door and collided with a man standing on the porch. Anna whipped her head up and took a step back, "I'm so sorry. I should've been paying attention to where I was going."

"No problem, Miss. I was just about to knock when the door opened."

Anna glanced at Colton, "Bye."

Anna squeezed past the man at the door and hurried down the walk. She looked up when she got to her car and noticed the man's car had blocked her in.

"Excuse me, sir, can you please move your car so I can leave?"

The man sneered at her and stomped down the steps toward his car. After the man passed by her, she threw Colton a look and mouthed, "What the heck was that all about?"

Colton yelled back, "See you Wednesday," and tugged his phone from his back pocket. Colton waited until Anna drove off and closed the door, locking the deadbolt. He searched through his contacts until he found Detective Bowen's number. He pressed the call button and waited.

"Hello, Detective Bowen speaking."

"Hey, it's Colton. My mom told me what you guys talked about today and that man is here. What should I do?"

"Is he in the house?"

"No, he's parking the car."

"Then how do you know it's him?"

He told the detective what had happened a few minutes ago and with the pictures. "Do I let him in or keep the door locked?"

"We don't want him getting suspicious, so let him in, but keep him occupied until I get there."

"Okay, I'll come up with something to distract him."

Colton peeked out the window to see where the man was. The man was trudging up the driveway, so Colton unlocked the door before the man could hear the loud click from the lock.

"I'm going to keep my phone on so you can hear what we're talking about," Colton told Detective Bowen.

"Good idea, son. I'm on my way. I won't say anything else— leave the door unlocked."

"Got it," Colton replied as he flipped the ringer off on the side of the phone and slipped it on the table next to the door.

Before the man could knock, Colton swung the door open wide and asked politely, "What can I help you with?"

"I'm here to see your mom. I'm your father's attorney, Mr. Keith McNeal. Your mom said she had something for me."

"Oh, well, she's resting right now. She gets exhausted after her radiation treatment. Is it possible you can wait awhile or maybe come back later?"

"Is that so?"

"Yes, sir. I'll go check on her if you'd like? I haven't seen her yet since I got home from school."

"Yes, do that." McNeal stepped forward, but Colton stood in the doorway, not letting him in the house.

"I'd prefer you wait out here while I check on her. Mom's not too keen on me letting anyone in the house I don't know," Colton said with a smile and a shrug.

McNeal huffed, not giving up. "It's quite hot out here today. I would really like to come inside and wait for her. She knows me. I'm your parent's lawyer."

I wish McNeal wasn't wearing a suit, Colton thought. The man looked too official to deny his request. Colton covered his hand over the phone on the table, cuffing it in his palm.

"Oh, you're right, it is rather humid out, and Mom knows you, I guess. Come in and wait right here." Colton moved aside allowing McNeal to enter and scurried down the hall.

Once inside his mom's room, he closed the door and pushed the lock in. He put the phone to his ear and whispered, "What do I do now?"

"I'm five minutes out. Just keep him inside until my men and I get the house surrounded."

"I'll try."

"Colton, who are you talking to?" Alexis asked.

Colton raced over to the bed and placed a finger to her lips, "That man you told me about is here. I'm on the phone with the detective."

She shot up, her eyes wide with fright. He could see she was trembling all over.

"Mom, I want you to go into the bathroom and lock the door. I'll keep him in the other room." Colton handed the phone over to his mom and helped her to the bathroom. "You keep the phone and let the detective know what's going on. I'm going back out there and tell him you're not feeling well."

Alexis nodded and did what Colton told her to do. Colton waited for her to lock the door and made his way back to the foyer.

"Sorry, Mr. McNeal was it?"

"Yes, that's correct."

"My mom is feeling exhausted and she's just not up to visiting with you at the moment. You'll have to come back later."

"That's not possible."

"Excuse me?" Colton questioned.

McNeal was starting to piss Colton off. What right did he have to come here and demand to see his mom? He knew McNeal wanted the pictures. Pictures they no longer had, except for the ones on his phone, but McNeal didn't know about those.

Colton needed to stall him. He moved towards the kitchen, hoping McNeal would follow. He did. "Would you care for something to drink?"

That was stupid. First, he'd told him that he'd have to leave and now Colton was asking the guy if he was thirsty. Colton could tell the man was agitated as he rubbed the back of his neck, and his face was turning red.

"Your mother said she had something for me. If you could just get what I need, I'd be happy to leave and be on my way."

"What was it you needed?"

"Mrs. Finley said she had an envelope with some photos in it for me. Something that could help your father stay out of prison."

"Really? She hasn't said anything to me. I wouldn't know where to look for this so-called envelope you're talking about."

McNeal started running his hand through his hair. If Colton continued to dillydally around, this man was going to get even more pissed off than he already was. Colton turned and opened the fridge, pretending to search for something, anything. Colton decided on a bottle of water and closed the refrigerator door, turning to face McNeal.

McNeal had a gun pointed at him. Colton took a couple of steps back, his butt hitting the stove and stopped. He had nowhere to go now and prayed Detective Bowen was outside.

"What the hell, man?"

"Look, son, I don't want to have to hurt you, so just give me the Goddamn pictures!"

"And if I don't?"

"Ah, so you *do* know what I'm talking about, don't ya'?"

Colton swallowed and set the bottle down on the counter next to him, his mind racing to come up with an answer. This man would kill him if he needed to and then what? Kill his mom too? He wasn't going to let that happen. Colton should just tell him the truth and maybe, just maybe, he'd leave without causing them harm. *Not likely*, Colton thought.

"I don't have what you're looking for, so just leave and I won't say anything."

McNeal howled, "You honestly think I believe you? I pull a gun on you asking for some crucial evidence you have on me, and you think I'll just let you live to testify against me? Do you think I was born yesterday? Come on son, give me the photos and I'll think about not killing you. Maybe just your mother."

Colton gasped, "I won't let you anywhere near her."

"And how will you stop me?"

Colton heard a car door slam outside and coughed in his hand to cover the sound. The cops were here, so now what? What could he do to keep McNeal from knowing what was going on? Colton relaxed his shoulders and stood tall.

"They're in my room, come upstairs and I'll show you." Colton hesitated for a second and then stepped forward, walking towards the stairs. He glanced over his shoulder to make sure McNeal was following him—he was.

Colton tramped up the stairs, feeling the man's presence behind him. Once in his room, he opened the drawer in his desk and pulled out the photos of him and his dad that he'd found months ago.

"I'll give them to you once we're downstairs and you're standing outside. No harm must come to us or I'll call the police and tell them everything I know."

McNeal contemplated and then spoke, "Sure kid, anything you say." McNeal's grin was anything but friendly.

They made their way back down the steps and stood in the foyer. Colton opened the door and waited for McNeal to stand in the threshold. The man held out his hand, waiting for Colton to slip the stack of photos into his hand. Colton took in a deep breath and held it in, wondering where Detective Bowen was, when he heard a familiar voice.

"Drop the gun and put your hands on your head," Detective Bowen commanded.

McNeal did as he was told. Detective Bowen grabbed his arms, twisted them behind his back, and slapped cuffs on.

"You okay, Colton?"

Colton blew out the breath he'd been holding. "Yeah, I'm fine. Glad you were here waiting for him."

"Thanks for doing what you did. We've been looking for this guy for a long time; we just didn't have a face or a name to go with it."

Colton nodded, "Glad I could be of help."

"Well, this should ease your mind—it's over now. Go check on your mom for me, while I read him his rights and take him to jail."

"Sure thing, Detective Bowen."

Colton closed the door and hustled down the hall and into Alexis's room.

"Mom, it's me…Colton, you can open the door now. The police have McNeal in custody."

The door clicked and then opened. Colton didn't stop his mom when she pulled him into her arms. Her body trembled beneath his grip. Colton reached down, lifted her into his arms, and carried her back to the bed.

Seventy-Five

Almost a full week had passed before Alexis heard any definite word about Jay. Detective Bowen called early this morning and told her Keith McNeal had been arraigned, brought before the Grand Jury, and was awaiting sentencing in a few weeks. Until then, McNeal would sit behind bars at a prison holding center. All charges against Jay had been dropped and he was acquitted for helping in the arrest of McNeal.

She'd learned from Colton, who had visited his father every day that McNeal had been working with Sergei Leonti making counterfeit money—the same money that was given to Jay in exchange for the art portraits and the same money he had given McNeal for his gambling debts. It had all been a scam hatched by the two criminals to get the counterfeit money out of their possession and replace it with valuable art pieces that were worth hundreds of times the amount of the debt. It had been set-up to prey on vulnerable, desperate gamblers.

Jay would not divulge his source's name; the man who had helped in faking his death.

Jay said he'd sent word to his friend about what had happened so he could protect himself. There was no need to get his friend involved since he technically didn't have a hand in the work Jay did with Sergei. More or less, all he had given Jay were pointers on what to do and how to cover his tracks.

The detective negotiated with Jay that by revealing the identity of the man involved in the apparent suicide, the detective will in turn get all charges dropped against Jay. Additionally, the detective swore no charges would be brought against the man who helped Jay with the apparent suicide.

Jay agreed to the deals only if his family was kept out of it. Detective Bowen made a sworn written statement to keep Jay's name clear of the investigation.

Along with a few bills of counterfeit money Jay had hidden away and the photos that were taken of Sergei and McNeal, this was the proof which verified the two criminals had worked together to scam him into participating in illegal transactions.

Jay provided Detective Bowen with the photos and the key to a safety deposit box where he'd kept the counterfeit money. Once their negotiations were complete, Jay awaited release.

Seventy-Six

Alexis stood in front of the mirror and adjusted her wig. Colton was bringing Jay home today, but she wouldn't see them until after her appointment with Dr. Brownski. She was getting an ultrasound and hoped all was well. She'd had five additional weeks of radiation treatments, and now the doctor wanted to check and see if the treatments had helped. If the cancer was gone she wouldn't have to continue the treatments, but if it wasn't she'd have to make some hard decisions about her future.

Dr. Brownski had already taken a significant amount of tissue from both of her breasts, and what was left made her feel less of a woman. Initially, she'd considered having a double mastectomy to eliminate the cancer, though; she'd still have to be checked throughout the year to make sure the cancer hadn't returned to any other parts of her body.

Back then, all she'd been thinking about was a quick-fix to hide it from NASA so she could be included in the next space shuttle mission. So much had happened since then that she didn't even feel like the same woman, and some things had been positive.

Alexis knew she needed to ask the doctor today and find out what her chances were of the cancer recurring or spreading after a double mastectomy. It had come to that point. She wanted to live!

The decision hadn't been easy for her to make to have the mastectomy if the cancer wasn't gone; it was the thought of having her family around that had swayed her. She'd taken Jay for granted the past twelve years and had denied love to her son. Things had changed this past year and she wasn't going to let life slip by her anymore.

Alexis had opened up to her friend Carla in Illinois and promised to come visit her and see the baby when she felt up to flying. Alexis had become close friends with Sarah and wished she'd done so many years ago.

Alexis ran her fingers down the sides of her hair, smoothing the fly-away strands. She took one more look, flicked the switch off in the bathroom, and for the first time in a long, long time walked out of the room and down the hall. She still held onto the wall every few steps, but it felt good to be on her own two feet.

The aroma of eggs and bacon lingered in the air making her mouth water. She turned the corner and saw Anna standing at the stove.

"Smells great!"

Anna whirled her head around and smiled, "I thought you'd like something different for breakfast this morning."

"Yes, thank you. A person can only eat so many saltine crackers."

"Ditto. Does this mean you have your appetite back?"

"Well, not all the way, but smelling this food is making my stomach growl."

"Good, I aim to please. Have a seat; I'll get you whatever you want."

"Thank you, but I think I can manage getting myself a cup of coffee."

Alexis rested her hip against the counter, poured a cup of fresh coffee and added cream and sugar. She placed a spoon in her cup, walked to the table, and sat down. She took a couple sips before Anna placed a plate with eggs and bacon in front of her. Anna walked away and came back with a plate stacked with pancakes.

"Wow, you really went all out this morning!"

"It's an exciting day. Your husband is coming home."

"Yes, I know. I can't believe it. Just shy of a year ago, I was mourning his loss and now he's going to be here with us. I wonder how many people wish they could have their loved ones back. The circumstances are different, but—"

"I know what you mean. If my mother reappeared, I'd be just as flabbergasted as you are."

"Just seems too good to be true."

Anna set a plate on the table and sat down. Steam rose off the eggs as she sprinkled some pepper on them. "Once in a lifetime dream. I'm so happy for you, though. You've been through quite a bit in the past few months just since I've been here, and I'm not only talking about the cancer, either."

Alexis nodded and started eating her eggs. "Oh my God, this tastes delicious, Anna!"

"Thank you, it's a recipe my mother taught me."

"You must share the secret with me."

"It's simple. You only need to add some cinnamon to the eggs as you're cooking them."

"Really?"

"Yep, that's all I do."

"Seems easy enough."

Silence filled the air as they both scooped eggs into their mouths and chewed pieces of bacon. Alexis paused, took a sip or two of her coffee, and then went back to her food.

"If you don't mind me asking, how did the talk go with Colton?" Alexis asked.

Anna waited until she finished chewing, and then washed the food down with a glass of orange juice. "The talk went fine. He actually wants to meet my daughter, Amanda."

"That's great news, right?"

"Yeah, I'm fine with him meeting her. Alexis, I really like your son. I more than like him. He's a wonderful person to be around, and he makes me laugh and feel good about myself. We have a lot in common, more than I can say about the other guys out there."

"Colton is one of the good guys. We've had our battles, but I can't think of anything bad to say about my son. But you should know, you're his first girlfriend, at least as far as I know you are."

Anna nodded, "I know, he told me. I was actually surprised when he mentioned it to me."

"Why's that?"

"Well," she giggled. "He's hot."

They both laughed out loud. "Yes, he is handsome, isn't he?"

Alexis finished her breakfast as Anna cleared the table. Anna put the remaining pancakes in a sealed plastic container, setting them in the fridge, then rinsed off her plate and placed it in the dishwasher. She turned, leaned against the counter, and looked around the room. The doorbell rang and she went to go answer it.

"Good morning, Sarah." Anna said cheerfully.

"Good morning to you too, Anna."

"Alexis is in the kitchen finishing her breakfast. Would you like some coffee?"

"I would love some, thanks."

Sarah wandered into the kitchen, while Anna shut the door and headed for the coffee pot.

"Have you eaten this morning?" Anna asked.

"Yes, I had a quick bite; thanks for asking."

Anna saw that Alexis had finished eating and grabbed her plate. She stood by the sink as the two women talked.

"So, today's the day we find out if the treatments worked?"

"Yes, and I wanted to ask you if you wouldn't mind sitting with me while they check? I could use a friend by my side."

Sarah reached out her hand, placing it on Alexis's arm, "Sure, anything you want. I know this is stressful, but if you need anything, please don't hesitate to ask."

"Thanks," Alexis smiled. "I just need to use the bathroom before we leave."

"Okay." Sarah turned in her chair, "How have you been, Anna?"

"I'm good. Been keeping busy with work and school."

"How are the classes going for you? If you need any help, I'm here for you. Some of those courses can be hard, but I'm sure I can help you through them."

"Thanks for offering. Right now, I'm at the top of my class, so things are going great."

"Are you and Colton all set for the prom?"

"I have my dress, and Colton told me he and Alexis went and picked up a tux. I just need to go shopping for shoes and then I'll be all set."

"Oh, I could help you in that department." Sarah stated. "I love shopping for shoes."

"Really? That would be wonderful."

"How about tomorrow or Sunday?"

"Tomorrow would be better; I have plans with Colton on Sunday."

"Great, I'll pick you up at your place, say eleven? And we'll go have lunch. Bring that sweet little girl of yours too."

"Okay."

Alexis entered the kitchen and stood beside Sarah, "I'm ready whenever you are."

Sarah stood and pushed her chair in and then walked with Alexis to the front door.

"Nice to see you without the wheelchair," Sarah commented.

"I know; I don't miss it one bit."

Sarah motioned Alexis to go first and then closed the door behind her.

Seventy-Seven

On the way to Anderson Cancer Center, Alexis got Sarah up to speed on Jay's release, which took her mind off the appointment. Sarah eased in between two cars and cut the engine. The two women talked as they walked to the building. The electronic doors slid open and they made their way inside. Alexis checked in at the desk, while Sarah took a seat a few feet away. Alexis joined her shortly.

Sarah dug in her purse, pulled out a book.

"What book are you reading now?"

Sarah angled the book towards Alexis, "*Discretion*," by David Balzarini. It's really good. You can read it when I'm done."

"Thanks, I'd like that. I was thinking of picking up an e-reader one of these days."

"Yeah, I have one of those, but there's nothing like the feel of a book in my hands. I guess I'm a little old fashioned when it comes to books. I use technology all the time at work; iPads have taken over the workplace. We use them to store patient files and test results; no more paper, if possible."

"Yes, I know. Working at NASA, we use nothing but technology. Everything is on computers and iPads—wouldn't know what to do if I didn't have them. I was actually there when the transition went through, and I wouldn't change it for the world. It has made my job so much easier to work with."

"I can see your point in something like that."

Sarah flipped to the bookmark and started reading.

Alexis sat, skimming the room. A few of the people in the lobby looked familiar to her, as she had seen them many times when she came here, but some faces were new.

"Finley," a middle-aged woman called out.

Alexis and Sarah stood at the same time and followed the nurse with chestnut hair through a set of doors.

"Second door on the right."

They went inside. Sarah drew up a chair next to the padded bed while Alexis settled herself on the bed next to her. Alexis sat with her hands in her lap and answered the questions.

"How have you been feeling, Alexis?" the nurse asked.

"Better, since the treatments have ended."

"No nausea, light headedness, or fatigue?"

"Yes, definitely fatigue." The nurse scribbled down her answer.

"Okay, let's get your weight,"

Alexis stood and stepped on the scale. She didn't want to look at the number to see how much weight she'd lost since the last visit.

"102 lbs.," the nurse said, as she wrote the number down in the chart.

After checking Alexis's blood pressure and jotting the number down in the chart as well, she handed Alexis a gown. "I'll leave you to change into this gown and then we'll start the procedure. Remember, opening in the front." The nurse placed a light-blue gown in Alexis's hand and left the room.

Alexis did as she was told and reclined back on the bed. She dropped her hand to her side and Sarah graciously gave it a squeeze. She couldn't believe she'd lost ten more pounds since her last doctor's visit. She was wasting away.

"Just take a deep breath and it will be over sooner than you think," Sarah reassured.

Alexis nodded and swallowed. There was a knock on the door and a different woman glided into the room.

"Hello, Alexis, my name is Mary. I'll be the technician doing your ultrasound today," Mary said with a southern slang.

Mary pulled a swivel chair in front of the machine and plopped down. Alexis stared at the ceiling as Mary prepped the machine and applied lubricate to the probe. The technician parted the gown, moved the probe over her right breast, stopping every few seconds to type something into the computer, and then began again.

"Do you see something?" Alexis asked, her voice shaky.

"Not sure yet. Right now, I'm just taking some pictures, and we'll have the doctor come in and look them over."

Mary finished with the right breast and started on the left. Minutes ticked by as Alexis watched with a concerned look. The technician finished, straightened, and hurried out the door.

Silence hung in the air. Neither Sarah nor Alexis knew what to say. Several minutes later, Dr. Brownski came in.

"Hello, Alexis. Let's see what we have, shall we?"

He held the wand in his palm and applied more lube. He motioned the probe the same way that Mary had just minutes before. He stopped, studied the photo, and moved on.

"Well," he cleared his throat, "It looks like there's a small mass around the side of your right nipple and then as I move the wand you can see the tentacles, sort of like an octopus, going around the lower part of the breast. Let's take a look at the other side and see what we have." His reaction was more the same as he continued his search. "See, here," he pointed to the screen. "This one isn't as large as the one on the right, but it should still be removed."

Alexis lay quiet, as she didn't know what to say. Had she expected them to find more cancer? What were her alternatives?

Did she really have a choice? She'd have to have another lumpectomy and definitely more radiation. On the other hand, she could call it quits, accept the decision she'd made days ago, and have the double mastectomy.

Sarah squeezed Alexis's hand, offering sympathy, but the last thing Alexis wanted was for someone to feel sorry for her.

"We can schedule you for a lumpectomy this Thursday and remove the rest of the cancer or…" Dr. Brownski paused. "Or we can schedule you for a double mastectomy. I'll leave that for you to decide. The radiation can be extremely hard on your body and eventually wear you down."

Before he could offer any more words, Alexis interrupted. "I want to have the mastectomy," she replied, fighting back tears. "I can't continue with the radiation. I just can't!"

"Sure, no problem. We can perform a breast reconstruction at the same time. I can replace your breasts with a silicone-gel implant, if you decide to go that route. Do you have any questions?"

"What are my chances of the cancer returning if I have the mastectomy?"

"Your chances are good that the cancer shouldn't return, but there is always that slim chance of the cancer returning in other areas. We'll still need to check you once, maybe twice a year. Are there any other questions you might be concerned with?"

"No."

Brownski nodded, "I'll have Mary bring one of the nurses in here and make the appointment for you. I'll see you in a few days or so."

"Okay," she said, disappointment weighing heavy in the one soft word.

Dr. Brownski stood and left the room.

Alexis replaced her shirt and sat down on the bed, waiting for the nurse. There really wasn't anything left to say. Neither Sarah nor Dr. Brownski had tried to talk her out of it this time.

Seventy-Eight

Twenty minutes later, they finished the paperwork and exited the building. Sarah remained mute until they were settled back in her car.

"Do you want me to be with you for the operation?"

"Oh, I don't know. Jay will be home, and he may want to be with me for that."

"Sure, I understand. If things change let me know."

"I will."

Sarah merged onto the highway, pressed down on the accelerator. They arrived at the house thirty minutes later. Colton's car was parked in the driveway, so Sarah hugged the curb and killed the engine. They both exited the car and silently went up the walk. Alexis turned the knob and stepped inside; Sarah followed two steps behind her.

Alexis saw Jay and Colton sitting outside on the patio and headed toward the sliding glass door. Colton opened it before Alexis did, and he joined Sarah inside so his parents could have some privacy.

Jay stood and Alexis practically fell into his arms. Tears poured out of her as if she hadn't cried in years. She gained composure and stepped back, wiping her face.

Jay held her hand in his as Alexis filled him in on what the doctor had said. Jay nodded when he needed to, but mostly listened.

"I go in next Wednesday for the surgery."

"I want to be there with you. I was gone for so long when you needed me, and I'm so sorry for what I've done."

"You did those things to protect us. I find no fault in that. I'm just glad you're here with us now."

"So am I, Alexis. Are we able to build a new life together? All three of us?"

"I wouldn't want anything less. It will take some time, but we will be a family again. Once the operation is over with, I'll sit down with my boss and decide what to do about work."

"Have you ever thought about retiring?"

"Jay, I'm only forty years old. We shouldn't be talking about retirement for at least another twenty years."

"Have you forgotten about the priceless art I have? It's worth more than we'll ever make in this lifetime. I'll do some research and find buyers. We don't have to sell them all, maybe one or two, here and there. We can travel around the world and see the things we've always wanted to visit. We can sell this house and buy any home you like. Colton will be in college; it'll be just the two of us. Whatever you want, I'll give it to you, just say the word."

Alexis smiled, "I only want you and Colton. Everything else will be a bonus."

"Then it's settled. I'll get started right away. All you have to do is feel better and have this surgery. I love you, Alexis. I'm sorry for all the problems I've caused. No more secrets, I promise. Things will be as if they never happened."

"I think I could live with no secrets. From now on, we talk about everything. Marriage is about love, trust, and honesty. No more untold truths between us."

They embraced one another and headed inside to talk to Colton and Sarah.

Seventy-Nine

Colton was in his room, getting dressed in his suit for the prom. He had rented a limo to take Anna and him to and from prom, a surprise for Anna. The limo was to pick Anna up at her home and then bring her to the house so his mom could take pictures. She was also to bring her daughter, Amanda, with her. His parents had begged Anna to let them babysit while they went to prom.

Colton adjusted his tie and grabbed the corsage and a small gift-wrapped box. He pelted down the stairs and entered the kitchen. His mom stood at the stove cooking, while his dad sat at the dinette, reading the newspaper.

"Well, don't you look dazzling?" Jay said.

Alexis spun around, her eyes shining bright as she smiled, "Look how handsome you are!"

"Thank you," Colton responded with a grin.

"Let me take some pictures of you before Anna gets here," Alexis insisted as she turned the burner on low and set the spoon on the counter.

She walked into the living room and grabbed her camera from the table. They all stood in the living room; she took pictures of Colton as if she were a professional photographer. Jay posed in some of the pictures, and then he took over so Alexis could be in some.

Anna arrived a few minutes later with her daughter. Alexis still gripping her camera took many more pictures and then Colton and Anna headed out the door to the limo. The middle-aged limo driver held the door open for the two of them.

Once inside, Colton pulled out the small box from the pocket of his jacket.

"What's this?"

"A gift for you," he smiled.

Anna removed the wrapping paper and lifted the lid of the box, "Oh my God, it's beautiful. You shouldn't have, Colton."

"Here let me help you put it on."

She leaned forward as he slipped the necklace around her neck and fastened the clip. The heart-shaped diamond pendant sparkled against her tan skin, just below her slender neck.

"It's a sign of my love for you, Anna."

"Thank you so much. I love it, Colton!" They kissed and then settled into each other's arms.

Minutes later, they pulled up to the banquet hall where prom was being held. Once inside the building, Anna's hand flew to her mouth, as she gazed around the room. The room was dark as if it was night, and the ceiling was covered with tiny lights that looked like stars in the night sky. Each table had candles and flowers decorated on them along with silverware and napkins.

To her left, students and their dates stood in-line waiting to have a photo taken. The background for the photo shoot had palm trees and several strings of lights hanging down. Colton and Anna merged into the line and awaited their turn.

When Colton and Anna finished, they walked around and found the dance floor. Music began to fill the air and he slipped his arm around her, swaying to the music as if they were the only two in the room. Anna rested her head on his chest, soaking in the moment.

When the song ended, they glided around the room in search of their table. They headed towards the front and stopped at a table where three girls were sitting. Colton gave a blonde girl his name, and she checked the sheet of paper.

"You're sitting at table four," the blonde girl replied, smiling.

Colton nodded and said, "Thank you," and they ambled around until they spotted their number. The table was positioned next to the dance floor. They relaxed in their chairs as the room began to fill with more guests.

Colton glanced around the room, spotted his friend Jake, and waved him over.

"Hey, bro', I didn't know you were coming," Jake said, smacking Colton on the side of the arm, jokingly.

"Yeah, thought I'd surprise you," Colton replied.

Jake looked from Colton to Anna. "So, are you going to introduce me to your date?"

"Jake, this is Anna. Anna, my best friend, Jake."

"Nice to finally meet you, Jake," Anna said.

"Same to you. I didn't even know my buddy here had a girlfriend. You're just full of surprises tonight, aren't you?"

"Well, what can I say, I'm a mysterious guy."

"I'll say. Hey, you remember Katie Burns? She's the captain of the cheerleading squad."

"What did you do to get her to come here with you?" Colton laughed.

"Very funny, dude. We've been dating for the past two months; where've you been?"

"Really?" Colton replied, his eyes wide. "Guess I've been busy with things at home."

"Guess so, bro'. How's your mom doing anyway?"

"She's doing great." Colton hurriedly changed the subject by interjecting. "Where are you guys sitting?" It wasn't the place or time to talk about his mom or the cancer.

Jake scanned the room. "Not sure yet."

"Did you check up front for your table number?"

"Nope, I guess we'll do that now. Catch you later, bro'."

Jake and Katie scampered away, but returned a few minutes later. "We're sitting with you," Jake laughed and plopped down in a chair next to Colton.

They ate their dinner and laughed with the group sitting at the table. As the night went by, Colton and Anna had danced almost every song in each other's arms. The DJ announced the last song of the night; Colton held out his hand to Anna.

Once on the dance floor, he embraced her in his arms as they swayed to the music. He whispered in her ear that he loved her and she replied the same. He kissed her and then pressed his forehead against hers. The night was more magical then he could have ever imagined. He held the girl of his dreams in his arms. What more could he possibly have dreamed of?

Eighty

Weeks later, Colton was in the gym locker-room adjusting his graduation gown. He adjusted the cap on his head, placing the tassel to the side.

"Are you ready, bro'?" Jake asked.

"I can't believe this day is finally here," Colton replied.

Jake and Colton walked out the door and headed to their seats. Colton glanced around the room, scanning the people in the bleachers. He smiled when his eyes found his parents and Anna with her daughter, Amanda, sitting next to them.

A year ago, he was sad and disappointed that his father wouldn't be here to see him graduate from high school. Today he felt nothing but happiness. His life after today would change, and he'll be an adult, heading off to college in the fall. He prayed his grades had improved enough and that the coaches from the University had accepted him for the scholarship.

He wanted nothing more than to play in the NBA, but that would be considered after he played college basketball. He knew he didn't need the scholarship to play, but he wanted them to pick him because he was a great athlete. Colton had been patient waiting for the letter of acceptance to arrive in the mail, but weeks had gone by and no letter had come.

Colton followed Jake down the aisle and they took their seats. Colton was a few rows behind Jake because seating arrangements were based on the student's last names. Once the students were seated, the principal came onto the stage and began his speech.

A half-hour later, Principal Hatton called out each of the student's name one-by-one. When Colton's name was called, he stood and walked up the aisle to the stage.

Colton walked across the wooden stage—Principal Hatton handed him his diploma and shook his hand. "Congratulations Colton Finley, for your hard work and dedication," Principal Hatton said.

Coach Martin walked over and stood beside the principal. When the principal finished speaking, he handed the microphone to the Coach.

"Colton, I want to thank you for all the wonderful years you played basketball on my team. Today, I'm proud to present one of my students with an Athletic Scholarship to Jacksonville University to play college basketball," Coach Martin announced. "Congratulations, I hope you succeed in everything you do in life."

Colton's eyes widened in surprise, "Thank you, I will definitely do my best. I'm going to miss you as my coach. Thank you for being hard on us and making our team play as well as we did."

"No, thank you, I hope I have more players like I had these past few years. I wouldn't mind winning more games."

"If you're their coach, I don't see how they can't win."

Coach Martin nodded and smiled. He handed the microphone back to Principal Hatton and walked with Colton to the steps.

"I'm glad to see your Dad is here with you today, and that he was finally able to come home and be with his family," the coach practically whispered.

Colton stopped in his tracks. He hadn't said anything to anyone, well except Jake, and Jake wouldn't have said a word. Colton wasn't sure if he was hearing things or if Coach Martin actually said what Colton thought he did.

Colton turned and looked his coach in the eyes. After everything with Sergei and McNeal, he now knew who had helped his father in faking his death. Colton's mouth opened then closed. Coach Martin nodded and smiled at him. Could the coach read his mind and know what he was thinking at that moment?

He'd have to talk to his father about this new information, but now wasn't the time or place. Colton nodded and walked down the stairs, making his way back to his chair.

Once seated, he looked up to where his girlfriend and parents were and waved his diploma and acceptance letter. Anna and his dad clapped as his mom wiped the tears from her face. Colton was glad his mom was finally feeling better and looked healthier. Her face had more color, and she didn't look as fragile as she did almost a month ago.

After all the students received their diplomas, the principal made one last announcement to the class of 2015.

"It has been a pleasure having all of you in my school, and I wish you all the best in your future to come."

The graduates all stood and threw their hats in the air, hollering and shouting, "Woohoo, we did it!"

Colton met up with his parents and Anna a few minutes later. His mom had her camera ready to take pictures of him with his diploma. When they were finished, they all walked to their cars in the parking lot. Colton peered over the roof of his mom's car. He saw Coach Martin climbing into his car—a dark-blue Honda Accord.

Eighty-One

After they arrived back home, Colton pulled his dad to the side and whispered, "Was Coach Martin the one who helped you?"

Jay looked around to see if anyone was listening. "Yes, son."

"But he's just a high school coach. What does he know about faking someone's death?"

"Go upstairs and change out of your gown and we'll go for a walk."

Colton nodded.

Several minutes later, Colton coasted down the stairs and met his dad in the kitchen. Jay told Alexis and Anna that he and Colton were going for a walk and would be back soon.

Once outside, they walked to the sidewalk and continued their conversation.

"Coach Martin's full name is Troy Martin. Before he became your coach, he was in the Army and worked in a military hospital. While he was there, he learned about medicines and what they were used for. After serving eight years in the Army, he came back here and got a part-time job and went to school to be a Physical Education teacher."

"How did you two know each other?"

"We went to the same high school and after graduation we went our separate ways. When he was discharged from the military, I saw him at the grocery store. We talked and made plans to meet up. That's when I found out about what he'd been doing all these years. I started talking to him about the trouble I was in. The rest you know."

"I take it this walk is so Mom doesn't find out? I thought there weren't going to be any more secrets between you two?"

"I'm not keeping this from her. If she asks, I'll tell her everything. She's had to deal with so much these past couple of weeks. Like I said, if she wants to know, she'll ask me."

"Do you promise not to gamble anymore?"

"Trust me. I've learned my lesson. No more betting on horses or dog races for me. I have everything I want right here." Jay stretched his arms out wide and turned in a circle.

Eighty-Two

The surgery for the double mastectomy had come and gone six weeks ago. Alexis was still sluggish, but the pain was starting to disappear. She felt almost like a new woman and decided to take Jay's advice, and took an early retirement.

She started reading books and joined the group *Blossom Buddies*. Women from all over the area came to the meetings and talked about what they had been through or were still going through with breast cancer, and how they'd struggled to get their life back on track.

Alexis gained back some of the weight she'd lost, and her hair slowly began to grow out. Since Jay was helping around the house, Anna returned to her part-time job at the hospital.

Jay only had to return three of the eight paintings back to the auction house, unaware that he had bought them with the counterfeit money. He had also found several buyers for a few of the paintings and made over five-and-a-half million dollars. Although, he had paid a lot less for the paintings, the buyers had the paintings appraised and Jay made triple what he had bought them for.

The remaining paintings he planned to hold onto and would sell them if they needed to. Jay wanted to leave them for Colton to do with as he pleased later in life. By then the portraits would double or triple in price as well, and would be a nice nest egg for his future.

Alexis placed the wig Sarah had given her on her head and left the bedroom. She poured a cup of coffee and joined Jay on the patio.

"I can't believe Colton is all grown up. I wish I hadn't missed so much of his life," she said.

"Don't dwell on what you can't change, my love."

"I know, but I can't help it sometimes. Seeing him receive his diploma last month made me remember all that I've missed."

"Don't be so hard on yourself. He has forgiven you and you should do the same. No sense holding onto the past. You have a future with him, now."

"Yes, you're right. I should let it go. I am thankful for surviving the cancer and being able to spend time with him and you."

"What time are you leaving for your meeting?"

"Around ten this morning."

"So, you're free later on tonight?"

"Yes, I suppose I am. Why? What do you have planned?"

"Oh, just something I've been working on these past few days."

"Really?" Alexis smiled. "What did I say about secrets?"

"I'm not hiding any secrets. It's a surprise for you."

"No hints?"

"You want a hint?" Jay tapped his chin with his forefinger, "Let me see. Okay, here's a hint. *Three.*"

"*Three,* that's my hint? What am I going to do with the number *three?*"

"Beats me, but you'll figure it out...or not," Jay smiled

She laughed then sipped her coffee, letting his hint soak in.

Eighty-Three

Later that afternoon, Alexis returned home from *Blossom Buddies*. She pulled into the driveway. From the driver's side window, she saw Jay standing at the front door with a man she didn't recognize. Her heart raced as her mind flew back to the months before. She didn't want to believe he was mingling with the wrong people again.

She turned off the engine and climbed out of the car. As she walked up the brick path, the man Jay had been talking with strolled past her without a word. She climbed the stairs; Jay welcomed her with open arms.

"So, who was that man you were talking to?"

"Oh, just someone who's helping me with some work," Jay replied, batting his hand in the air.

She waited for him to say more, but he didn't. They walked inside and went into the kitchen.

"So, how was your meeting?"

"It was fine," she replied, feeling glum. She wanted to know what he was up to. Who was that man that had just left? Should she come right out and ask Jay? Or, think positive and pray he wasn't getting back to his old habits of gambling. She'd hoped he was done with that and would focus on them.

"Good. I have to grab something from the office and then I want to take you somewhere."

"Okay." She opened the fridge and grabbed a bottle of water.

Jay returned, holding a blanket in his arms.

Alexis smiled, "Are we going to the beach? Just like old times?"

"Yes, that's part of my surprise."

Jay motioned her to follow him. He opened the front door and waited for her to step out, shutting and locking the door behind him. Once in the car, he backed out of the driveway and drove towards the beach.

Fifteen minutes later, he pulled into a vacant lot and parked the car. Jay said nothing and climbed out of the car. He opened Alexis's door and held out his hand for her to take.

A warm breeze rattled her hair as she tagged alongside him. They strolled down the sandy path and onto the beach. Alexis followed as he led the way, stopping to unfold the blanket. Alexis grabbed one end and helped place the blanket on the sand. She sat down first and then Jay beside her, except he was facing the opposite way with his back away from the ocean.

"Why are you facing that way?" she asked, tilting her head to the side.

Jay leaned over and kissed her on the lips, "Turn around; I want to show you something."

She did as he asked and sat searching his face, "Is this my surprise?"

Jay said nothing. Leaning slightly back, he stuck his hand in the front pocket of his jeans and pulled out a single piece of paper. He unfolded the paper and handed it to her.

"What's this?" she asked as she scanned the picture. "This is a blueprint of a house." Alexis tilted her head, her brows making the skin on her forehead crinkle as she studied her husband.

"Yes, it is."

"Can you tell me more?"

Jay raised his hand and pointed to a wooden sign.

She followed his finger to the sign hammered into the ground. On the sign was written, *Lot three, SOLD*. Alexis glanced at the paper in her hands and back up at the wooden sign.

Before she could say anything, Jay spoke. "That's what our house will look like after it's built."

She was speechless for a moment. "A house?"

"You always wanted a house on the beach. I drove by a few weeks ago, saw it, and called the number on the sign. Once the house is nearly complete, we'll put our home we live in now on the market."

"Oh, Jay," Alexis smiled. "I can't believe you did this. Oh my God, this is so amazing. You are amazing."

Everything she'd thought earlier had slipped away. Why did she assume the worst and think he was doing something illegal? She'd have to trust him if they were to start over.

Jay pulled her into his arms, and she smiled up at him, "I love you, Alexis, and I will never leave you again."

"Oh, Jay, I love you too." She pulled back and stared into his eyes. "This is a wonderful gift and a surprise, but how did you know I wanted to live by the ocean?"

"Colton. He said he overheard you telling Sarah. We both have been through so much, and I want us to start over and be a family. Neither of us has to work anymore. We can grow old together, right here. We can wake up to the sound of the waves slapping the sand and watch the sun poke over the horizon every morning."

Alexis smiled as he pulled her close, holding her tight. She couldn't think of anything she wanted more than to be in his arms at this moment and all the moments to come. She knew without a doubt that traveling to outer space couldn't replace the feelings of love and happiness she felt inside at this moment.

ACKNOWLEDGMENTS

I would like to express my many thanks and appreciation to Deborah Bowen Stevens, my editor, who believed in FAMILY SECRETS enough to take it on, and who gave me incredibly thoughtful, insightful feedback, helping me make it an even stronger, more powerful book. I so appreciate how you also allowed me to follow my heart and intuition as I edited along with you. Thank you so much for all the hard work you put into making this novel complete. I owe you so much for all you did, and I'm so glad that I met you on Linkedin.

Last but not least, I want to give many thanks to my husband and daughter for their patience while I'm writing.

I give many thanks and love to all of you in your support as I begin my long lived dream as a writer.

ABOUT THE AUTHOR

Donna M. Zadunajsky was born and raised in Bristolville, Ohio, and resides in Homer Glen, Illinois. She has written seven children's books and two novels. Available on Amazon and http://www.littletscorner.com

Besides writing, she enjoys spending time with her daughter and husband, their dog and two cats. She enjoys reading and working on crafts and scrapbooking. She graduated from The Institute of Children's Literature, in spring 2011.

More about the author go to:

http://www.donnazadunajskymalacina.blogspot.com

http://www.facebook.com/donnamzadunajsky

http://twitter.com/72Zadunajsky

FIRST NOVEL
BROKEN PROMISES

Two years after their marriage, Jim Culback wasn't the man Clare thought he was. How many more broken promises could she accept? After packing and moving everything they owned from Ohio to Naples, Florida, she actually thought their marriage would improve. But as time went by, she couldn't take the beatings, lies or cheating any longer. But could her husband be capable of homicide? Is Jim responsible for the murders of two women?

A detective from Chicago is put on the case to help solve the murders and has an encounter with Clare. What develops between them? Can Clare trust another man? Or does Jim have other plans for Clare?

NOT FORGOTTEN

Twenty-six years later, Deanna Iris and her son Brent move back to the town she grew up in—back where her secret began and when her life changed forever.

She receives a call stating her sister and son have been taken to Mendota Community Hospital after being critically injured in a car accident.

Sitting with her son who is unconscious and her sister Sheila who is in a coma, Deanna meets their doctor who reminds her of someone she once knew.

After meeting an old friend who knew about her secret, Deanna receives a note in her mailbox telling her to leave town or she will suffer the same fate.

What transpired all those years ago and who is the mysterious woman she spots as she drives by her sister's house?

Will Deanna ever allow herself to be loved and to let go of the past? Or will searching for the answers lead to her death?